HOLLAND FAMILY NOVELS

Lay Down My Sword and Shield
Two for Texas
Cimarron Rose
Heartwood
Bitterroot
In the Moon of Red Ponies
Rain Gods
Feast Day of Fools
Wayfaring Stranger
House of the Rising Sun
The Jealous Kind
Another Kind of Eden
Every Cloak Rolled in Blood

OTHER FICTION

Half of Paradise
To the Bright and Shining Sun
The Convict and Other Stories
The Lost Get-Back Boogie
White Doves at Morning
Jesus Out to Sea

EVERY CLOAK
ROLLED
IN BLOOD

JAMES
LEE BURKE

ORION

An Orion Paperback

First published in Great Britain in 2022 by Orion Fiction,
This paperback edition published in 2022
by Orion Fiction,
an imprint of The Orion Publishing Group Ltd,
Carmelite House, 50 Victoria Embankment
London EC4Y 0DZ

An Hachette UK Company

1 3 5 7 9 10 8 6 4 2

A CIP catalogue record for this book is
available from the British Library.

ISBN (Paperback) 978 1 3987 0789 4

Printed in Great Britain by Clays Ltd, Elcograf S.p.A.

www.orionbooks.co.uk

In memory of Pamala Roberta Burke

Chapter One

I GAZE UPON THE season from my veranda and know all too well its gaseous vapors and fading colors and deceptive embrace. An orange sun hangs in the cottonwoods down by the river, backdropped by the razored peaks of the Bitterroot Mountains. For me, the sun's lack of warmth is a harbinger of our times, or at best a sign of our collective ephemerality. But please don't be taken aback. Age is not kind, and it leaves a mean stamp on an elderly man's perceptions.

A red Ford F-150 pulls to a stop on the dirt track between my barn and the river. There's a bullet hole in the back window, frosted around the edges like a crisp of ice. A gangly teenage boy vaults over the tailgate and can-sprays a black swastika on the door of my barn. His stomach is flat as a plank, his hair grown over his ears. He pisses in my cattle guard while rotating his head on his neck, his urine flashing in the sunlight.

I walk down the slope, the air damp and tannic from the decomposition of leaves. The boy climbs back into the bed of the pickup and bangs his fist on the cab's roof. The driver wears a red cap. A man in the passenger seat turns his head slowly toward me, his salt-and-pepper hair scalped around the ears, his face insentient, perhaps hardened by the elements or a life ill chosen. A beer can rests on the dashboard. The truck drives away, swaying in the potholes.

"You don't belong here!" the boy shouts, trying to keep his balance, a childlike grin on his face, one that seems incongruent with the nature of his visit. "Go somewhere else!"

He shoots me the bone, his free hand cupping his package.

A HALF HOUR LATER a state police trooper gets out of her cruiser with a clipboard and fits on her campaign hat. She brushes her nose with the back of her wrist, as is our wont during the virus that has changed our culture. She can't be over five-two. Her hair is thick, the color of slate, her skin tanned, her eyes recessed and bright and happy like those of a young girl who is curious about the world. She asks me to tell her everything that happened. When I finish, she makes no comment, and I wonder if I have overestimated her.

"My description doesn't help much?" I said.

"You didn't get a tag number?"

"There was mud on the plate."

"The dispatcher said you've had trouble out here before," she says.

"Kids who threw a sack of pig guts in my yard."

"Why would anyone want to paint a swastika on your barn?" she says.

"They don't like me?"

She puffs one cheek, then the other, as though rinsing her mouth.

"I called 911 because I'm required to do so by my insurance company," I say. "I appreciate your coming out. I doubt anything will come of this, so let's forget it."

"How about giving me a chance to do my job?"

"Sorry."

"How old are you?"

"Eighty-five. Why do you ask?"

"You don't look it."

"It's Dorian Gray syndrome."

She looks into space, then at the two vehicles parked among the maple trees in my front yard. "You live with others?"

"I'm a widower."

"That's not what I asked."

"I live by myself."

"You look like Sam Shepard. You know, the actor?"

I don't reply. For many people who have had a recent personal loss, superficial conversation has an effect like an emery wheel grinding the soul into grit. The swastika on my barn door seems to become uglier and more intrusive as the day grows colder and more brittle, like winter light on a grave.

"Hello?" she says.

"Yes?"

"I mentioned Sam Shepard as a compliment. Know any white supremacists hereabouts?"

"I've seen some people at the grocery and the PO with AB tats."

"Where did you hear about the Aryan Brotherhood?"

"Bumming around."

"You didn't try to take a picture of the truck or the kid shooting you the finger?"

"I don't have a cell phone."

"You're the writer, aren't you?"

"I'm 'a' writer."

"I think there's something you're not telling me, Mr. Broussard. I think you stirred up some white supremacists. I've seen your letters to the editor."

"White supremacists don't read the editorial page."

"Can I make a suggestion?"

"Why not?"

"Stay away from these guys. They're not just racists. They mule the meth that gets brought into the res from Denver and Billings. I don't think the high number of murdered and missing Montana Indian women is coincidence, either. Are you listening, sir?"

"These guys who sprayed my barn weren't dope mules. They're leftover nativists. They think their time has rolled around again."

"Nativists? You're not talking about Indians?"

"Nope."

She takes a business card from her shirt pocket and writes on it and hands it to me. "That's my cell number on the back."

"Why the special treatment?"

"You read Oscar Wilde."

"Pardon?"

"You mentioned Dorian Gray. I assume you know who wrote the novel."

The skin on my face shrinks.

"I read one of your books," she says. "I think you're a nice man, Mr. Broussard. But you need to take care of yourself. There's some mean motor scooters down in the Bitterroots."

The name on her card is Ruby Spotted Horse. "Officer, I didn't mean—" I start.

She gets in the cruiser and starts the engine and hooks on a pair of yellow-brown aviator glasses, then rolls down the window. "Did you lose your daughter recently?"

"Yes, I did."

"I'm sorry for your loss, sir." She looks in her outside mirror. "Watch out. I don't want to run over your foot."

I nod but don't speak, which is what I do when others mention my daughter's death. I still haven't dealt with her loss, and I probably never will.

Ruby Spotted Horse makes a U-turn and drives down the dirt lane, the sun's reflection wobbling like an orange balloon trapped inside her rear window.

Chapter Two

THE WORST DAY in my life began the first of August and has continued as though it has no end, no direction, no resolution, no meaning, no purpose. My daughter's name was Fannie Mae Holland Broussard. She was fifty-four when she died. Her body was not discovered for three days. The medics had to put on hazmat suits before they entered the house.

In the early hours of each morning I wake with that image in my mind and a hole as big as a pie plate in the center of my chest. I cannot breathe. I feel I'm living in a nightmare that belongs in the mind of someone else. I close my eyes and see through the hole into a blue sky that offers no respite and is filled with the cacophony and the fury of carrion birds, like a dirty infection of the firmament itself.

Fannie Mae's mother was killed in a car accident when our daughter was three. Fannie Mae had no siblings and I never married again. She never loved a man; she married one and lived with others and remained friends with some but, for good or bad, had no romantic feelings toward any of them. She loved animals more than human beings. Regardless of her age, she remained a girl and never grew completely into a woman. The interior of her home was coated with animal fur and smelled like a barn; birds flew in and out the doors; the counters and tabletops were chained with seat smears from her cats and sometimes the dogs. She brought a pair of goats, Okie and Dokie, into the living room to watch television with her. An industrial cleaning service burned out its machines trying to vacuum the rugs and couches. Her favorite song was "Me and Bobbie McGee."

That's the anecdotal story, the one that makes everyone smile. Her life was made forfeit by alcohol and Ambien and, when that wasn't enough, by sojourners who posed as friends and took from her every dollar they could.

AFTER THE OFFICER has left, I walk up the slope through the maple trees that are both yellow and aflame with the season and cross the veranda and go inside, the wind following me, the joists and walls creaking. In the hallway is a glass cabinet where I keep the guns I have collected since I was a boy, although I no longer shoot them. That does not mean they lack power over me. I like to touch the coldness of the steel and smell the gun oil in the dark grain of the wood. The same with the heft of the stock against my shoulder. The same with wrapping the sling around my left forearm and aiming through the peep sight of my M1. Sometimes I touch my guns and bite my lip in a salacious way and feel a tingle in my loins.

I drink a can of soda in the kitchen in one long chug without sitting down and throw it harder than I should into the trash. There are snow clouds above the Bitterroots, bristling with electricity, and I hear a sound like the rumbling of bowling pins.

Fannie Mae was buried with a solitary rose clutched in her

right hand, a framed photo of me and her two cats tucked face-out under her forearm. The surrounding hills were green and bare and beautiful as velvet. In the sunset I could see the Rattlesnake Mountains and wisps of red and purple clouds strung across a valley. I wanted to rope Fannie Mae's casket on my back and take the two of us deep into the wilderness and never return. I did not want condolences or handshakes or food or flowers brought to my house. Nor did I wish Fannie Mae's fellow dead binding her to the earth, robbing her of the life that should have been hers and maybe was still available for her, perhaps even for *us*.

Please don't think me mad. I have been among the dead. Legions of them. Their quilted uniforms pocked with machine-gun rounds, their faces bloodless and waxy under the trip flares swaying above them, their eyes eight-balled by a marching barrage of 105s. I will tell you what I have learned about the dead. They are not to be feared. In fact, they are sad creatures, and the silence in their faces begs for our pity, but sometimes I long to sleep among them, even those I killed.

I will not accept my daughter's death. I will find a way to pull her back through the veil or untether myself and lie down in the bottom of a boat that has no oars and float down the Columbia and into the Pacific, where she will be waiting for me somewhere beyond the sun.

I WAKE ON THE sofa in the morning, still dressed, and sit in the coldness of the dawn and try to catch my breath, as though I spent the night running uphill. I try not to have thoughts about my daughter's physical preparation for an open-casket viewing. I try not to think about the men who gang-raped her when she was nineteen, and the couple who more recently beat her outside a nightclub and went unpunished.

I drink a pot of coffee and eat an egg sandwich in the kitchen and think about the boy who vandalized my barn while two adults waited in the cab of the pickup truck.

Where had I seen the boy? The rural post office? A place where some of the recalcitrant and the unteachable refuse to wear masks no matter how many warning signs are posted by the employees? In fact, they take pleasure in tearing the warning signs off the glass doors.

Several of them live in a dip on a back road down in the Bitterroot Valley, among a tangle of half-dead trees and ancient outbuildings and dirt-floor garages too tight for contemporary vehicles, their houses eaten by carpenter ants, the lawns choked with dandelions and pieces of rusted cars and piles of moldy debris the garbage service will not pick up, the windows flapping with torn sheets of lead-colored plastic.

I was there last week, returning from a fishing trip, and saw a house in a grove of pine trees and a bare-chested young man shooting arrows at an upended hay bale, the muscles in his back knotting when he pulled back the bowstring, his face filled with delight when his arrow smacked the paper bull's-eye. I also remember a red truck in the yard.

I wash my dishes and dry my hands and thumb-pop the business card given me by the trooper. My telephone is on the kitchen counter. A column of light is shining on it through the window. But I do not call the trooper. Instead I drive into the Bitterroot Valley, a warning bell clanging and a red light flashing at the train crossing near my house, although no train has burnished the rails in years.

IT'S ALMOST TOO easy to find the kid who pissed in my cattle guard and shot me the bone, and I wonder if I am on the edge of making an irreversible mistake over a minuscule issue, the kind that haunts your days and steals your sleep for the rest of your life. The boy is trying to handsaw a broken tree limb that has crashed on the roof of a desiccated frame house and now lies wedged inside the shingles like a giant celery stalk. The red Ford F-150 is parked on the grass, the pocked hole in the rear window. I turn into the yard and get out of my Avalon.

"Hi," the boy says, looking down.

"Got a minute?" I reply.

"Yes, sir."

"I look familiar to you?"

He squints one eye and muses on the question. "No, sir, I don't think so."

"I own the barn you decorated."

"Decorate for Halloween or something?"

"You painted a swastika on the door. Why would you do that?"

He tugs on the bill of his olive-green cap; his eyes seem full of light, yet they're empty of thought. The rows in the corn-field next to the house look dry and unmaintained and hard as iron, and the stalks whisper when the wind gusts. "Got to get back to work. We had mighty high winds last night."

"I know," I say. "My barn door slammed all night. The one with the Nazi swastika on it."

A muscular man wearing a floppy wide-brimmed hat comes out on the porch and lets the door slam behind him. He lifts his chin, allowing the sunlight to expose his face, and I realize I'm looking at the man who was in the passenger seat of the Ford pickup that visited my house. The wood steps squeak under his weight; his hand slides down the rail as audibly as emery paper. He takes my measure, a faint smile on his mouth, like a man deciding whether he should peel a tangerine. "He'p you?"

"Is that your boy up there?" I ask.

"Was when I woke up this morning."

"Do you know why he would want to vandalize my barn?"

"I didn't catch that."

"Late yesterday evening. I think you were with him. Is that your pickup yonder? You were in the passenger seat."

I'm speaking too fast. I have no doubt I've borrowed trouble from the wrong man.

"I know who you are," he says. "You own that big ranch the Mormons used to own."

"That's correct."

"The Mormons are good people." He says it with a merry light in his eyes, and I'm reminded of many a confrontation where the accent was the same, the disingenuousness equally corrosive, the venomous suggestion on the tip of the tongue.

"You went right past me," I say.

He screws a cigarette in his mouth but doesn't light it. "Come down here, Leigh."

"What's your name, sir?" I say.

"John Fenimore Culpepper. My friends call me Johnny B. Goode. That's because I'm not too bad on the guitar." He smiles as though sharing a joke. His son climbs down the ladder and wipes his face on his sleeve, although the morning is too cool for him to be sweating.

"Tell this man what we was doing last night," the father says.

"Went to the men's-only Bible class."

"I said 'yesterday evening,' not 'last night,'" I say.

Leigh's cheeks are as red as apples, his eyes shiny from either fear or embarrassment. He looks at his father, unsure what he should say. "It's all right, boy," his father says. "Go in the house. Tell your mother she can start lunch."

"Yes, sir."

The father doesn't speak until he hears the screen door bang shut behind him. "You had your say. Now get moving."

"What have you got against me, Mr. Culpepper?"

He fishes a Zippo out of his slacks and lights his cigarette, taking his time, the flame whipping in the wind, singeing his cupped palms. He lets a wad of smoke the size of a cotton boll float from his mouth. "Who says I got anything against you?"

"I won't file charges if you'll promise to repaint my barn door. How about it, partner? Let's get this out of our headlights."

I can hear him breathing. "You ask me what I have against you? My boy has special needs. I had to sell off most of my acreage so he could get on Medicaid. Maybe that's the way it's supposed to be. But you got a fine ranch you probably bought with your credit card. Your Hollywood friends tell jokes about us on *Saturday Night Live*. That's why we don't like you. Does that seem unreasonable to you?"

"I'll be going, Mr. Culpepper. I hope all good things come to you."

"Talk down to me like that again, I'll take a switch to you, old man or not."

I feel my face twitch, as though a bottle fly has settled on it. I open and close my hand against my thigh. I try to look through him and not indicate any animus toward him. The phenomenon I'm experiencing has been with me for many years, and it leads me into blackouts and places I never want to visit again.

I step backward, my eyelids stitched to my brow. But my expression has no connection with the images in my head. A twig breaks under my boot. I hear a stream swollen with melting snow and roaring with torrents of water and eroded earth and pebbles and loosed stones and broken beaver dams and uprooted trees that cascade and bounce over boulders like pogo sticks. I experience these images because if I allow their symbolic representation to become real, I will commit deeds I cannot undo. The violence of the Hollands is well known, both to others and to them, often by gunshot. And all the thoughts I just described have occurred within five seconds.

"You look like you're fixing to do something both of us might regret," Culpepper says.

I cough into my palm. "I have a number of serious character defects, Mr. Culpepper."

"You have what?" he says, a fleck of his spittle striking my face.

"Holes in my memory, almost six years of them, but I don't drink. I was in a southern prison when I was eighteen. I wasn't a criminal, but I was genuinely insane. My greatest enemy is sleep. I see the men and boys I killed many years ago in a foreign land, and I'm filled with sorrow. Have you had those experiences, sir? Please tell me that is indeed the case and that you wish to get them out of your life. Can you do that for me, sir?"

Chapter Three

Four days later, on a cold Sunday morning, I drive up a long, steep-sided pass that opens onto the Flathead reservation and the Jocko River and mountain peaks that pierce the clouds and stay snowcapped year-round. The valley is elevated above Missoula, as though it were scooped out of the sky and created separate from the rest of the earth, a place where the moon and stars hang atop the hills even as the pinkness of the morning rises to meet them.

I fill my gas tank, the pump spout like a chunk of ice in my bare hand, my eyes watering in the wind, then I rumble across a wood bridge and follow a dirt road along the Jocko, the boulders steaming in the current, the gold leaves of the willows floating like fish eels on the riffles. The remoteness of the countryside, the sparsity of human structures, the absence of traffic and commerce, and the hush of the morning leave me in awe and make me wonder if the traces of Eden are not still with us.

I pull into a driveway and park in front of an old two-story house surrounded by birch trees, half of the house lit by the sun, the glass in the dormers as black as obsidian. A cruiser is parked in the barn, the front end pointed out. There are no other vehicles in sight, not even a tractor. My tap on the door sounds like a gunshot.

Ruby Spotted Horse opens the door, keeping the chain on, in a blue robe with a towel wrapped around her head.

"What are you doing on my porch?" she asks.

"I'd like to speak with you."

"Have you heard about calling someone before you go to their house, particularly early on Sunday morning? How'd you get my address?"

"I fish up here with the tribe lawyer."

"How convenient," she says. Her eyes have a purple tint, and I cannot tell if it is because of the shadows or because they are deeply recessed in her face. "Sir, you're staring at me."

"Sorry."

"Mr. Broussard, I respect you, but you shouldn't have done this."

"What if I come back in a few hours and take you to lunch?"

"This isn't about the swastika, is it?"

"Not directly." The grass in the lawn is brown and stiff with frost. I can smell a smokehouse and meat dripping into the ash. I hear bugles blowing and echoing out in the hills, sounds that are imaginary but which I never rid myself of. A fat tabby cat walks down the porch rail and jumps with a thud by my foot, then begins doing figure eights on my legs.

"A man named John Fenimore Culpepper threatened me," I say. "He also goes by the name Johnny B. Goode. I strung a tripwire full of aluminum cans around my house."

"So?"

"Montana is a stand-your-ground state."

Her jaw tightens. She takes off the chain. "Get in here, Mr. Broussard."

The living room wallpaper is water-stained and cracked, the design faded into extinction, the carpet threadbare. The couch and chairs look as though they have never been vacuumed. The woodwork in the trim and the staircase is probably mahogany or walnut and a hundred years old. A solitary light fixture hangs from the ceiling, the tiny yellow bulbs flickering inside the fluted shades.

"Why are you looking that way at my house?"

"I didn't know there was a Victorian home on the reservation. I've never noticed it."

"So now you know. Let's get back to the man who threatened you."

"I bear an animus toward people who preyed on my daughter, and I'd like to shorten their life span. So instead of doing that, I started thinking of ways to take out my anger on an ignorant man who probably forced his son to vandalize my barn."

She looks sideways, then back at me. "You're actually talking about capping someone? And you're telling this to a police officer in her home?"

"I guess that sums it up."

"One of us has a problem, Mr. Broussard. Either you're insane or I have shit for brains, meaning I just let you in my house."

"Goodbye," I say.

My shoes leave wet prints through the frost on the lawn as I walk toward my Toyota pickup. I bought it twenty years ago when I had far less money than I have now. Back then I lived a simpler life with my daughter, and now I would burn every dollar in my possession in order to get her back. The sun is yellow and cold above the hills, and snow is blowing off the peaks of the Mission Mountains. I feel a loneliness that is almost unbearable.

I pull open the driver's door of the truck, my hand dead to the cold of the handle, my stomach flopping for the fool I have made of myself.

"Come back, Mr. Broussard!" Ruby Spotted Horse calls from the porch.

I smile and shake my head.

"I was too hard on you! Please, Mr. Broussard. I don't want you on my conscience."

I retrace my steps and reenter the house. The cat goes inside with me, tail straight up, stiff as a broomstick.

"I need to get dressed," she says. "There's some muffins and coffee in the kitchen."

"That's very nice of you, Miss Ruby."

"You're from the South?"

"Why do you think that?"

"Your manners."

"Thank you, but the South is a state of mind rather than a place. Much of it is good, but much of it dark, thanks to our replication of original sin in the form of the Middle Passage. John Calvin and Cornelius Jansen spat in the punch bowl as well."

She seems to examine my words inside her head, then picks up the cat and drops him heavily in my arms. "Meet Maxwell Gato."

She goes upstairs and I go into the kitchen with the cat. Through the window I see lambs playing in a shed built on the side of an unpainted barn, stacks of baled hay, a swayback mare with a blind eye and skeletal ribs, a blue roan in a pen (part of the treatment for laminitis), a fawn without a mother at the stock tank, a cat with a pasty pink medicine smeared on a patch of mange, an Old English sheepdog, its eyes buried deep in its fur. I pour some dry cat food in a bowl for Maxwell

Gato. He crunches a few pieces, then jumps on the counter and stares out the window.

"Want to go outside with your pals?" I say. "Well, let's go out there and see what these fellows are up to."

I cradle Maxwell Gato in my arms again. I can hear him purring and feel his warmth against my chest. Then I start toward the back door. To my left is a stairwell that descends into the cellar. Maxwell Gato is tensing in my arms, trying to straighten his body, digging in wherever he can.

"What's wrong, Maxwell?" I say.

One claw almost takes off my right nipple; he tumbles on the floor, then bolts for the living room. I let him outside and watch him run past my truck into a field of unharvested pumpkins that resemble deflated basketballs. I return to the stairwell and the back entrance. I have no idea why the cat became so frightened. I click the stairwell light on and off. Nothing happens. In the gloom at the bottom of the steps I can make out a door and a steel U-shaped padlock hanging from the hasp.

I unconsciously touch my shirt where Maxwell Gato hooked me and realize I have dropped a gold ballpoint given to me by my daughter. I descend the stairs in the semi-darkness, one hand tight on the rail, feeling each step with the heel of my shoe. The air is cooler now and smells like a cave.

Something slams into the wood from the other side of the door, rattling and stressing the padlock, knocking dust into the air. After a pause, there's another blow against the door, this one even harder. The object on the other side of the door, one that is obviously mobile, has weight and density and a ferocious level of self-destructive energy and is driven by an intelligent source, one that may possess arms or legs or fingernails or claws, because I heard scraping sounds against the wood.

I go up the stairs two at a time, my heart pounding. Ruby Spotted Horse is at the top of the stairs. "What are you doing down there?" she says.

"The cat scratched me and I dropped my ballpoint."

She clicks the light switch up and down. "The bulb must have burned out. Come up here before you hurt yourself."

"What's in that cellar?"

"Preserves and canned goods. Why?"

"Something hit the door."

"Sometimes my fruit jars blow up." She motions for me to keep coming up the stairs. "Those steps are not reliable. You're about to give me a heart attack."

She's wearing jeans and a cowboy shirt unsnapped at the top; her hair is damp and uncombed, the towel gone. I know she is lying about the cellar and that she heard the same sounds I did, which caused her to hurry to the back of the house.

"Did you hear me, Mr. Broussard?"

I reach the top of the stairwell, breathing as evenly as I can, the floor solid under my feet, the rectangular world of predictability at the ends of my fingers. "I know what I heard and what I saw, Miss Ruby."

"I think you're a little confused."

"That's not flattering."

"Then I don't know what to tell you."

"How about the truth?"

She chews her lip. "I can't believe I'm doing this. Okay, wait here. I'll get a flashlight. I'll also try to find the key to the padlock. I misplaced it a couple of days ago. If I can't find it, I'll bring a crowbar, and we'll rip off the hasp and break anything else of your choosing."

"I'm sorry to make trouble for you," I say.

"For a few minutes, can you just say nothing at all?"

She goes into the kitchen, and I hear her opening and shutting drawers and cabinets. A phone rings, and she begins talking and walking deeper inside the house. I hear her footsteps coming back toward the brief hallway that leads to the cellar stairs. "You still there?" she says.

"Take your time," I reply.

She walks away again. Finally she returns with a flashlight and a key. The key is threaded onto a long ribbon of gingham tied in a loop, and I wonder how anyone could lose it.

"Excuse the delay," she says. "That was my ex. If you have a telephone pole up your ass and want to drop the hammer on a genuine sack of dog turds, let me give you his address. Oh, I forgot. You're tied up with a swastika on your barn door.

"Anyway, we need to get your ballpoint. You also have blood on your shirt. We need to get that fixed, too. Now get behind me. This is still my house."

Chapter Four

A T THE BOTTOM of the stairs she picks up my ballpoint and drops it in my shirt pocket. "Okay, we've got that out of the way. Here, hold the flashlight."

She inserts the key in the padlock and twists slowly until the shank pops free from the locking mechanism. She takes the flashlight from my hand, then pushes the door back on its hinges and shines the light inside. The interior is more than simply a cellar. The floor is concrete, the walls an aggregate of subterranean boulders filled in with hand-stacked stones taken from a riverbed. The air is cool and dry, the way cave air is, like a reminder of a pre–industrial age or maybe a monastic wine cellar. The flashlight beam dances on shelves lined with preserve jars.

"Where's the light switch?" I ask.

"On the back wall."

"I'd like to turn it on."

"Enough is enough, Mr. Broussard."

"What do you mean?"

"Look on the floor. I think that's what you heard."

She points the flashlight between two rows of shelves. Three piles of broken glass mixed with a green-and-red mess twinkle in the flashlight's beam. "Tomatoes," she says.

"I have a hard time buying that."

"Well, I'm sorry."

I do not want to give it up. But my life is not a study in rationality. I have another problem. I do not enjoy my role as an old man in a nation that has little use for antiquity and even less for those who value it. I touch the surface of the cellar door. It is three inches thick and made of oak and rusted metal plates and iron spikes, the kind of door Vikings broke their axes on.

"This could have come out of the castle," I say.

"Ready to go?" she says.

Accidentally the beam of her flashlight bounces off a piece of hand-carved blond wood into which a deep-brown glass eye has been inserted.

"What's that in the corner?"

"My niece's rocking horse."

"She plays down here?"

"She died a few years ago."

"I see."

"I have to go, Mr. Broussard. I'll put a Band-Aid on that scratch before you leave, okay?"

Just before she clicks off the flashlight, the beam lights up a page of tightly folded yellow notepaper on the concrete. I can see threads of green ink on the paper, the strokes as thin as a cat's whisker. I pretend to sneeze and take my handkerchief from my pocket, then drop it. When I pick it up, I scoop the notepaper inside it. Before we go, Ruby Spotted Horse locks the cellar door, her face thoughtful. "The Culpepper man you mentioned earlier? He's on a list at the Southern Poverty Law Center. The FBI knows him, too."

"Culpepper is a terrorist?"

"An imperial wizard in Alabama. I don't know if he's active now. Let's get some peroxide and bacitracin on you."

She had brought up Culpepper out of nowhere and just as quickly and mysteriously dropped the subject. I follow her up the stairs. "I'll skip the first aid, Miss Ruby. How about dinner sometime?"

She walks ahead of me into the kitchen, glancing over her shoulder as though making sure I'm with her. I wait for her to speak, but she doesn't.

"Do you eat dinner with old people?" I ask.

"Sure, give me a call."

"One more thing?"

"Oh, boy," she replies.

"I'm still deeply disturbed about that cellar."

"Then I don't know what to say," she says. "Steamed vegetables and fruit packed in airtight glass jars can explode as loudly as an M-80. You saw the mess on the floor. How about giving it a rest?"

"I saw dust fly off the door."

"All right, you asked for it. This is the res. Things happen here that don't happen in other places. The same on the Marias River and at the Big Hole and the Custer battlefield. Don't question the power of the dead, Mr. Broussard."

"You're saying you have spirits in your house?"

"Look for them and you'll find them. Don't look for them and you won't."

Her thick dark hair is prematurely gray in places, her eyes mysterious, her petite stature and full bosom the kind that causes a mixed form of desire that men seldom untangle.

"Why do you keep looking at me like that?" she says.

"I don't want to give you any grief. I'll say goodbye now."

"Listen, my great-grandfather was Nez Perce and at the Big Hole. My great-grandmother was Blackfeet and killed at the Baker Massacre. I get the feeling you think you have the right to invade my privacy because you sympathize with Indians. If that's so, lose the attitude right now."

"You got it," I say. "I love your cat."

I walk back to my truck and drive along the side of the Jocko, the spray on the boulders iridescent in the sunshine, the waterfalls high up on the Missions frozen like the teeth of animals. A moose with a huge rack is grazing in a grove of cottonwoods, the ground wet and green and shining. I try to take solace in the beauty of the day and the time on earth that I shared with my daughter, Fannie Mae. I think of her every day, over and over, and pray that she is with me and that one day she will contact me in an undeniable fashion and tell me that's she safe from all the evil.

I almost forget the folded page of yellow notebook paper I picked up from the cellar floor. Could it be from Fannie Mae? Why can't I receive a sign today rather than in the future? I hold the steering wheel with one hand and unfold the note-paper with my thumb and read the words that are written in a frail hand, perhaps by a child, perhaps by an elderly person: *Help me. Please. I don't want to die.*

Chapter Five

THAT NIGHT I SIT alone in the darkness of my kitchen and try to think my way out of the situation I have stumbled into. No, "stumble" is not the word. I'm the creator of my troubles, and I entered into them with enthusiasm and forethought. I confronted an ignorant and probably dangerous man and took the consequences to a woman who, to all appearances, cares for abused and neglected animals. Now I must decide if I should keep silent about my experience when I neared her cellar door. Even more distressing, what should I do about the plea on the notebook paper? The childlike penmanship belongs to someone very young or frail or very old. To deny that person help could blacken my soul forever, and I mean *forever*. The message is so simple and earnest that I cannot get its plaintive desperation out of my head. But must I report Ruby Spotted Horse to her superiors—the same police officer who gave me her phone number because she worried about my safety?

Had not her people paid enough dues? She said her ancestors had been at the attack on the Nez Perce at the Big Hole and at the Baker Massacre on the Marias, two of the cruelest and most unwarranted examples of inhumanity in our national history. In January 1870, a drunkard named Major Eugene Baker attacked a sleeping village of innocent Blackfeet in subzero weather. The soldiers slew them without mercy, and the ones they slew in largest numbers were women and children. The suffering and misery imposed on the survivors has no equal in the Plains Wars. They were driven into freezing water, their wickiups and clothes and food burned. That afternoon, prisoners who tried to escape were chopped to death with axes to ensure the others did not attempt the same. Others had to find their way in arctic conditions to Fort Benton, seventy-five miles from the massacre site. When it came to fighting the Indians, General Sheridan had formally instructed Baker to "hit them hard." Baker was hailed as a hero and never charged for his crimes or the sadistic and mindless way in which he committed them. Is it surprising that Hitler made use of our racial attitudes in support of his own in *Mein Kampf*?

Chief Joseph was one of the most gentle and spiritual people among the Indian nations, to say nothing of his moral superiority to the politicians and land-grabbers who promoted the extinction of the buffalo herds in order to starve the Indians onto the reservations. Joseph's only crime was his desire to take his people into Canada—called "Grandmother's Land" by the Indians—and live close by Sitting Bull and the Sioux, who had fled the country after the Battle of the Little Bighorn.

The Nez Perce fought a running battle of eleven hundred miles across Washington State and Idaho and into Montana and outwitted the army at Lolo Pass and, in the dark, filed across the land my house is built on, the women carrying their babies on their backs, the wounded and the sick dragged by travois and Appaloosa ponies. Then they entered the wide magnificence of the Bitterroot Valley and, for the first time since they left Washington, began to feel they had eluded the army or, better yet, the army had tired of them and given up. They even bought clothes and supplies from the white traders in the valley without incident. Perhaps the warm late-summer haze on the meadows and the silence in the hills were signs that the war's ferocity had burned itself out.

They headed for the Big Hole, a high-country paradise of rolling foothills and meadows filled with game and arroyos strung with fir trees where they could hunt grouse. The countryside seemed magical. The mountains in the distance were capped with snow and turned as red as a jewel in the sunset, and the riffles in the Big Hole River so cold among the rocks that the broad lateral stripe on the rainbow trout was a brilliant purple.

At dawn on August 9, 1877, General Gibbon's men waded quietly through the fog on the river and, once on dry ground, formed into squads and knelt on one knee as though about to pray. But the white man's most favored prayer was a gun, in this instance a single-shot trapdoor .45–70 Springfield rifle. The Springfields were heavy and cumbersome and had been converted by the army from Civil War muskets to save money, and they did not have the rapidity of fire that the Henry did. But on the perimeter of an unsuspecting people wrapped in warm dreams, they would do just fine.

In unison the soldiers fired three volleys blindly into the wickiups. The effect was devastating. Women clutching as many children as they could ran for the cover of downed cottonwoods or dunes along the riverbank or a gap in the rocks above. The slaughter was on, aided by a howitzer. The braves stood and fought, and the women and children ran. And ran. And ran. The oddity was their silence. They were obviously terrified, but they fled in groups like desperate shadows on a rock wall, without sound, as though they already knew their fate because they had already lived it. They ran anyway, until they were shot down and their children thrown wide-eyed from their grasp, the .45–70 rounds whining into the distance.

These thoughts and images do not give me rest. I know they are associated with depression. I pace my living room floor. I want to drink, and I think about women, and I think about death and wonder if it isn't a better choice than the life that has become mine. I speak out loud to Fannie Mae. When I hear no response, I ball my fists until my nails cut my palms. The moon is high above the Bitterroots and streaks the yard with shadow and paints the veranda the color of tarnished pewter. I can see the aluminum cans in which I poured pebbles out of my palm and strung through the trees three inches above the ground. They might tinkle when the wind blows or a rabbit crosses the yard, but I know the difference between the innocent work of the wind and animals and an ankle or a boot catching on the wire and rattling cans all over the yard. When the latter does not happen, I'm disappointed and at the same time feel shame for the secret fires that have been with me since Pork Chop Hill. A car passes on the highway, probably a late-Sunday-night drinker on his way down to Ravalli County, where the saloons and casinos stay open until two and no one worries about distancing or masks.

Where are you, Fannie Mae? Why are you not with me in my darkest hour?

I unlock my gun cabinet and remove my M1 and push back the bolt with the heel of my hand and, with my thumb, press an eight-round clip into the magazine, then remove my thumb quickly so it doesn't get caught when the bolt snaps shut. I try to convince myself that my behavior is thespian. True, I hate the violent history of the Holland family, and I hate the martial mentality of those who love wars but never go to them. Why am I arming my M1? I fit the front sight under my upper teeth and touch the roof of my mouth; I can taste and smell the oil and the coldness of the steel. My heart is beating, my thumb on the trigger. *Oh, God, don't let me do this.*

I pull the barrel from my mouth and prop the M1 against the divan and call a friend in the Missoula Sheriff's Office named Jeremiah McNally. He's in his late thirties, educated, taciturn, unmarried, handsome, genteel, a former DEA agent, although no one knows why he gave up his position. He wears a suit wherever he goes and doesn't use profanity and plays bingo at a Catholic church.

I ask him to meet me tomorrow at a café near the courthouse.

There's a pause. "What's going on?" he says.

Before I can reply, I hear a woman's voice speak in my left ear: *Don't tell him.* I not only hear the voice, I also feel it, like the tickle of a feather against my skin. I look around me and open and close my mouth to clear my hearing. "It's about meth on the res," I say.

"Small creatures with no eyes are living in my in-basket," Jeremiah replies. "Can you just tell me what the problem is?"

"Not over the phone."

The wind buffets the house, and a pinecone pings on the roof of the veranda and bounces into the yard. *Tell Jeremiah he's the only friend you have in the courthouse*, the female voice says, and this time I have no doubt whose voice it is. My mouth is dry, my windpipe like a hose someone just stepped on.

"Are you all right?" Jeremiah says.

"Sure," I lie. "I need to see you. In person."

"The CIA has a tap on your phone?"

"You're my only friend in the courthouse."

That one works. "Okay, ten o'clock at the café across from the courthouse," he says. "Who's that with you?"

"No one."

"Really?"

"You actually think you heard someone?" I ask.

Chapter Six

IT'S MONDAY MORNING, and the crowd at the café is thinner than I have ever seen it. The pandemic is taking its toll in many ways. In rural areas all over Montana, a majority have refused to practice respiratory protection. Many of the quarter million bikers traveling to and from the Sturgis Motorcycle Rally left their fluids and fouled air for us to deal with.

Down the street, kids in Black Lives Matter T-shirts and masks are singing "We Shall Overcome." Twenty yards away, a counter-group wearing red MAGA hats has gathered around a flatbed truck flying the Stars and Stripes and blue-and-white Trump flags. Individuals from each group stray to the other and chat or shake hands. This is Missoula. The year is still 1968 and the flower children are everywhere. The symbol most associated with the city is the peace sign that overlooks the downtown area and the university campus. Jeannette Rankin, the first woman to hold federal office, and Elizabeth Gurley Flynn, the sweetheart of the IWW, are patron saints. When Donald Trump came to town during the 2020 campaign, the word "liar" was spelled out in large white letters on the side of the mountain behind the university so the president could have a good view from Air Force One.

In front of a pawnshop across the street from the court-house is a different kind of group. They have long rifles. At least one is carrying an AR-15. Jeremiah and I are sitting by the café window with a view of Broadway and the daily traffic and the Doughboy statue on the courthouse lawn, one hand hefting his '03 Springfield with the bayonet fixed, the other hand frozen above his head, bringing up his squad, men who may have disappeared inside clouds of mustard gas over a century ago. I think of my father, who went over the top at both the Marne and the Somme.

It's a bluebird day, the kind that shouldn't go wrong, the kind you want to lock in a safe as proof that the earth abideth forever. The boy with the AR-15 has his back to me; he's tall and wears a camouflage jacket and half-top boots and a flop hat; his hair hangs over his ears. A thirty-round magazine juts from the well of his weapon. With a bump stock, he could spray down dozens in under one minute.

Jeremiah and I order, then he follows my line of sight. "We're watching them," he says.

"Watching whom?"

"The Second Amendment crowd."

"They're not out there about the Second Amendment, Jeremiah," I say. "They're there to menace and intimidate."

"How do you prove it?" he replies. His hair is dark, freshly clipped, lightly oiled, his skin without blemish. His features make me think of a 1930s leading man. He's wearing a cheap suit with a checkered shirt and a navy blue tie. He looks more scholar than cop, more outlier than joiner. His eyes brighten in the hope that I won't comment anymore on the latitude given to people who belong on an ice floe south of the Aleutians. "What did you want to tell me?" he asks.

"Know a state trooper named Ruby Spotted Horse?"

His eyes are flat. "Lives on the res? Yeah, she got some ink about three years ago."

"For what?"

"Shot and killed a guy at a rest stop on I-90. He'd busted out of a holding cell in Washington. He raped and murdered two children."

Since Fannie Mae's death, every coarse or cruel word or image I hear or see is a serpent that curls around my heart and then slithers away and goes to work on another organ, all of this before I can process what I've seen or heard. "Give me the short version, okay?"

"She smoked him in the dark," he says. "No witnesses. She thought he had a gun. He didn't. She popped him four or five times. It looked like a bad shoot to me. But she didn't use a throw-down, so that was on her side. You didn't read about it?"

"Fannie Mae developed seizures about three years back. Her feet curled up like claws. I didn't pay much attention to local news for a while."

I just became the martyr with his tragedy on his sleeve. I've done it before. Why? To get even with the world.

The waitress puts plates of waffles and scrambled eggs and hash browns and bacon for Jeremiah in front of us. She's stout and in her late thirties and has pale red hair with streaks of blond in it. She leans across the table to put a fresh ketchup bottle with the salt and pepper and hot sauce; her hip brushes against Jeremiah's shoulder. "You guys need anything else?"

"We're fine, Betty," Jeremiah says.

"Just holler," she says, and winks.

"Go ahead," he says to me, although his eyes are on the waitress's rump.

"I got into a situation with a man named John Fenimore

Culpepper. He had his son paint a swastika on my barn door. I should have let it go. Instead I went to Culpepper's house. Ruby Spotted Horse had been the responding officer when I made the 911 call because of the swastika. So I went to her home yesterday morning to tell her I had shown bad judgment."

Jeremiah's eyes are veiled. He drenches his waffles with maple syrup and parks a fork-load in his mouth. "That was the only reason you went there?"

"Sunday is a bad day to be alone," I reply.

He tries to smile and is probably embarrassed by my candor. "I know what you mean," he says. "But I'm kind of lost here. What can I do to help?"

I can't concentrate. Someone is shouting through a megaphone. The Trumpers, the BLMs, and the people with guns are looking down the alley on a side street. Two uniformed policemen are running through the traffic toward the alley. Jeremiah drops the blind on the window glass and says, "Forget those guys. What happened at the res?"

I tell him everything: the incongruity and Gothic ambience of Ruby Spotted Horse's nineteenth-century home, her care of injured or neglected animals, the field of pumpkins left to rot when her neighbors could probably use the food, the lock on a cellar that supposedly contained only preserves, the huge object that thudded twice into the door like the heavy bag in a boxing gym, worse, the scraping of claws, her disingenuous explanation about preserve jars exploding.

"You searched the cellar?" Jeremiah says.

"No, the light switch was in the back."

"There was no sign of anyone in the room?"

"Not that I saw."

"I'd just blow it off," he says.

"Blow it off? Whatever hit the door must have weighed over two hundred pounds. It knocked dust in my face."

"Did you talk to the tribal police?"

"I don't want the lady to look bad in front of her people."

He squeezes his temples. "I don't know what to say. Maybe she keeps a crazy relative down there."

"One that has claws?"

"Look, Aaron, there are times in our lives when we shouldn't trust our senses. Maybe this is one of them."

"Say again?"

"It's just a thought."

I try to control my feelings. People of my generation have few confidants, because there are fewer and fewer people who understand the America we grew up in. Most would not recognize the names that to us were as important as Bunker Hill. I carried my best friend down a trench in a place called Pork Chop Hill and dropped him when a 105 burst ten yards from me. My friend may have ended up a lab rat north of the Yalu. The Communists transported four hundred POWs with them into China, perhaps even into Russia, for use in medical experiments. I will never find out the fate of my friend, and thinking about it is for me a perfect hell.

I stick two fingers in my shirt pocket and remove the folded piece of yellow notepaper I picked up from Ruby Spotted Horse's cellar floor. I unfold it and press it flat on the table and slide it toward him. I can see the ink and the wispy penmanship clearly on the yellow paper and almost hear the voice of the poor soul who wrote the message. "I took this from the cellar."

"What is it?"

"Read it."

He glances at the page. Then picks it up and turns it over. "What's going on here, Aaron?"

"What's going on? Someone's life is in peril."

"There's nothing on this paper."

"Cut it out."

"Look for yourself."

"I don't have to."

He lets out his breath slowly. He looks at the waitress, and I know he wants to be with her and not me. Or with anyone except me. "I think you need to rest, Aaron."

"Look me straight in the face and tell me again there's nothing on that paper."

He makes a sucking sound with his teeth. A crowd has formed by the alley. A thin Black kid with gold-peroxided hair is sitting on a bicycle, talking to the cops. Three white kids have taken the position against a brick wall inside the alley, leaning on their arms, their feet spread, all of them in tight, dirty jeans and biker boots, a cop shaking them down. One of the kids is the boy who was carrying the AR-15, although he is not carrying it now. He's also the same kid who painted the swastika on my barn door.

I get up from the table and refold the notepaper and return it to my shirt pocket. I remove a crisp bill from my wallet and lay it on the tablecloth. "You think Jackson's face should be taken off the twenty-dollar bill?"

"Haven't given it much thought."

"You ought to. The Indians were his loyalest allies. He betrayed them and put them on the Trail of Tears. On the way to Oklahoma, they were raped, starved, and murdered."

"Sit down, Aaron. We'll work this out. What would Fannie Mae want you to do?"

"Don't you or your colleagues use her name."

I feel naked, as in a dream. The sounds in the room slow to a crawl, then drain through the floor. The people at the tables are frozen in place and stopped in midspeech. Our waitress gives me the blank look of a mannequin, her face distorted, her tray about to spill. Jeremiah has also become painted on the air. I leave the room hurriedly, bouncing against chairs that seem bolted to the floor.

OUTSIDE, THE WORLD shifts back into overdrive, cacophonous, blaring, the sun eye-watering bright. The BLM kids are play-acting a giant arrest, lying facedown on the sidewalk and the courthouse lawn, their wrists crossed behind them as though cuffed. The situation at the alley is winding down. The Black kid on the bike says the three white kids stopped him and demanded he show them identification. He also says they accused him of carrying a gun and being a member of Antifa. He didn't have a gun and claims he has lived in Missoula since he was four months old. He's obviously frightened.

The cops give citations to the three white kids, who walk away grinning at one another. In the background I see John Fenimore Culpepper, Leigh's father, coming fast across the courthouse lawn, his face as tight as a drumhead. I'm sure he's on a collision course with me. I start to raise my hand in caution. He goes right past me and grabs his son's arm so hard I think he's going to lift him in the air and shake the teeth out of his head.

"What'd you do, boy?" he asks.

"Nothing, Daddy."

"Where's your rifle?"

"Locked in the truck."

"Why'd you single out the boy on the bike?"

"He's a nigger. I thought—"

The father slaps him so hard that spittle flies from the boy's mouth. "You don't use that word. Not now, not ever. Who are those boys with you?"

"Guys from school."

"They use that kind of language?"

"I didn't mean nothing, Daddy."

Culpepper's face is filled with conflict, like that of a man who knows his best efforts in life will never be enough. "I understand, son. But there's other ways. Don't be ganging up on the colored boy. That ain't our way."

A towering uniformed policeman walks up, his shoulders huge, the back of his neck pocked with scars that look like they were burned into his skin. He removes his shades, his expression amiable. "Everything all right?"

"This here is family business," Culpepper says.

The policeman gazes at the street. "When you hit people, it becomes my business."

"Yessir," Culpepper says.

"Have a good day," the police officer says, and walks away. Culpepper's nostrils are white around the rims, his breath audible. His eyes remain fastened on the policeman's back, his jawbone flexing. Then he notices me. "You mixed up in this?"

"No."

"Then why are you here?"

"Good question," I say. "Mr. Culpepper, you correct your boy for using racist language and bullying a Black kid, but you sic him on me. Can you explain that?"

"It's your kind that cause the trouble."

"I'm glad you cleared that up."

"I'll send a painter out to your house, Mr. Broussard. Now let us be."

But I can't, and he knows it just as I do. An aberrant social contract in America was created when the first British ships set sail with their cargo of slaves packed like spoons belowdecks, a repository of bilge and rotted rations and the stench of sweat and feces and corpses and stillborn infants and raped women who killed themselves by chewing open their veins. My ancestors, an elite group, profited from those ships. Culpepper's Cockney ancestors did the dirty work. They threw their souls over the gunwales, along with the corpses they pulled with ropes out of the hold every morning, and later were the custodians of the whip and the branding iron in the sugarcane fields where I grew up, and forever after were taught by the oligarchy that Black people were their enemy, lustful, subhuman, idle, and mendacious, respondent only to the pillory: the only human beings lower than themselves and, at the same time, the only creatures over whom they could have total power, and none of that has changed, no matter what we tell ourselves.

"You got something to say?" Culpepper asks.

"I'd like for you to look at a piece of paper for me."

"*What?*"

"Look at this piece of paper. Tell me what's on it."

"Did you get loose from a crazy house?"

"Just tell me. I'll leave you alone."

He takes the notepaper from my hand, drops his eyes, then stares into my face, barely able to contain his anger.

"What's wrong, Mr. Culpepper?"

"I know the devil's work when I see it. Take it." He tries to hand me the notepaper.

"What did you see?" I ask.

He throws the notepaper at me. A gust of wind blows it end over end across the courthouse lawn and into the street. I run after it, but it's sucked under a truck and disappears. Culpepper has cupped his hand around his son's arm and is walking him as fast as he can down Broadway. I go after him, bumping against people on the sidewalk. Culpepper turns around, his mouth twisted, the gaps between his teeth exposed. "I got a knife," he says.

I raise my hands in surrender, then see Jeremiah McNally watching from across the street, his face sad, as though a dear friend has departed from his life.

Chapter Seven

IT'S STILL MONDAY. The moon is up, white and cold and ringed with vapor, the current of the Bitterroot lit by its reflection and running hard, the middle of the river bladed with small waves. I take a 1911-model army .45 from my gun cabinet and slip an eight-round magazine in the handle, push it into the back of my belt, and walk along the riverbank and then through the cottonwoods whose leaves are above my ankles.

I have beseeched Fannie Mae to contact me. She died in a strange fashion. She was finally clean and sober. Her anti-seizure meds were working; she was looking forward to another trip to Hollywood, where she had negotiated a film adaptation of my work, now in production. The heart attack seemed to come out of nowhere. She was watching television in bed and eating cherries from a bowl on her night table. Her death was probably instantaneous, although she bit her lip severely and bled heavily on the bedclothes. Three days later, when the medics broke into the house, she still had a cherry stem between her thumb and two fingers. Since then I have believed this was Fannie's way of telling us she did not suffer.

The day after her funeral, I found a cherry stem on the stairs in my house. I had no cherries in the house and could not re-member when I had bought any. Other peculiar phenomena began to happen. Fannie Mae used to make what I called "ani-mal safety tours" around the ranch. She hand-molded chicken wire around the edges of my three stock tanks so gophers and chipmunks could climb out of the tanks if they fell in. She also made sure all empty buckets or feed tubs were turned upside down so no small animal could get in and die of starvation. One night recently an electrical storm flashed its way down Lolo Pass and blew one of my barns apart and brought down a ponderosa on my brooder house. Poultry feathers, horse tack, buckets, split feed sacks, and Fannie's tub of alfalfa treats for the horses were scattered everywhere. I looked at the wreckage through my bedroom window and promised myself I would start a cleanup by nine and went back to sleep.

I woke to a dripping dawn and a barnyard that had been cleaned and cleared of any hazard to the animals. There were no footprints in the mud. The alfalfa treats had been put in a gunnysack and hung from a peg inside the barn. The stock tank was filled to the brim, the water as clear as high-country snowmelt, the surface ringed with raindrops. Chicken wire taken from a new roll was snugged around the sides of the tanks with clips and plastic ties.

As I stood in the midst of the barnyard, the horses and sheep motionless inside the mist, I knew that Fannie Mae was perhaps no more than twenty feet away. I called out her name again and again, but there was no reply.

Now I walk up the slope through ponderosa and fir trees whose elongated shadows resemble shaggy animals stretched out on the ground. On this same slope I have found frac-tured chert that was probably the detritus of Nez Perce work mounds. I have also found traces of mercury where members of the Lewis and Clark party almost certainly urinated, tattooing their venereal disease and its primitive curative into the soil. In the middle of the night, out in the trees, I have seen entities that glow like phosphorus and are humped like bears, but they are neither bears nor monsters. I believe they are part of Chief Joseph's people trying to escape the army, the women and infants wrapped in the fur of animals, the pain and passion of their struggle no less an agony than the path up Golgotha.

At the top of the slope is a spring that usually dries out in the summer. But this year has been a wet one, free of forest fires, at least around here, and water is swelling like liquid silver out of the ground, pooling over the rocks that Fannie Mae stacked in a circle when she was a little girl, which is why I named this place "Fannie Mae's Little Altar."

The fog is blue and hangs in the trees and puffs along the ground, and inside it I can see the gnarled horns and glassy brown eyes and wet noses of the deer who come here to drink. The air is heavy with the smells of pine needles and mushrooms and lichen on the rocks and fallen trees that have rotted and been reduced by worms to the weight of balsa wood.

I stand by the spring and toss a pinecone up the hill and watch it roll back down. "Fannie Mae?" I say.

There's no answer.

"It's your old man, and he's in a mess of trouble."

No response.

"Don't be like this, Fannie Mae. Give me a sign."

The wind is not a good companion. It courses through the canopy and sprinkles my hat with droplets of water that run down inside my long underwear. "It's not right to leave me in the lurch."

Fannie Mae invented stubbornness. If you tried to influence her behavior, she would make a religion out of doing the opposite.

"I know you're out there. You left the cherry stem on the

stairs, and you cleaned up the barn and the yard after the storm. I know it was you."

In truth, I *don't* know that it was Fannie Mae. It could have been a neighbor. A local religious group is constantly doing anonymous good deeds for others, paying checks in restaurants and even at the Lolo Dairy Queen, whether the recipients like it or not.

The fog is thicker and grayer now and clings to my skin like moist rags, reminding me of my childhood home in the bayou country of southern Louisiana. I remove the .45 from my belt and stick it in my boot, and sit on the boulder by the spring and feel the coldness of the stone seep through my trousers. In moments like these I cannot separate reality from madness, and in my sickness I often reach out to dead members of my family. It is not a good way to be.

My father always referred to death as the Great Veil. He believed you could put your hand through it and touch not only the dead but the unborn; he also believed that all events occur simultaneously rather than sequentially. As a boy, he had seen Confederate soldiers in the early-morning fog on Spanish Lake, outside New Iberia, and Saxon warriors in a cloud above the German fortifications on the Somme. But if these visions were real, why has my father not tried to contact me, or appeared in a dream, or simply whispered, *Keep a brave heart*? I have no answer. And I feel myself teetering on the edge of despair.

Then I hear the voice: *Why did you bring the .45, Pops?*

I feel like an icicle has just been driven through my chest.

You're not thinking about doing the Big Exit, are you?

"You knocked the breath out of me, kiddo. Where are you?"

Up here, in the tree. She drops to the ground. She's wearing jeans and sandals and a faded Mike the Tiger LSU T-shirt I gave her, and she looks like she did just before she died, which was always youthful.

"Aren't you cold?" I ask.

I'm not the problem, Pops. Answer my question. What's with the gun?

"I thought you might need it."

You're still the worst liar on the planet.

I tell her about the Indian trooper and the possibility of a prisoner in her cellar, and about the note I took from the cellar on which Jeremiah McNally denied seeing anything but which enraged an unlettered, violent former Klansman who called it the devil's work. "Why could he see the writing but not Jeremiah?" I ask.

We're not all from the same tree. There's more than one gene pool. Some of them got pissed in.

"Who told you that?"

It's common knowledge on this side of things. Your father is here. He's been here since you were eighteen.

"What?"

He's a real gentleman.

"Why doesn't my father give me a sign he's all right?"

He thinks he let you down. The drinking and whatnot.

"He shouldn't feel that way."

You got it turned around, Pops. He feels that way because you haven't forgiven him.

"That hurts, kiddo."

Quit it with the names. I've got to run.

"Come down to the house."

I don't make the rules.

"Did you suffer?"

I was afraid. Then I saw your cousin Weldon and I was all right. He said to tell you hello.

I lose control. Weldon was my first cousin, but I thought of him as my big brother. He was at the liberation of Dachau and came home with the Silver Star, two Bronze Stars, and three

Purple Hearts. I stumble and almost fall and grope behind me until I can steady myself on a boulder.

Don't cry, Pops. We're happy here.

"What's it like?"

A green valley. There's animals grazing in it and a rainbow overhead and wildflowers on the hillsides.

"Stay just a little longer."

Don't fret, Pops. You were always my best friend. You never let your little girl down.

My knees buckle, then I try to enter the fog with her. Instantly I feel like I have been dipped in ice water. The fog rises into the canopy and is burned into a thousand droplets by the sun. Fannie Mae is gone, and I feel as though she has died a second and third and fourth time. I walk downhill with the abandon of a drunk, my heart thudding, my coat and shirt ripped on a tree, my rib cage gashed by a broken tree limb, a scream rising from my throat, my hands raised at the sky. "Why have you done this to me?" I shout. "Why? Why? Why?"

I cross the barnyard and the veranda and crash through the door and into the living room. I see my reflection in the glass on the gun cabinet. My head could as well have been severed and placed on a tray. My eyes are out of focus. I smash my reflection with my forehead and watch my expression shatter in shards on the stocks of the rifles lined erect in the cabinet.

But a greater pain is that I cannot undo the loss of my daughter, and the greatest pain is that it didn't have to happen. It didn't have to happen. It didn't have to happen.

How do you live with it, family and friends ask. The answer is I don't. When you lose your kid, the best you can hope for is a scar rather than an open wound. I feel I'm in a house of mirrors, and I want to break every one of them.

Chapter Eight

I's THREE P.M. Tuesday. I'm in Pablo, Montana, pulling into the Flathead Tribal Police headquarters way up on the res, almost to Flathead Lake. The vastness of the country, the enormity of the Mission Mountains, is literally breathtaking. The ranches, particularly the old ones with giant slat barns, seem miniaturized and clinging to the earth.

I called earlier and told the dispatcher I wanted to make an appointment and report an event that occurred at the home of a resident on the Flathead Reservation. It was not an easy call to make.

"What kind of event?" the dispatcher asked.

"One that might involve a kidnapping. Or worse."

"What's the name of the resident?"

"Ruby Spotted Horse."

"She's a state trooper," the dispatcher said.

"That's why I'm troubled."

"Well, you sure came to the right place."

His comment sounded strange. I would soon find out why. I introduce myself to an officer at the counter by the entrance of the building. He points at a uniformed officer at a desk in the corner. "That's Ray Bronson," he says. "He'll be glad to take care of you."

I walk to Bronson's desk. He's drinking coffee and looking out the window either at the mountains or two young women who have parked their camper in the police parking lot and are photographing a pasture with llamas and horses in it. The wind is up, flattening the long stretches of yellow and brown grass, blowing the young women's hair back in their faces.

"I'm Aaron Holland Broussard," I say. "Do you know Trooper Spotted Horse?"

"I should," he says. "Have a seat. You want some coffee?"

"No, thank you."

He has brown hair and a narrow face and the biggest, most unnaturally white teeth I have ever seen. "Ruby's in trouble of some kind?"

I don't know where to begin. "I was at her house Sunday morning. I think somebody was locked in her cellar."

"It doesn't surprise me."

"Sir?"

"She's a little crazy. Was it a guy down there?"

"I don't know."

"You didn't see anyone?"

"No, but I—"

"You heard the person?"

"Yes. I also found a note on the floor. The person who wrote it was begging for help."

"The note was on the floor of the cellar?"

"Correct." I notice a strange mannerism in him. His gaze is invasive, as though others are public property.

"You were inside the cellar, but you didn't see anyone?"

"Yes," I say.

"I'm getting kind of confused. You have the note with you?"

"It got blown away in the wind. In the traffic in front of the Missoula courthouse."

He has a ballpoint in his hand and a legal pad on the desk but has written nothing down. "What happened to your head?"

"It's just a little cut."

"Fall in the bathroom? That's where most home accidents happen. I mean with older people."

"Who cares?"

"You're telling me some strange things here, Mr. Broussard."

"Maybe I'm talking to the wrong man."

His gaze wanders around on his legal pad. "No, you got the right man. I'm Ruby's former husband. Eight years ago her niece was raped and murdered. Nobody was ever in custody. Three years back she shot and killed the same kind of guy who killed her niece. Ever since, she's developed a few kinks in her head. Unless you subscribe to that artsy-fartsy stuff that goes on in Arizona."

My temples are throbbing. "Two things, sir. Number one, you shouldn't be interviewing me, and number two, I don't know what the state of Arizona has to do with any of this."

"They got these cults around Sedona. They think corn came out of a hole in the ground. That's where they say the gods live. I'm not making this up. You want me to talk to Ruby or not?"

"I didn't mean to encumber your day."

"What did you say your occupation was?"

"I'm a novelist."

"Science fiction?"

"How'd you know?"

I get up and go out the door. The dispatcher catches me outside. He's very young and has a tight haircut and earnest eyes and the kind of innocence I hope he will never lose. "Got what you needed?" he says.

"Yes, thank you," I reply. "Why did you send me to Officer Bronson?"

"I didn't. He heard me and you talking on the phone and said he knew you and he'd take care of whatever was going on at Ms. Spotted Horse's place. That was okay, wasn't it?"

"You bet," I say.

I CROSS THE BITTERROOT River and rumble across the cattle guard and park among the trees by my veranda. My home was built in 1903, and I added two barns and a chicken house and created three pastures that I rotate. I love the main house for its dowelled woodwork and dormer windows and the little second-story balcony that protrudes from Fannie Mae's bedroom. But it's a lonely place now, and the silence can be like entering a bathysphere. For that reason I am guilty of sometimes wanting any intrusion of any kind that will free me from the moment a cop knocked on my door and told me my daughter was dead. Down the slope, someone is hammering on my barn, smacking nails with a sound like the clean crack of a pistol.

As I walk through the trees, I can see the Ford-150 that has a bullet hole punched crisply in the rear window. A broad-shouldered woman wearing a red baseball cap and cargo pants and a long-sleeve corduroy shirt and nylon vest is nailing a board in place on the barn wall. There are three cans of paint or stain on the ground. The entire barn door has been repainted; the swastika is gone. She turns around, her face as blank and rough as pig hide. Her hair is bleached the color of fresh sawdust and wadded under her cap.

"I mixed a couple of cans to match the original," she says. "It's got the same brownish-red shine now. You also had a board busted loose. I didn't have a replacement, so I put some storm latches on it."

"Thank you," I say. "Can you tell me who you are, please?"

"My last name is Stokes. I live in Victor."

"Since that's Mr. Culpepper's Ford, I assume he sent you here."

"You assume wrong. That's my truck, not his."

"Why do you have this interest in me, Ms. Stokes?"

"I don't have any interest in you at all."

"I'm confused. You're standing on my property, but I'm of no importance to you?"

"That notepaper you showed John Culpepper. Something about kidnapping and somebody getting killed. We believe in the Bible. We say, 'Get thee behind me, Satan.' You upset a member of my congregation."

"You have a church here'bouts?"

"That's none of your goddamn business, is it?"

"No, ma'am, it's not."

She drops her hammer in a toolbox and plants her hands on her hips and straightens her shoulders, her chest almost popping her shirt. "Got anything else you want to say?"

"Yes, there's no need for you to come back here," I reply.

She huffs air from her nose and raises her eyes to my forehead. "You got blood coming out your bandage."

"Thanks for telling me." I start walking uphill.

"Hey!" she says.

"Yes?"

"You trying to be a smart-ass?"

I try to reach the trees before she starts in again.

"Don't turn your back on me, mister," she says.

I keep going. She says something, but her voice is lost in the wind. The horses are nickering in the pasture, the light fading in the pines. I know genuine hatred when I see it. I grew up in a culture that nursed it for generations. Ten miles from my home on Bayou Teche, a twelve-year-old Black boy was sentenced to death on the basis of a confession he gave with no counsel, and he was electrocuted not only once but twice because the executioners were drunk. I get to the veranda and mount the steps slowly and open the door and go inside, the muscles in my back as tight as knotted rope. I lock the bolt and look through the curtain. Ms. Stokes is standing by her truck, talking into her cell phone. She thumbs the phone into her cargo pants and loads her toolbox and paint cans on the truck bed and slams the tailgate and drives away, her windows down, obviously indifferent to the rawness of the wind and the dust funneling from her tires.

I SHOWER UNTIL MY skin is red and put on a fresh bandage and clean, soft, unironed clothes, then cook pancakes and scrambled eggs for my dinner. I have never done well with vegetarianism, and twice have gotten food poisoning from salad oil, but the day after the policeman came to my door and told me Fannie Mae was dead, I changed my diet to hers. The irony is I cannot taste what I eat or even remember what I had for lunch, if anything.

The sun is below the mountains now, the sky sprinkled with white stars, the surface of the Bitterroot glazed with moonlight. Through the kitchen window I see a pair of headlights coming up the dirt lane. The six o'clock local news carried a story about two armed men who committed three robberies in the Lolo area. The images on a security camera showed the two suspects in a darkened parking lot, wearing hoodies and breathing masks, each with a pistol. The headlights turn into my drive. I pick up my .45 and click on the porch light and look through the curtain on the door glass. The vehicle is a state police cruiser. I push the .45 between the cushion and arm of a stuffed chair and open the door and step outside. "How you doin', Miss Ruby?" I say.

She gets out of the cruiser and walks up the steps, her face shadowed by the brim of her hat. She doesn't speak.

"Would you like to come in?" I say.

"I'm not sure what I'd like to do."

"Is this about my conversation with Officer Bronson? I didn't single him out to speak with. When I went to the tribal headquarters, I was told to sit down at his desk. When I found out who he was, I told him he shouldn't have been interviewing me."

"You have no idea of the harm you've done."

"That was not my intention."

"I'd like to shoot you."

"Well, I can't help that. I'm fixing to eat. Why don't you join me?"

"Mr. Broussard, I think you're from the other side of Mars."

There are many social problems that come with age. One is you know what people are going to say before they say it, but if you have any wisdom, you will not interrupt them or attempt to change their mind.

"You're not going to say anything?" she asks.

"I feel like I betrayed you, but I had to talk to someone. I picked up a note on your cellar floor written by someone begging for help. What was I supposed to do?"

"I didn't know about that. What did the note say?"

I tell her. Her hands are opening and closing as though

she doesn't know what to do with them; her eyes are lost in thought. "Why didn't you tell me this?"

"Because nothing you told me about that cellar made sense."

She looks sideways at me, her face softening. "What happened to your head?"

"I used it to break the glass on my gun cabinet."

"You did what?"

"It was an emotional moment."

"It's cold out here. Let me talk to you in the cruiser, Mr. Broussard."

"I don't like sitting in cop cars. Come inside."

"No."

"A woman named Stokes was here earlier," I say.

"Virginia Stokes?"

"She didn't give her first name. She painted my barn door. The whole door, not just the swastika. She also repaired a board in the wall. You know her?"

"If she's Virginia Stokes, she did a five-bit in Idaho. Second-degree homicide. She ran over a guy outside a bar, then backed over him. You didn't get her mad at you, did you?"

"Maybe a little."

She looks at her watch. "I'm off the clock in nine minutes, so I guess no one will object too much if I go into your house. I'm going to tell you a few things that might make you uncomfortable. You can believe them or not. But don't you ever come to my home again without calling first. Also, you will never discuss me with my ex-husband."

The swing on my veranda is empty and weightless and rhythmically squeaking in the wind. The moon has moved into the southeast and, I suspect, hangs over the great barren emptiness of the Big Hole, where history ended for the Nez Perce.

"Why do you hesitate, Mr. Broussard?"

"I fear the content of your knowledge, Miss Ruby. I don't know if I want to be in possession of it. That said, please come inside."

"You want me gone from your door, don't you?" she replies.

"No, I would never say that to you." I push open the door and let her walk ahead of me.

She removes her hat in the living room. The chandelier is lit above the dining room table, the Irish lace tablecloth snow-white, the two place settings I've kept for Fannie Mae and me immaculate and untouched by others and ultimately macabre if not perverse. "You have a nice home," she says.

"Sit down, Miss Ruby. I'll get our food."

"You'd better hear what I have to say first."

I have long called myself a believer, but even to myself I have never quite defined what I believe. I think the universe is infinite, but the terms "infinity" and "eternity" are abstractions that have no physical correlation. The possibility that matter can act as its own architect and create the human eye or brain strikes me as irrational. The great mystery for me has always been the presence of evil in the human breast. Animals kill in order to survive. The record of humankind is so bad we cannot look at it squarely in the face or dwell on its memory lest we become subsumed by it. No? Try watching the 1937 Japanese footage of their own crimes in Nanking. Or the footage from Auschwitz or Dachau or photographs from My Lai. Or read medieval accounts of disembowelment and burning of a condemned man's entrails, followed by the drawing and quartering of his body, all of it performed alive.

Ruby Spotted Horse asks me to tell her everything I told her former husband. I do as she asks. When I finish, she says, "Ray Bronson is the most selfish human being I have ever known. He's also a dirty cop, one with no bottom. Am I getting through to you?"

"I think I get your drift."

"The cellar isn't just a cellar, Mr. Broussard," she says. "It's a conduit into a cavernous world that has never been plumbed. The people there are dead, but they have the power to come back among the living. You've heard of the Baker Massacre on the Marias?"

"Wait a minute. Say all that again."

She repeats the same statements. They obviously embarrass her.

"Yes, I know about the massacre," I say. "The leader of the village was a Blackfoot named Heavy Runner."

"Major Eugene Baker, the officer who murdered all those innocent people, is under my house. Or a spirit who looks like him." She watches my face. I try to show neither belief nor disbelief. "What did you do with the note you picked up from the cellar floor?" she asks.

"Showed it to Jeremiah McNally. He's in the sheriff's department."

"Yeah, I know him. What did he say?"

"That there was no writing on the page."

She nods passively. "What did you do then?"

"Showed it to John Fenimore Culpepper. He read the message and got upset. Why can an ex-Klansman see the handwriting and not a sheriff's detective?"

"Spirits like Baker belong to a group called the Old People. They can manipulate good people and use their virtues against them, but they can't possess them. People in the system are a different matter. McNally is in the system. So am I."

"I don't follow."

"The Old People plant themselves in the system. They need

a banner above their heads. Religion, country, anything that justifies kicking lots of butt."

"How about Culpepper? He saw the writing on the note. Just like I did."

"Culpepper is probably more complex than we think."

"I'm having a little trouble with this, Miss Ruby. No offense."

"But you don't dismiss it?"

"My father was the most intelligent man I ever knew. He used to say that science and art are nothing more than the incremental discovery of what already exists. He also believed the material world is an extension of an unseen one."

We are sitting at the table, her hat crown-down on the lace tablecloth. Her eyes are moist.

"Did I say something wrong?" I ask.

"You have to forgive me. There aren't many people who have your attitude. There's one other thing I have to say." She gazes at a silver-framed photo of Fannie Mae and me on our cherrywood sideboard. "The Old People can mask themselves as family members who have recently died. Has anything unusual happened around your property recently?"

Chapter Nine

At two a.m. I hear the wind, and pine needles sifting off the roof, and the clicking of tiny pieces of snow against the windowpanes in my upstairs bedroom. I stare at the ceiling, unable to sleep, wondering if I have given myself over to a bizarre frame of reference for those who cannot contend with the realities of ordinary life. I lay my forearm across my eyes and try to keep my mind empty and am almost on the edge of sleep when I hear a clinking sound in the yard. Then I hear it again, this time louder.

I put on my slippers and go to the window. The moon is bright, the remaining leaves on the maples stiff with frost, the ground frozen and definable, empty of movement. Then I see a wood rabbit hop through the yard and disappear in the shadows. The wind begins to gust, strong enough to rattle my window and bounce a cardboard box across the yard, but there is no sound from the cans I strung between the trees. There's a rail fence between the yard and the barn. I tied the trip string to one of the posts. The string is broken, and the cans and string lie on the ground like a broken worm.

I move to the edge of the window so I don't silhouette.

Two men are standing by the chicken house in the moonlight, evidently undecided about their next move. They seem out of context, inadequately dressed in hoodies and tennis shoes and thin khakis that flatten against their legs in the wind.

I have no telephone on the second floor. I go downstairs and take my .45 from the stuffed chair and go into the kitchen. Through the glass in the back door, I can see them crossing the yard, one gripping a chromed semi-automatic with two hands, the other carrying a hammer whose head is wrapped in cloth, a roll of duct tape, and a handgun with the squat ugly lines and extended magazine of an Uzi. Both men are thin, young, with narrow, pale faces and dark hair that bunches up inside their hoodies.

I can call 911 and report what is happening at my house while I lose the visual advantage over the intruders. I dial the emergency number, leave the phone off the hook on the drainboard, and go into my office, which gives me a side view of the men as they approach the kitchen door.

The moon slips behind a bank of snow clouds and drops the backyard into darkness. I pull back the slide on the .45 and ease a round in the chamber. My adrenaline has kicked into overdrive; a brass band is playing in my head; my saliva tastes like WD-40.

In one way or another, all the things I love are within my touch: photographs of my daughter and my parents, at least a thousand books on the shelves, my first editions and those of friends in a glass case, my Gibson acoustic guitar, my Fenwick fly rod, my father's baseball glove from his time in the Texas bush league, my boyhood collection of baseball cards and arrowheads and coins and Civil War bullets, all symbols of the America I grew up in, whether Norman Rockwell invented it or not.

Only a few feet and a wall separate me from the young men in the yard. But the difference in our worlds and cultural experience is enormous. In my teens I was on a road gang with a dozen boys my age, slinging gravel from cain't-see to cain't-see behind a truck that sprayed tar in our faces, oversight courtesy of a mounted gunbull like a black cutout pasted against a molten-red sun, our reflections shrunken inside his mirrored sunglasses. The boys I stacked time with were inured to pain and abuse and tougher than I, but I was spared, and most of them probably fell by the wayside. Perhaps the young men on the other side of my wall are like those boys of years ago. Did their parents love them? What a laugh. What kind of orphanage were they in, one that made them polish the floors by wrapping rags around their knees? A tiny tick of a dial in the back of their heads could have made all the difference. Am I willing to take their lives? By the same token, am I willing to let them take mine?

One of them begins taping the window on the kitchen door, preparing to break it with the cloth-wrapped hammer and ease the shards out of the frame. I put on a battered Stetson and a canvas coat that hangs on the back of my desk chair, unbolt my office door, and step out on the flagstones.

"How you doin', fellows? I'm the owner of this house, and I have an army .45 pointed at your backs. It is my belief that you are breaking into my home with the intention of doing me harm. That means I can blow you all over the yard and go back to sleep and in the morning hose you off the walk, and the authorities will yawn when I call in the 911. Very gently set down the hammer and tape and the chrome job and the Uzi. Do it all at once."

Both of them are motionless, their eyes on each other.

"You have two seconds, then I'll shoot both of you," I say.

They half-squat, putting down their weapons with the care of two aerialists balancing themselves on a high-wire.

"Now step backward, please."

"No problem," one of them says.

"Now get on your knees and pull out your wallets and place them on the ground."

Again they obey.

"Are you the guys who have been terrorizing Lolo?"

No reply.

"Let's see your ink."

They look at each other.

"Want me to say it again?" I ask.

One is a little taller and older than the other. "It's cold," he says.

"It's a lot colder when you're six feet down," I say.

They pull off their hoodies and roll up their shirtsleeves. The moon has broken free from the clouds. Both boys are unnaturally pale and have pits in their cheeks. Their arms are like pipe stems, their skin almost luminescent, twined with blue serpents and sprinkled with SS lightning bolts and small death's-heads.

"Did anyone ever tell you the Nazis lost the war?"

My words seem to bounce off them. I doubt they could find Germany on a map.

"You look like brothers."

No response.

"Who sent y'all?"

"Nobody," the taller boy replies.

"I got it. Just passing by," I say. "Put your jackets on. We're going to go inside the barn, and you're going to tell me what I want to know. If you don't, I'm going to bury you up to your necks in my compost pile. Lace your fingers on top of your heads."

I suspect neither of them is over twenty. Their tats represent the symbology of the dumbest people on earth. Their histories never change: petty theft, joyriding, possession, intent to sell, probation, juvie, reform school, then an adult facility where they are either raped or they rape others. We cross the yard into the barn. I jerk the chain on a bare bulb that hangs from the ceiling.

"Sit on the floor."

"Yes, sir," the taller boy says.

They slide down the wall and pull up their knees. I stick the .45 in the back of my belt. The safety is on. The eyes of the boys are like glass. "We weren't gonna hurt anybody," the taller one says. He tries to smile. "We thought maybe we'd get some food."

"With an Uzi and a cannon?" I say.

"It's just to scare," he says. "The Uzi is semiauto. I mean, it's legal. Right?"

"Where'd you get it?"

"Boosted it," he says.

"Where?"

"A pawnshop in Idaho."

"You guys just attempted an armed robbery," I say. "That can get you twenty years. You're willing to risk twenty years for some food?"

They stare at the lightbulb, the pupils of their eyes dilated to the size of dimes.

"Did you fellows see that news story about somebody putting swastikas on the Anne Frank memorial in Boise a couple of days ago?"

"The *what* memorial?" the younger boy says.

"Y'all didn't stick a little meth up your nose, did you?" I say.

Their eyes travel all over the barn, as if the conversation is of no more interest. Their trousers are smeared with hay and chicken excrement. They smell like urine and look like they might fall asleep.

"You know a woman named Virginia Stokes or a man by the name of John Fenimore Culpepper?"

They shake their heads as though they have just searched their souls and cannot say, to save their lives, they have ever heard those names before.

"I bet Ms. Stokes has an interesting background," I say.

"We don't know anybody by that name," the smaller boy says.

"You're both lying, but I suspect you've been doing that all your lives," I say. "Here's my problem, fellows. I don't want to turn you over to the police. I'd rather shoot you and dump you up in the high country and let the griz have a picnic. Know why that is?"

They shake their heads, this time in earnest.

"I had a daughter named Fannie Mae Broussard. She got hurt by some bad people, but they skated. So I've got a bias about the system."

They look at each other. The younger boy lifts his eyes to mine. "Fannie Mae was your daughter?"

"You knew her?"

"Just around. Concerts at Caras Park and shit," the older boy says. "She was big on animals. She'd bring her pups to the concert and feed them Popsicles."

I stare at them a long time. "If you guys feel that way toward her, why are you robbing and terrifying people?"

They drop their eyes.

"It's not a difficult question," I say.

The older boy picks at his nails; both of them are sullen, as are all recidivists when forced to examine the vacuity of their lives. I kick the older boy in the foot. He flinches. "You're here to pop me, aren't you?" I say.

"No, sir," he replies. "We don't hurt people."

I kick the other boy in the foot. "How about you? You think it's manly to kill people?" He doesn't answer, and I kick him again. "You want me to submerge you in the stock tank?"

He looks up, his face pinched. The thinness of his voice makes me think of a stiletto: "Then do it, you arrogant son of a bitch."

I step back. He wipes his nose on his sleeve. The older boy tilts his head forward and spits a long stream of tobacco juice between his legs.

"Tell you what," I say. I open the tack-room door and click on the light and gaze at the bridles and halters and coiled ropes and saddle blankets hung in a row on wood pegs, and also at the snow shovels and garden rakes and pickaxes and posthole diggers and hayforks propped against the wall. The two boys can see me through the door. I pick up a hayfork and touch the tips of the tines, ground into conical points. I lean the hayfork against a snowblower and reach into the shadows and remove a broom from a steel hook.

I step back outside the tack room and close the door behind me. "Get up and lean against the wall," I say.

"What are you gonna do?" the older boy says.

"You're about to find out."

"Look, man—" he begins.

"Don't address me as 'man.'"

The younger boy says nothing. His eyes are fixed on mine, liquid and brimming with malevolence. With my left hand, I pull the .45 from the back of my belt.

They get to their feet and prop their arms against the wall.

"Spread your feet," I say.

"Sir, what are you doing?" the older boy asks.

"Shut up," I say.

The younger boy hangs his head as though he's nodded off

or is long inured to abuse. The older boy twists his neck and tries to see what I'm doing. He starts to cry.

"Who sent you?" I ask.

"Santa Claus, asshole," the younger boy says. "Do whatever you're gonna do. And fuck yourself while you're at it, you cocksucker."

"You might regret that," I say. "But look at things another way. If you're stand-up, why take somebody else's fall?"

"Oh, you're con-wise," the younger boy says. "We're really impressed."

"You guys are a lot of laughs," I say.

I sweep their clothes clean of hay and chicken manure, from their shoulders down to their heels, slamming them against the wall when they resist, jabbing the broom end into their necks and faces. Both of them roll up in balls.

I blow out my breath. "That's it, fellows," I say. "You just got reborn."

"Reborn?" the younger boy repeats.

"You got it, partner. Your weapons and your hammer and tape and your wallets stay here. You're free. The next time you're in church, burn a candle for Fannie Mae."

"What's the catch?" the older boy says.

"You'll figure it out," I say.

I walk back into the house and bolt the door and leave them stupefied in the yard. The cops come by later, but I tell them my 911 was a false alarm and apologize for bothering them.

Chapter Ten

At the kitchen table in the light of day, I put on rubber gloves and unload the Uzi and the chrome job, a .40-caliber Smith & Wesson, and shake the contents from the boys' wallets. Both boys have Idaho driver's licenses. The older boy is Clayton Wetzel. The younger is Jack Wetzel. Jack has a Missoula library card. Clayton carries a condom. Their wallets contain a total of thirty-seven dollars. Their names don't show up on Google or Facebook.

I put their tape and hammer in one reinforced plain paper bag and their weapons in another. Today is still Wednesday, and I do nothing of consequence until sunset, then dig a hole behind my barn and bury the boys' wallets and the bullets from their weapons and drive to the main post office in Missoula and park in front. Because of the pandemic, few people wish to enter the building and instead use the drive-by boxes to mail their letters. I put on a mask and my rubber gloves and wait until the building is empty, then walk through the glass doors to the parcel drop, pull the handle, and slide the paper bags inside. They make a clunking sound when they hit the bottom of the receptacle.

SUNDAY MORNING I put on a gray suit and dress shirt and bolo tie and a six-X black Stetson and a pair of pointy-toed, spit-shined oxblood Tony Lama boots, and I drive twenty-three miles straight south into the heart of the Bitterroot Valley and the town (population eight hundred) of Victor, Montana. Other than the motorized vehicles and the electrification of the structures, the town could have been teleported from the year 1875. The streets are lined with trees, the mountains immediately west of town massive, stretched across the sky; they seem to tumble into the tiny backyards of the neighborhood.

Not far from the center of the town is a small white church called the New Gospel Tabernacle. It has a faux bell tower and the soft, immaculate color and lines of a freshly iced wedding cake. There is a glassed-in welcome and information sign by the front entrance. Services are at seven p.m. Wednesdays and ten a.m. Sundays. The pastor is Sister Ginny Stokes.

The sun is straight up in the sky when I arrive. A row of shiny motorcycles is parked on the side lawn. A tarp suspended on poles ripples and pops above a table covered with a checkered cloth and piles of food; smoke leaks from the closed lid of a barbecue grill. No one wears masks. The men's beards are the size of shovels; they have hair like Mongolian warriors and chests like beer kegs. Their hands are rocks. They're hobnailed, strung with ornamental chains and stomp-ass tats, and wear leather or denim stiff with dirt and grease. Most of the rockers on the back of their vests suggest visions of either hell, the devil, or primitive tribes who were dedicated to tearing down civilization stone by stone.

One of their favorite songs is Jerry Jeff Walker's "Up Against the Wall, Redneck Mother," with an emphasis on the phrase "kicking hippies' asses." Their vocal cords sound chemically fried or soaked in Drano. To them, misogyny is a given and accepted as such by an inexplicable strain of women who, of their own volition, will cling to the back of a sociopath at eighty miles an hour without a helmet, knees spread around his hips, hair whipping them blind. The greatest virtue of out-law bikers is their ferocity in a gang fight. Even when they lose, they eat their pain and glow with a bloody aura and refuse to dime the people who put them in a hospital.

I put on a mask before I get out of my truck. Leigh Culpep-per is tuning an electric cherry guitar on a wood stage, the feedback screeching through a loudspeaker. His father stands next to him, a Japanese acoustic hanging from his neck; he and his son are dressed in hundred-dollar lavender suits, their neckties crusted with sequins.

Virginia Stokes comes from the back of the church with a ham on a tray. She sets the tray on a buffet table and begins slicing the ham, one eye on me, ignoring two bikers who are telling her a joke of some kind. She's wearing Santa Claus boots with bells and designer jeans and a light mackinaw. Her hair is spread on her shoulders and looks attractive.

I take off my hat to her and put it back on. She stops cutting and puts down her butcher knife and meat fork and wipes her hands with a towel, her eyes locked on mine. The two bikers follow her line of vision and stop talking. One has a gray beard, fluffy like Spanish moss and streaked with red, the other a face like a hatchet, a Stars and Bars kerchief twisted into a rope and tied tightly around his head.

Then I hear Fannie Mae's voice in the wind: *Don't let these guys write the script, Pops. Get on it.*

How? I respond in my head.

Do what they don't expect.

The sun has tilted toward the west. I walk toward the serving table, the brim of my hat pulled down to keep the glare out of my eyes. "How do you do, Ms. Stokes?"

"It's Sister Ginny," she says.

"You have a real nice building here."

"It's a church, not a building," she says. "What do you want?"

"I thought I'd catch your sermon."

"That's why you arrived after it was over?"

"Maybe I can come back on Wednesday night."

"Is this guy causing a problem, Sister?" the bearded man asks.

Her eyes take me apart. "No," she says.

"How much for the buffet?" I ask.

"I didn't hear anyone invite you," she says.

The tarp is flapping overhead in the quiet. The mountains are blue and deep green and wrapped with black shadow and long stretches of thickly wooded forests on the slopes.

"It's fifteen dollars," she says. "There's a tin box on the table."

"Can I talk with you?" I ask.

She rubs her hands as though she's putting lotion on them. "I'll think about it."

I pay for the meal and go through the line and fill a plate with slaw and beans and potato salad. An elderly woman in wool slacks pours a cup of Kool-Aid for me. "You're not going to have any barbecue?" she says.

"Have to watch my cholesterol."

"Sister Ginny keeps it lean for us seniors. Where might you be from?"

"Up toward Lolo."

"Well, it's nice to know you and to see you here. We hope you come back."

"You, too, ma'am," I say.

It's obvious she's a kindly lady, and being in her late seventies, she's very vulnerable to the virus. Why is she with a bunch like this?

"Ma'am?" I say.

"Yes, sir?"

She waits, her blue eyes glassy with cataracts, her face seamed with harsh winters, maybe up on the Highline, where Canadian storms leave both livestock and wild animals clanking with strings of ice.

"This is the best Kool-Aid I've ever had," I say.

It's warm in the sunshine, and I sit by myself at a plank table and listen to the Culpeppers and three women play country and bluegrass spirituals. My favorite is "I'm Using My Bible for a Roadmap." John Culpepper plays mandolin and banjo as well as guitar and has a fine voice. After a half hour, someone shouts out, "Johnny B. Goode!" Others start yelling, too.

"Cain't do it," Culpepper says into the microphone.

"Hell yes, you can!" someone yells.

"It's Sunday," Culpepper says.

"Not in Afghanistan," someone else yells. "Play it for them boys over there!"

Everyone laughs and claps. "I guess that won't hurt nothing, will it?" Culpepper says into the mike, looking at Virginia Stokes. She smiles approvingly.

He borrows his son's electric guitar and kicks it off in a barre C major way up on the neck, then does some magic on the treble strings with F and G7th the way Chuck Berry did, sliding his fingers down the frets into a conventional C chord, suddenly bridging into a driving four-four beat that has the crowd going wild.

I wonder if I have misjudged the congregants or been too hard on them. Minutes earlier the Culpeppers and their friends were singing and playing the songs of Ralph Stanley and Don Reno and Red Smiley with the same level of skill, the same nineteenth-century Appalachian purity, the same serenity in their faces. Now a former Klansman is paying tribute to a Black man who was the most influential musician in the history of rock and roll. I want to stand up and clap with the others, but I don't. Why? Because I remember the years of distrust, growing up in the South, and the disappointment I felt when I convinced myself that the adoration of the Lost Cause was gone, and that the valor of the boys in butternut somehow undid or at least ameliorated the sin of slavery. Even today I want those things to be true, and I cannot watch footage of the mob flinging ropes on Lee's statue and in seconds reducing it to rubble.

Culpepper goes into Berry's duckwalk across the stage. It's as good a representation and as funny as Michael J. Fox's in *Back to the Future*. Then someone throws a plastic Obama mask on the stage, and Culpepper scoops it up and puts it on and continues his duckwalk, except the innocence is up the spout and the hilarity of the crowd is of a different kind—atavistic, raw, their faces gleeful and vindictive as if they're drunk, a fecal shine in their eyes.

I get up to go. Then a hand settles on my shoulder. I look up at the face of Sister Ginny Stokes. "You still want to talk?" she says.

I follow her into the building. The hallway is painted from floor to ceiling with a portrayal of Yahweh raging above the red and black flames of an inferno. In gilded letters at the top of one wall are the words "The Wrath of God."

"Like it?" she says.

"Who painted it?"

"Me."

"You're pretty good," I say.

She pushes open a door. "This is my office. Sit down. Don't give me any bullshit, either."

The office is small, the desk made of metal, a solitary book-shelf above it. Among the titles are *Little House on the Prairie* and *My Ántonia*. There is a glass jar full of candy balls on the corner of her desk. I sit on a hard chair. Hers is a swivel, padded with leather.

"I had a visit in the early a.m. Wednesday from two kids named Wetzel," I say.

"Yeah?"

"They seemed to know you."

"Well, I don't know them."

"I think they came to pull my plug."

"You *think?*" she says.

"They're from Idaho. I hear you did a five-bit there."

Her eyes contain no emotion, no sign of injury or even thought. "You fuck around?"

"Pardon?"

"You heard me."

"I cut those kids loose, Sister Ginny. That means I put potentially dangerous people on the street."

"You don't like to talk about fucking?"

"I think I'd better go."

She twists the swivel chair back and forth. "Got you off guard? Hang around. Maybe we'll take a drive somewhere. Have a few drinks. Afraid I'm going to shake your peaches?"

I get up to go. "You've got a lot of artistic talent, Miss Ginny. So does Mr. Culpepper. Why waste it running a hate group?"

She unscrews the lid on the glass jar and puts a candy ball in her mouth. "Want one?"

"No, thank you."

"Google says you're worth sixty million dollars."

"Writers like me don't make that kind of money."

She takes a book from the shelf on the wall. It's a hardback copy of my most recent novel. "You do all the shit that's in here?"

"The character defects are mine. The rest is fiction."

"Want to sign it?"

She pushes it toward me, her face whimsical, her eyes peeling off my skin. I write on the title page and tuck the flap into the page and close the cover and hand the book back to her. She opens it and reads the inscription. "'To a lady who does it her way'?" she says. "What the fuck does that mean?"

"You don't take prisoners."

"Got a question for you. You turned your back on me the other day."

"Yes, I did."

"Where do you get off with that?"

"You scared the hell out of me."

She rolls the candy ball around in her mouth, letting it click against her teeth, then writes a phone number on a scrap of paper and gives it to me. "Don't treat this in a casual way. I don't make the invitation to just anybody. Get my drift, sweetcakes?"

She cracks the candy ball with her molars.

Chapter Eleven

ALL THE WAY home, Fannie Mae will not let me alone.

Have you lost your mind, Pops? That woman belongs in a cage.

"People are always better than we think," I say. "That's from George Orwell."

That was just before he got shot through the throat in Spain and almost executed by the people he was fighting for.

"Will you give it a rest?"

Those people are evil, Pops. If they had their way, we'd go up the chimney.

"What about the Wetzel boys? You think they're Nazis?"

No, they're meth heads. They'll be used by others, then thrown away. They're not your responsibility.

The sun is yellow and low on the horizon, dust rising in strings from the fields. Up ahead is a ghost ranch, with a house and barns and loading chutes that now consist of boards as wind-hewn and weightless as air, tumbleweeds bouncing through them, the original red paint barely visible.

You're turning sad on me, Pops.

"You were always my little pal."

Don't go down that road, Popsie. It really sucks.

"I'm angry at you for dying."

The inside of the car becomes silent. A semi goes flying by, air horns blowing, the trailer swaying. I'm on the yellow stripe. I overcorrect and swing onto the shoulder.

"I probably dozed off," I say. "But we're okay."

Tell that to the guy in the Mack shaking his fist out the window.

When I return home, Ruby Spotted Horse is parked in front of my veranda, seemingly preoccupied with paperwork, her windows sealed, the engine running. I park below her and walk up and tap on the window. Her face jerks, then she rolls down the glass. "You gave me a heart attack," she says. There's nothing funny about her manner.

"What's going on?" I ask.

She unlocks the doors. "Get in," she says.

"I told you, I don't like sitting in cop cars. Tell me what you're doing here."

"Know a kid named Clayton Wetzel?"

My stomach turns to water.

"That's what I thought," she says. "Are you going to get in or not?"

I walk around to the passenger side. The inside of the cruiser is warm and comfortable, but my heart is tripping, and a pressure band is tightening around the side of my head. She's wearing her campaign hat and a Kevlar vest; she has a clipboard propped against the steering wheel and a large envelope full of eight-by-ten photos on the dashboard. "Am I right?" she asks. Her voice is neutral, perhaps too friendly, perhaps deceptive. "You know a kid named Wetzel?"

"What about him?"

"This," she replies. She pulls one of the photos from the envelope and hands it to me. "That's what's left of his head."

A half-cup of bile rises from my stomach. I can hardly hold it down.

"Take a look at the other photos," she says. "He was torn apart, literally, his arms and legs ripped off. He was also disemboweled."

I force myself to look at each photo and have to keep clearing my throat to get through them. I hand them back to her and unconsciously wipe one hand on my trouser leg. "Where did this happen?"

"By the railway track on the res."

Be careful, Pops, Fannie Mae says.

"How is Wetzel's death being treated?" I ask.

Spotted Horse hesitates. "There's been no decision on that."

She begins telling me details about the body's proximity to a nightclub, the blood scatter in the weeds, the trouble she had obtaining crime-scene photos from someone at the Flathead police station. But she keeps avoiding the most probable explanation for the boy's death and the violence done to his body.

"You don't think he fell under the train?" I say.

"No, I don't. Did you know this kid or not, Mr. Broussard?"

"I had a confrontation with him."

"'Confrontation' won't cut it. You're going to have cops at your door either tonight or tomorrow morning. Since this is Sunday and the DA is out of town, they'll probably be here in the morning."

"Why me?"

"Wednesday night, some guns and a hammer and tape were dropped in the parcel chute at the main post office in

Missoula. One of the guns was an Uzi, like the one used in the Lolo robberies. The guy with the Uzi in the security-camera videos was wearing a jacket just like the one Wetzel was wearing when he got torn apart."

I make no reply. I can't think straight. I wish I had turned in Wetzel and his brother. The heater in the cruiser is hot against my leg. My armpits are sweating and I can smell my own odor. I think she's determined to turn an accident into a homicide. I also wonder if she's really a friend. Then she drops it on me. "Guess who was seen leaving the post office Wednesday night?" she says.

"If you're talking about me, I go there about three or four evenings a week. Let's get back to Wetzel and the possibility that he tried to jump on the train and fell under it. Were the body parts *on* the track or *by* the track?"

"They were scattered."

"Coyotes or wolves could have gotten to him."

"This is the same crap I've gotten from several of my colleagues. Some of Wetzel's entrails were shoved down his throat. I don't think animals do that to each other."

"I'd better not say any more, Miss Ruby."

She presses her wrist to her forehead as though she has a migraine. The sun begins its descent behind the mountains, and in a blink, shadows fall across the valley and the river and through my yard and trees and into the house, as though the elements are colluding against me. I wonder what happened to the younger boy.

"I'm not here to get on your case, Mr. Broussard," she says. "I want to help you. I already know who killed the Wetzel kid."

"Who?" I say, although I know what's coming.

"Somebody who lives under my cellar."

"Nope," I say. "I'm not going down this highway again."

"You insisted on learning about my cellar. You're going to listen whether you like it or not. The death of that boy also involves Jeremiah McNally."

"What does he have to do with this?"

"Probably more than you want to know. He came to my house because he was concerned about you. Or at least that's what he said. I think he wanted to put moves on me. He said he'd been at the casino. He wanted to take me back there."

"That's not his style," I reply.

"Believe what you want, Mr. Broussard. We were in the living room and something began crashing against the cellar door. McNally demanded to know what was down there, just as you did. Then we heard a voice come from the staircase. A little girl's voice. All my animals started going crazy."

I put my hand on the door handle. "Miss Ruby, that's enough. I'm done. It's obvious I've gotten myself in a mess. But that doesn't mean I want to get myself deeper in it."

"The horses trampled my English sheepdog. Mr. Droopy. I could hear him whimpering in the lot. I ran outside and shielded his body and tried to calm the horses before they broke his neck." Her eyes were wet, her voice wired. "Then I saw McNally, that son of a bitch, coming out the back door and heading for his car. I didn't know what he was doing. I thought maybe he was going home. Mr. Droopy was in such pain that I couldn't move him, and I couldn't leave him alone. The horses were breaking down the rails. What was I supposed to do?"

"Why did McNally go to his car?"

"He got a jack handle and went down to the cellar. I started running for the house. I was too late. He broke the lock on the door. The girl got out."

"What girl?"

"That one I call 'the girl.' She doesn't have a name. She lives with the Old People. Or they make use of her. I don't know. I left her my niece's rocking horse to play on."

"What did McNally do after she got away?"

"Nothing. He's an idiot. He said there was no girl in the cellar. Or anybody, for that matter. He said some neckers or dopers were playing their boom boxes out in the woods, and that's what we heard. I took him into the back of the cellar and showed him the entranceway."

"Entranceway?"

"It's the conduit to the prison where the Old People are confined. They've been there for thousands of years. There're petroglyphs on the wall that tell you how to roll back the stone that covers the corridor tunnel."

"You've opened the door?"

"No, there's others who do that. The Guardians catch the Old People and bring them here."

I wonder if she's insane. Or am I insane for listening to her? "You showed McNally the petroglyphs?"

"He said the petroglyphs were nothing more than the scales of hellgrammites."

"Who's the girl, Miss Ruby?"

"Who do I *think* she is?" she says. "I think she's my niece. But her body has been taken over by an evil spirit. Do you know which evil spirit I'm talking about?"

"No, I don't, and I'd rather you not tell me."

"Major Eugene Baker."

"The soldier who slaughtered the Blackfeet on the Marias in 1870?"

"Yes."

I take a breath. "Okay, will you show me the petroglyphs?"

The cruiser's overhead light is on. The sun has descended behind a black mountain, as though the light is sliding down the shingles of the world. Is this the lot of mankind? I ask myself. Are we indeed trapped in the Doomsday Book, dressed in sackcloth with ashes on our brow? Oh, dear God, deliver me up from my own thoughts, may I abide in the joyous fields of your Son.

I feel as if I have manufactured a cocoon inside the cruiser and am trying to borrow security that doesn't exist on the other side of the window glass. I think this is what people mean when they talk about primal fear and the poor embryo waiting for the flash of light that will release him or her into a world of anacondas and tigers and hyenas and, most destructive of all, the forked creature who reaches for the infant with hands that, not long ago, were fins on a fish.

I ask again to see the petroglyphs.

"No, I don't think I should show them to you," she replies. "I think I've made a mistake. You pretend to be a believer, Mr. Broussard. But you're not."

"You're talking about theological belief?"

She taps on the photos. "This was done by a monster. You heard the sounds in my cellar. Quit lying to yourself."

"Who made you the jailer of all these evil spirits?"

"One of the Guardians."

"Why you?"

"Because my ancestors died on the Marias and at the Big Hole. I think the job is about to go to someone else, though." She tilts her head up so I can see her face. "Get my drift?"

"If you're talking about me, forget it." I open the door and get out.

"What did you and Virginia Stokes talk about today?" she asks.

"Say that again?"

"You know the lesson every long-term cop eventually learns?" she says.

"No."

"Most of the time, the system only punishes the people who are available, the kind who stick their neckties in the garbage grinder. That's why we have recidivists. They're the only people we can catch."

"I don't wear neckties," I reply.

"Funny man."

I walk up the steps onto the veranda and go inside. Fannie Mae is lying on the couch watching television, except there's only white noise on the screen.

Learn anything from Short Stuff?

"More than I wanted."

Anything outstanding?

"She made a slip. They've got a wire inside Ginny Stokes's church group."

Chapter Twelve

I DID NOT MEAN to seem cynical about belief. Age has brought me little if any wisdom. I knew more at twenty-one than at forty. Why is that? Because at age forty I was dumb enough to believe I knew anything at all. The only lesson I've learned in life is that the human personality does not change, and our propensity for destroying the earth and our fellow man is stronger and more wanton than it has ever been, and if the incineration of our cities and civilians and the increased lethality of our weapons during the last one hundred years has not taught us that, nothing will.

I cannot envision eternity or infinity. I cannot understand the concept of endlessness. Nor do I understand how a primeval swamp can produce life-forms that can plan their own evolution and become sentient and functioning creatures with eyes and neurological systems and the ability to survive on a planet that had not cooled and whose skies were streaked with smoke from volcanoes as numerous as anthills. And for those reasons I try not to discount or reject possibilities of any kind, including the possibility that unseen entities exist just the other side of our fingertips.

The great inventions and geographical discoveries have often come about because of the inventor's or the explorer's blunder. The same applies to my life. The greatest events or changes in it were not planned and have occurred in an unpredictable and illogical fashion. That's a humbling thought. I would like to claim power and personal direction over my life. But a day does not go by that I do not experience a reminder of an event that left me at the mercy of strangers. The trigger can be one of many: the sound of rushing water, the press of bodies inside an elevator, a piece of food sticking in my windpipe. In seconds I'm back to a wintry day in 1935, three months after exiting my mother's womb and about to be baptized by immersion in the San Antonio River, not far from the Alamo.

Model T cars were parked on the mudbank, and people had put on their best clothes and, in spite of the weather, had brought picnic baskets and pitchers of lemonade to celebrate the occasion. As would be expected in that time period, all of them were white, uneducated, and very poor; better and more respectfully said, they were people who cut their own hair and sewed clothes for their children from colorfully stamped Purina feed sacks and thought corn pone with maple syrup was a treat. They also thought a baptism was a big event, one that took the congregation away from the endless privation that seemed to characterize their lives.

It should have been a grand day, except the preacher was drunk and stepped in a deep hole and dropped me in the current.

In seconds I was whisked away. The wool blanket I was wrapped in turned to lead. Thirty yards downstream, a fat Black woman who had no name except Aint Minnie was washing clothes in the cattails. Her only family was her thirteen-year-old daughter, who was as big as her mother and known as Snowball.

Aint Minnie turned her washtub upside down and dumped the clothes in the water and waded into the current, using the tub as a buoy, her dress floating above her hips. In the meantime I had gone under. I was not told that. I know it because I still have nightmares filled with enclosure, graves, tunnels, entrapment in a sewer pipe, a cold liquid darkness that seeps into the bone. I try to flee the blanket, but my arms are pinched against my sides. In the dream I know I'm about to die, and I know that no power on earth can save me.

Aint Minnie clutched my blanket, then my diaper, and lifted me from the water and placed me in the washtub and pushed me ahead of her into the cattails. Snowball grabbed one side of the washtub, and she and her mother slogged in men's work boots through mud that was up to their calves until they were on high ground. My grandfather was the first person to reach us. He was a Texas Ranger and owned a sizable ranch, although the drought had burned up his cotton and blown away a third of his topsoil. He picked me up and wrapped me inside his coat.

"Aint Minnie, you and Snowball got a home at my ranch the rest of y'all's lives," he said. "I swear that before the throne of God."

Grandfather kept his word and then some. When he died, Aint Minnie and Snowball were in his will. Aint Minnie lived to be ninety-seven years old, and Snowball became a professor at Texas Southern University in Houston. For years members of my family called me "Aint Minnie's little boy." And that's why I try never to reject the perceptions of others or the stories they might tell about their lives, no matter how improbable the account might be, and that includes Ruby Spotted Horse's stories about monsters and rogues who are imprisoned under the earth.

Chapter Thirteen

It's MONDAY MORNING, the pinkness of the sun buried inside the fog that shrouds the Sapphire Mountains. I feed the horses and chickens and fill all three stock tanks on the property. Dawn in Montana, no matter the season, is like a rose opening unto the light. As John Steinbeck said, Montana is not a state; it's a love affair. I'll go a step further: The rising of both the sun and the moon in Montana are moments either a Druid or a genuine Christian would recognize as sacramental. In my opinion, to treat them as anything less is to exile oneself into the land of Nod, east of Eden, where Cain was forced to live after he murdered his brother. I know that's grandiose, but Paradise is real; it's right here in the northern Rockies, and the winds that blow down the slopes, I'm convinced, have a mystical source.

With these kinds of unusual thoughts in my head and Spotted Horse's advice to leave the house early in the morning, before the police arrive, I drive north through Missoula, then give my old truck the gas and climb the long green-black, cliff-shaded slope called Evaro Hill and find myself once again in Indian country and the sunlit grandeur of the Jocko Valley.

I find the place where Clayton Wetzel died and am almost sorry I did. Wetzel was a criminal, maybe even a hit man, but he was also a kid who deserved a second chance. Blue clouds of wood smoke hang over the hills, and a train track curls along the highway into a billowing bank of fog as thick and white as cotton. Not far away, I can see the neon on the night-club that Spotted Horse mentioned. There's only one car in the lot. The grass in the field between the nightclub and the train tracks is waist-high and wet with dew. There's no crime-scene tape anywhere. The grass is crisscrossed with tire impressions, probably from the emergency vehicles. There's blood spatter on one rail tie, then more in the grass, where tiny yellow flags have been stuck in the ground.

I go inside the nightclub. The bar and red stools and booths are wiped down and glistening, the jukebox and beer signs and pinball and gambling machines all lit. "We're closed," the bartender says.

"What time do you open?"

"It depends."

"On what?"

"I haven't quite processed that."

"My name is Aaron Broussard," I say. "I'm a writer. I wonder if I can ask you a couple of questions about the accident that happened by the tracks."

He's a big man. He wears pigtails and a sparkling white snap-button shirt and a rodeo champion's belt buckle. His sleeves are rolled. "Yeah, I know who you are. I don't know anything."

"I knew the kid who was killed. He had a brother. I was interested in talking to him."

The man leans on his arms. His triceps ridge like rolls of quarters. "You've made movies, haven't you?" he says.

"The scripts were adapted by someone else. I was never a screenwriter."

"You ever see *My Darling Clementine*?"

"Multiple times," I reply.

"Henry Fonda says to the saloon keeper, 'Mack, you ever been in love?' Mack says, 'No, I've been a bartender all my life.' I love that line."

"The brother's name is Jack Wetzel. He'll last about five minutes in Deer Lodge."

A truck has pulled into the lot. Two men and a woman get out. They look like they've had a hard night. The woman cups her hand over her eyes and stares through the nightclub window, then says something to the men. They get back in the truck and leave. The bartender picks up a dishrag and tosses it into a sink.

"I cost you a customer?" I ask.

"This isn't a country club."

"Sorry." I get off the stool.

He blows out his breath. "Three months ago the Wetzel boys were slinging dope behind my building. I told them I'd break their necks if they came around again. But they came back two nights ago, driving a junker, no plates. They probably boosted it. They were selling dope out the car window. I can't figure it."

"Figure what?"

"I went outside and was gonna slap the shit out of them. Then the younger kid, what's-his-name, he says, 'Go fuck yourself.'"

"Jack Wetzel?"

"Yeah, that's it. The one the cops had a mug shot of. But I think he was all show, like he wanted to get involved with me, like I was a safer bet than somebody else."

"What about Clayton, the older brother?"

"Stoned. His head was glowing in the dark."

"What time did this happen?"

"About one-thirty in the morning."

"You think Clayton fell under the train?"

"If you fall under a train, you stay under the train," he replies. He starts to walk away from me.

"You know where the younger boy might be?" I ask.

He walks back on the duckboards and rests one hand on the bar. "No, I don't. But you know what you haven't asked me about?"

I shake my head.

"The cops had the younger kid's mug shot and not the older kid's. I thought maybe that was because the older kid was dead. The younger kid looked like a shrimp to me. But the cops said the shrimp set fire to his house when he was twelve. The father was locked in the bedroom."

"What happened to the mother?"

"They didn't say. I didn't ask."

THE SKY IS a translucent blue and the tops of the Mission Mountains are streaked with fresh snow as I drive up to the Tribal Police Department in Pablo. I go inside and am welcomed by the same young officer who helped me previously.

"Officer Bronson is at the café in Ronan," he says. His eyes are merry, full of goodwill. "He eats lunch a bit early sometimes."

"Which café?" I say.

"Oh, sorry," he says, and gives me the name and directions. "Officer Bronson said you'd be along."

"I wonder how he knew."

"One thing you can say for sure about Officer Bronson?" he says, as though he's about to break a great secret.

"What's that?"

"When he gets on it, he's on it."

I look at his name tag. "I'm sure you're right about that, Officer Hackman. Thanks for your help."

"You betcha," he says. "Any time."

It's six miles to the café in Ronan. When I pull to the curb, I realize I'm not alone. Fannie Mae is on the sidewalk by the corner of the café, petting a Labrador that is on a leash and held by a man who's looking at a plane as it flies overhead. The Labrador's tail is flipping back and forth like a spring. The owner automatically shortens his hold on the leash and looks up and down the sidewalk as if someone is approaching him and causing the dog to wag. But he sees no one else on the sidewalk.

I have seen Fannie Mae several times that I have not told you about: standing by the highway on Evaro Hill and looking at a nineteenth-century railroad bridge built across the canyon; last night in a dream, barefoot at eight or nine in a wash-faded dress too big for her, blowing a dandelion into a balloon of white fuzz; and crossing against a red light on a street in Missoula earlier this morning.

The reason I did not mention these other visitations is my fear that I am having a nervous breakdown. All the signs are there: suicidal thoughts, depression, insomnia, psychoneurotic anxiety, and the ennui and daily misery that can put you in the white-coated custody of people whose gloved hands you will not forget.

But I do not want Fannie Mae to go away. If she does, I know I will want to go with her. In fact, if I'm allowed to bargain, I will ask that I be allowed to step aboard the same vehicle and go somewhere among the stars, maybe in the cold white smoke of the Milky Way, far from where moth and rust doth corrupt and where thieves break through and steal.

A bell rings when I walk into the café. Ray Bronson is sitting at the counter, telling a joke to five men who have formed a half-circle around him. It doesn't take long to catch the content. I grew up with it. It always begins with a grinning, shared perception of groups who are a threat to the man telling the joke and a threat to his listeners. Their eyes crinkle, their chins and necks seem to shrink inside their shoulders, like turtles pulling their heads inside their shells. Briefly, there is a warm look of glee and confidence that heats and lights the circle they have drawn around their fears, using ridicule instead of fire to burn the woman or the Jew or the Black man who has robbed them of their God-given superiority. Then they walk away, re-empowered, assured they are not alone, that the armies of the night are actually their liberators, a grand awakening about to happen any day now.

Bronson's listeners laugh in unison, their voices guttural and heavy with phlegm, enough so they have to cough in their hands, proud of their indifference to masks, their gaze already turning on a stranger at the gate whom they haven't noticed, a threat to the morning that was going so well.

Ray Bronson gets up from the stool and sees me. His mouth flexes, and his perception shifts inward, as though he's trying to remember the last words he said.

"Hello," I say. "I heard you were expecting me."

"I didn't quite get that," he answers, his grin broad. "What's up, bud?"

I ask him to sit down with me in a booth. "If you're buying," he replies.

Fannie Mae is looking at me through the window. She mouths the words *Watch yourself.*

The waitress brings me a menu; Bronson is already looking at his watch. "Ever hear of a kid named Jack Wetzel?" I ask.

"Yeah, we're looking for him."

"As a witness to his brother's accident or homicide?"

"Let's be honest, Mr. Broussard. You got a thing for my ex. I can't blame you. But Ruby is crazy as batshit."

"The question stands."

"No, it doesn't. The Wetzel brothers are our concern, not yours. I'm about to order a hamburger. You want one?"

"You ever hear of Major Eugene Baker?"

He looks sideways at nothing, then back at me. His eyes are misaligned, one higher than the other, his eyebrows untrimmed and tangled. He props his elbows on the table and knits his fingers together and points them at me, like a man interrupted in the midst of prayer. "I know you've had a loss in your family. But stay out of other people's business, starting with the tribal police. The Wetzel brothers are part of a meth investigation. That's all I'm gonna tell you."

"How long did you live in Ruby's house?"

"Man, you just don't quit."

"Did you ever see any rocks in the cellar that had petroglyphs on them?"

"The only thing I ever saw down there was rotten fruit that stunk up the place and carpenter ants eating up the wood in the ceiling."

The waitress takes his order, then looks at me. She has a few streaks of gray in her hair. I can smell her perfume. "Coffee," I say. He stops her before she can walk away. "Irene, we're still on at six?" he says.

"Roger that," she says.

He gives me a grin featuring his big teeth. It's like a rictus.

I get up from the booth and place two one-dollar bills on the table. "For the coffee," I say. "Whoever or whatever killed

Clayton Wetzel wasn't human. Every one of you bastards knows that, but you're not going to do anything about it. That's why you're cruel."

Through the window I see Fannie Mae give me two thumbs-up as I walk out of the café.

Chapter Fourteen

At EXACTLY MIDNIGHT a gale shakes the entire house. I had fallen asleep watching the late news on the couch. The inside of the house is black, the television screen dormant. Through the kitchen window I can see flashes in the trees way up the hill, like ball lightning splintering in a swamp. At first I think I'm seeing the reflection of Missoula in the clouds. But the blue clouds on the hill resemble smoke more than fog or impending rain, and also they are too low to reflect the city lights that are over ten miles away.

There's a quaking under my feet. The pots and pans hanging above my stove are clinking. The handle on the faucet in the sink squeaks and twists by itself and splashes water on the counter and floor, then stops as quickly as it started. The horses are nickering and blowing in the corral, clattering against the rails, the way they do when they smell wolves or a forest fire. My trip string is broken in many places, the aluminum cans scattered by the wind.

I take the gun-cabinet key from my pocket and start to insert it in the lock, then realize the cabinet is already open. I have no explanation. I paid the glazier to replace the glass I broke, watched him leave, then locked the cabinet and have not touched it since. I pull the door open and remove my M1 and pull back the bolt and push an eight-round clip into the magazine. My thumb has barely cleared when the bolt snaps shut. A great brilliance bursts inside the trees up the hill, lighting the barn, the backyard, a small statue of Saint Francis that Fannie Mae had since she was a child, the horses walleyed and terrified and running and kicking each other.

I put on my canvas coat and step into the backyard. The light up the hill seems to emanate from the ground and extend over an area half the size of a football field. I can hear the popping of small-arms fire and smell burned gunpowder and a stench like offal or animal hair going up in flames. I circle around my barn and keep going up the grade. I can hear infants crying and women screaming and horses squealing, maybe going down with their riders or being shot in large numbers.

I splash through half-frozen ice in a streambed, the gunfire growing louder and more sustained until it is one sound rather than many. I can see wickiups burning, blue-jacketed soldiers with fur caps shooting at close range, Indian women tearing open their shirts and exposing their breasts in the hope that they and their children will be spared. An officer with a drawn revolver is pacing back and forth in the firelight. He's a mustached, grim man and wears a mashed flattop hat and shoulder straps framed in gold. His free hand is knotted in a fist, propped primly on his hip. He watches as an enlisted man shoots an infant through the head.

I kneel behind the trunk of a ponderosa tree and aim through the peep sight at the officer's back and begin firing, the stock snugging into my shoulder, six inches of flame leaping from the barrel, the ejected shells sticking like darts in a patch of soft snow. Then the bolt locks open with a *ping*. The magazine is empty. The officer has shown no acknowledgment of my presence.

I take another clip from my coat pocket and press it with my thumb into the magazine and roll the heel of my hand from the bolt. The officer seems to hear the bolt feed the round into the chamber. He turns and looks at me in a quizzical way. Behind him, his men are piling buffalo robes and blankets and clothes and bundles of food on a giant fire. A cone of sparks and heat and smoke and ash twists into the sky and flattens like a greasy stove lid on the tips of the trees. I have the officer's chest locked inside my peep sight. I begin shooting and do not stop until my second clip ejects.

My right ear is ringing. There's a coppery taste like blood in my mouth. My back aches when I stand up. But I have changed nothing in the equation. The officer grins at the corner of his mouth and beckons for me to join him. His junior and noncommissioned officers are already gathering around him, as though posing for a historical photograph.

"Never," I say. "Let your cloak be rolled as fuel for the fire. Let hell be your home."

I begin backing away, my sniper's nest scattered with empty cartridges, smoke billowing skyward in huge curds. I cannot keep the screams of the infants out of my ears, or the wails of the wounded and dying. I weep and stumble down the hill, the sparks and ash and the chorus of suffering and pain rising into the darkness, the soot soiling the heavens.

Chapter Fifteen

Jeremiah McNally is at my house at 8:37 a.m. I open the door and let him in after looking past him to see if anyone is in his vehicle. I close the door behind him. "What's up, partner?" I ask.

"I'm going out on a limb. You'd better have an explanation for dropping those guns in the parcel chute at the post office."

"Who says I did anything at the post office?"

"Only you would do something like that," he replies.

"You went out to Ruby Spotted Horse's place and gave her a bad time, and you used me to do it."

"Wrong," he says. "Spotted Horse can't accept the death of her niece and needs to see a psychiatrist. I hate to say this, Aaron, but I think you've got the same problem."

"Get out," I say.

He looks at the couch. "Is that an M1?"

"What about it?"

"I think you're a threat to yourself."

"Really? Take a walk with me," I say. "I'll get my coat." He can't make up his mind. "Afraid?" I say.

The sky is blue, the sun warm, the frost on the barn roof

sliding in sheets off the edge. We walk up the hill, Jeremiah behind me, his breath fogging, his irritability growing. "No more of this," he says, "I've got to get back to work."

There's a rectangular flat rock in front of us, wet and striped with lichen. "Have a seat," I say.

He's wearing an expensive overcoat. He remains standing. "Has this got something to do with Fannie Mae?"

"Maybe. I've seen her up here. I saw fires here last night. And Indians being killed."

"I think I'll head back to the office now."

"See the snow in the trees? I was there last night. I burned two clips on the back of a United States army officer from the nineteenth century."

"Yeah, there are a lot of those kinds of guys running around these days."

I walk another twenty yards up the slope to the stand of trees where I knelt and aimed through iron sights at an officer I believed was Major Eugene Baker. "Take a look." My brass casings are scattered in the snow, half-buried, gleaming in the sunlight.

"You did some target shooting here? That's the big story?"

The sun is shining on the clearing where I saw the massacre of the Indians and the burning of their wickiups and their clothes and blankets and bearskins. I walk to the spot where the biggest fire was and pick up a stick and start gouging the dirt. The stick breaks and I get another one and dig harder. "Come look," I say.

"This is embarrassing, Aaron."

I get down on one knee and scoop up a handful of dirt and hold it up to him. "Smell it."

"It's carbon. You know how many forest fires we've had here?"

I bring the dirt up to my face and blow on it. "Look."

"Those are berries," he says.

"No, they're beads."

"I think you should see a counselor, Aaron. I'm going now."

I get down on both knees and scoop up with two hands what looks like particles of wood and bone and ash and antler and animal hide that have calcified into stone, all of it mixed with black silt.

"Give me your hands," I say.

"No."

"Do it, Jeremiah. Honor your namesake."

"What?"

"Shut up and do what I say."

The pain in my hands is more than I can bear. My eyes start to water. "Take this or I'll rub it in your face."

He turns up his palms. I drop everything from my hands into his. His eyes pop. "Jesus!" he says. He flings his hands into the air, then stares at them, his palms and the undersides of his fingers puffed with welts. "What are you messing with, Aaron? What in God's name have you gotten into?"

"I think we're standing on dead people."

But he's already halfway down the hill, his necktie streaming over his shoulder.

Chapter Sixteen

On SATURDAY MORNING there is a story below the fold in the *Missoulian* about the discovery of a woman's body by hunters in a dry creek bed under a bridge outside St. Ignatius. The woman was single and had been missing for four days. The sheriff's office and the Tribal Police Department have now confirmed that the deceased is Irene Barr, age forty-two, who was employed as a waitress in a Ronan café fifteen miles from St. Ignatius. The county medical examiner has not revealed the cause of death.

There is something wrong with the story. Every newspaper journalist knows that in police reporting, the issue is not the content of the story but what is left out. People fall from high places and die of a broken neck. No mystery. They have heart attacks and float down a stream, or accidentally shoot one another. They drive their cars off cliffs. The visuals tell most of the story within five minutes of discovery. Was she bruised? Was she naked? Was she without warm clothes? Did she have on shoes or have a purse? Single women don't wander out in rough country in cold weather without telling anyone, particularly their employers, and then lie down on rocks under a bridge and die of natural causes.

Regardless of the story's content or noncontent, I have a sick feeling in my stomach and also a problem of conscience, because I do not want to get any deeper in my relationship with Ray Bronson, with whom I drank coffee Monday morning in the café where Irene Barr worked. Ray Bronson said he was picking her up at six o'clock that evening.

I dial Jeremiah McNally's cell phone number. He must look at his caller ID. Without preamble, he says, "I'm through with that problem behind your house, Aaron. Whatever is up that hill isn't my business."

"I'm not calling you about that," I reply. "Do you know anything about the woman who was found dead in a ravine outside St. Ignatius?"

"That's Lake County, that's the res, it's not my business."

"I was in her place of employment Monday morning. I was with Ruby Spotted Horse's former husband. The waitress's name was Irene. He told her he was picking her up that evening."

The line goes silent.

"That's the first you've heard about Bronson's possible involvement?" I say.

"That's right."

"What are you not telling me?"

"Both Lake County and the tribal cops are sitting on this one."

"Why?"

"The woman was moved under the bridge. After she fell two hundred feet and bounced on rocks all the way down or somebody chain-dragged her behind a car or truck. Bronson was taking her somewhere Monday night?"

It takes me a couple of seconds to get the implication. "Bronson hasn't told anyone he had a date with her?"

"Check it out if you want. I haven't heard Bronson's name mentioned in the investigation."

"He said it in the café. He was picking her up at six. She said, 'Roger that.'"

"Yeah, I got it. Talk to Lake County or the tribal police. They'll appreciate it."

"That's it?"

"It's called good citizenship. It beats anonymously dropping off guns and other shit in a post office box and muddying up a homicide investigation."

"I've never heard you use profanity."

"The pope gave me a dispensation." He breaks the connection.

I call the Tribal Police Department. The young dispatcher, Officer Hackman, answers.

"How you doin', partner?" I say.

"Is that you, Mr. Broussard? I just started one of your books."

"I hope you like it. Is Officer Bronson there?"

"No, sir, he's off today. Can I help you?"

"I wanted to talk to him about that woman who was found in a ravine outside St. Ignatius."

"Yeah, she worked at the café I sent you to," he replied. "She was a nice lady."

"Is Officer Bronson taking this hard?"

"Sir?"

"I mean they were pretty close friends, right?"

"I guess he knew her from the café. Heck, I don't know. You'd better ask him."

"Know where I can find him?"

"He likes to whitefish in late fall. Up at Alberton, where Fish Creek dumps into the Clark Fork. Mr. Broussard?"

"Yes?"

"Officer Bronson might could use a friend."

I DON'T WANT TO see Ray Bronson. But what are my alternatives? I drive fifty miles to Alberton Gorge. Even though winter is at hand, the Clark Fork is still running fast and wide between steep mountains that drop directly into the current and form a canyon whose whitewater turbulence is not for the weak of heart. Gray boulders spiderwebbed by large-leafed, plum-colored vines lie half-submerged in the water by a sandy beach at the entrance to the gorge, the slate-green current undulating smoothly to the next bend and the bend after that, the sun's reflection floating like gold coins just below the surface.

Down the slope from the two-lane asphalt road that goes through the tiny town of Alberton, I can see Ray Bronson casting with a spinning rod on a slab rock in the shadow of a giant boulder. No one else is on the stream. I park among the willows and put on a mask and walk through brush until I'm behind him. He's dressed in khakis and a checkered shirt and a fishing vest but without a hat, although the wind is cold when it blows across the water. A holstered chrome-plated snub is clipped on his belt.

"It's Aaron Broussard, Officer Bronson," I say. "I didn't want to give you a start."

He retrieves his line but doesn't turn around. "I saw you. What do you want?"

"The waitress named Irene at the café in Ronan? She was killed?"

He lifts his lure out of the water. It's a Mepps spinner, one with a treble hook. He flicks it over the riffle and lets the weight of the lure tighten the line, then begins to retrieve it. "It's my day off."

"It's a yes-or-no question."

He slowly winds the monofilament line onto the spool and turns around. There're deep bags under his eyes. "There's an investigation in progress. Mostly by Lake County."

"You had a date with her the night she disappeared. Correct? Does Lake County know about that?"

He props his rod against a willow tree and takes a mask from his pocket and hooks it on his ears. "We were going out to eat, but she canceled."

"You reckon her death was an accident?"

"I don't know what it was."

The wind changes and I can smell his odor, a mixture of nicotine and last night's beer. And maybe fear. The kind that wets the armpits and leaves a stink like soiled kitty litter.

"I talked to an investigator," I say. "To his knowledge, you didn't tell anyone you were picking up the lady at six p.m."

The skin under his left eye twitches. "You trying to do a number on me?"

"Nope."

"Hell you're not. You want in my ex-wife's bread, you son of a bitch."

I have no way of knowing where the hatred in his eyes comes from. But his vitriol is not of an ordinary kind. It has a question mark in it. As a child he was probably rejected and abused at the same time he was told he was loved and the pain he was enduring was for his own good. It is a masterpiece of deceit and guaranteed to cause the victim conflict with himself and the world for the rest of his days.

"I'm waiting," he says.

"On what?"

"Did I call it or not? You'd like to get in her pants?"

"You ever have your jaw broken by an eighty-five-year-old man?"

His face is like a death's-head. I've crossed a line. I see Fannie Mae standing in the shallows wearing a cute cap and a Garfield sweatshirt and pink tennis shoes without socks. She wiggles a finger of caution at me. But it's too late. You don't push a flawed man like Ray Bronson in a corner.

"Trout are out of season," I say.

"What?"

"It's catch-and-release on trout now. Why hurt them with a treble hook? Put some salmon eggs on a single hook and catch you a mess of whitefish." I try to smile at him.

He shoves me in the sternum.

"Please don't do that," I say, and step back.

"This?" he says. He shoves me again, harder.

I take another step back. "I didn't mean that about breaking your jaw. I'm sorry."

He makes a fist and hits me in the center of the chest, twisting his knuckles into the bone. The air goes out of my lungs.

Time to deck him, Pops, Fannie Mae says.

"Okay, Buster Brown," I say. "You called it. You're fixing to be the deadest bucket of shit that was ever poured in the ground."

"What did you say?"

"Put your hand on me again and I'll punch your ticket. I've done it to people I didn't have anything against."

"I don't care if you do," he says.

"Say again?"

"I saw the photos that were taken under the bridge," he says. "I can't get them out of my head. Somebody—"

"Somebody what?"

"Twisted Irene all up. Sanded off her skin. She didn't look human. Like her eyes were pasted on raw meat."

The image is hard to deal with. I clear my throat. "You believe the guy who did this also killed the Wetzel kid?"

"The Wetzels are Mexican 'breeds from Albuquerque. They're after the hundred grand that's buried on the res."

"What are you talking about?"

He wipes his eyes with his forearm. "I got to go."

"Tell me about the hundred grand."

"It's just one of those urban legends, that's all. Forget everything I said. Forget I put my hand on you. I'm sorry."

His breath is bilious, his throat printed with blue veins, his face as bloodless as china. The illogical state of his mind is a given, his potential anywhere between either sobbing hysterically or shooting people in a church. But I no longer believe the dark energy in his eyes is generated by hatred of his fellow man. That's too simple an explanation.

"You have a meth problem, partner?" I ask.

He points one finger between my eyes. "Stay away from Ruby. Touch her and you'll deal with me."

He throws his rod and reel in the current and marches up the slope to a brand-new Toyota RAV4 parked in the trees.

You gave it your best shot, Pops, Fannie Mae says.

"He's a dangerous man."

So are you. But you didn't hurt him. That's what style is all about.

Chapter Seventeen

THREE DAYS HAVE passed. I have not been bothered by the authorities regarding the drop-off I did at the post office with the Wetzel belongings. I suspect this is because Jeremiah McNally has already told his colleagues I intend to stonewall whatever questions they ask me. When they have evidence, they'll come after me with a chainsaw.

Tuesday morning I call Ruby Spotted Horse on her cell phone. "What is it now?" she answers before I can speak.

"Has your ex been sticking anything up his nose besides virus swabs?"

"You had trouble with him?"

"He thinks I have an agenda."

"An agenda with me?" she replies. "He's paranoid. He always has been."

"Do you have any information about the murder of the waitress in Ronan?"

"No one has called it a homicide. The body was found on a federal reservation, so the FBI may have gotten involved."

"You ever hear about a hundred thousand dollars being buried on the res?"

"Where'd you hear that?" she asks.

"From your ex."

"It's one of those legends. Except I heard five hundred thousand. Some dealers drove in a house-trailer load of crank that'd been cut with lithium and hydrochloric acid, and there was a big firefight with the mules and a lot of people got killed and the money got buried in an iron box, and the only guy who knew the location got capped. It's the kind of crap Ray would believe."

I feel my attention draining. "I saw Eugene Baker. I looked right into his face. I saw him burn the village. I pumped sixteen rounds into him with no effect."

"You saw this in a vision or what?"

"On the hillside behind my home."

"When did this happen?"

"Six days ago."

"You're just telling me now?" she says.

"I'm cautious about what I tell people. So are you, Miss Ruby."

There's a long silence. Through the window I see a yellow rust-eaten battered Mazda with no hubcaps, oil smoke welling from under the frame, come up the drive and stop. John Fenimore Culpepper gets out and peers at my windows, the car door open, one foot still on the floor, as if he's afraid to disengage from his portable fortress.

"I'm a little hurt, Mr. Broussard," Spotted Horse says. "I've trusted you. You should have told me you had an encounter with Baker."

"There's one other thing I need to tell you. Your former husband said I shouldn't come around you. In fact, he used the word 'touch.' "

"He did, did he? Well, fuck him."

"I'd better run."

"Did you hear what I just said?" she asks.

"You mean fuck him? Yes, that came through pretty clearly."

"Meet me at Applebee's at noon."

"Ten-four on that," I say, and ease the phone receiver into the cradle. When I turn around, Fannie Mae is standing three feet from me. *Bad Da-da,* she says.

"Stop giving me those stupid names."

How about "Parental Unit"?

I go through the front door and greet Johnny B. Goode Culpepper before she can say another word.

CULPEPPER IS WEARING a plain billed gray cap and a rumpled white shirt and a suit coat that doesn't match his trousers. I walk down the grade to his car. "What can I do for you, sir?"

"You mind if I come on your property and talk?" There's a tremolo in his voice.

"No, sir, I don't mind at all."

"I heard you taught at the university here."

"I was an instructor many years ago."

"They got a vocational program. I wondered what you thought of it."

"I think it's good."

His foot is still propped on the floor of the car, his arms stretched across the roof, his face windburned, his eyes almost colorless, the pupils like burnt match heads. He studies a sparrow hawk gliding above the trees. "My boy is a little slow, but he's a good worker," he says. "His hobby is bow-making. They got anything like that out there?"

"I can find out for you."

"It's the dyslexia that holds him back. It runs in our family. Both sides." His eyes go away from mine.

"You looking for a tutor?"

"Yessir, one that don't cost a lot."

"I'll see what I can do."

"I got to ask you something. That note you give me at the courthouse, somebody was asking for he'p. I said you was doing the devil's work. I did that because I was scared. Was somebody really wanting he'p?"

"I'm not sure, Mr. Culpepper."

But there's no relief in his face, and I have the conviction that I'm talking with a man who will never find peace.

"There's things I just don't understand," he says. "The way the world is. The way nothing adds up."

"Have you thought about getting away from Sister Ginny's crowd?"

"Judge not, lest you be judged."

"Using common sense is not a judgment on others, sir."

My words break across his face. He takes a piece of paper from his shirt pocket and hands it to me. "That's my phone number. If you can he'p Leigh, I'll be in your debt. I didn't treat you right, Mr. Broussard. You're a man of principle, and I admire you for it."

I watch him drive away, a blue-black cloud of oil smoke trailing him, then go back into the house. Fannie Mae is waiting for me. "Why are you giving me that look?" I say.

I don't trust Culpepper. If he was a wizard in the Alabama Klan, at the least he had to know the friends and families of the men who blinded and killed the little girls in the Birmingham church bombing.

"We don't know that."

Stop it.

"People change, Fannie."

You used to say people grow into what they always were.

"I was a cynic."

No, you refused to lie to yourself. You said it was the one sin we never forgive ourselves for.

I will not reply.

Where are you going?

"To take a shower."

Having lunch with Short Stuff?

Even as a little girl, Fannie Mae could be jealous when my attention went to others. "I won't listen to this."

Sorry, Pops. I get lonely when you're gone. Give her my best.

BECAUSE OF VIRUS restrictions, Applebee's is working at half capacity, and Spotted Horse and I are able to find an isolated table at the back of the restaurant. She's in uniform and her cruiser is parked on the other side of our window. I have never gone out in public with a woman who is fifty years younger than I. It feels strange and a little embarrassing, and I wonder if my discomfort indicates a degree of hypocrisy in my behavior—namely, I had no problem when I was alone with her.

There is another factor at work. Forty feet from me is a neatly dressed middle-aged mustached man eating with two other men of approximately the same age and dressed with the same level of neatness. The first man is looking straight at me, not with anger, not with recognition or even curiosity, but like a man looking at a dream or a memory or a mirage on a tar-patched desert highway or perhaps a decaying film negative about to flicker and light up in a space no bigger than a match flame and disappear into the world of inconsequence, leaving behind no trace of pain or irreparable loss.

I pick up a breadstick and bite off a small piece and chew it slowly and sip from my iced tea, my gaze focused on neutral space. "You're a quiet one today," Spotted Horse says.

"Officer Bronson said the Wetzel brothers were from Albuquerque. I thought they were from Idaho."

"Why do you want to know?"

"A lot of crank is coming out of Albuquerque. A bartender told me the younger brother burned up his father. Where's the mother?"

"I don't know. You know how many boys like the Wetzels are running around?"

Her voice is thinning out on me. I cannot resist looking at the middle-aged man at the table forty feet away. I pick up my bread knife with the tips of my fingers and set it back down. Spotted Horse looks over her shoulder and back at me. "That's Joe Latour. He's a detective with the sheriff's department. He's from Boston originally."

"Yeah," I say.

"You know him?"

"I met him the night my daughter was beat up."

"Latour caught the 911?"

"Yeah, he was in uniform then. He wouldn't allow her to sit in his cruiser. She had lost her coat and was cold."

"Maybe it was the end of his shift. Maybe he didn't want someone throwing up in his vehicle. Sometimes you just don't know."

"He didn't dump the cameras at the nightclub where she got beat up. He was going on vacation the next day."

"I don't want to say the wrong thing, Mr. Broussard, but from what I hear, your daughter had a few problems."

"Want to order?" I say.

"Sometimes cops have their problems, too."

"I got the message. Don't worry about it."

We order, then the food comes. My taste buds are still shot. I might as well be chewing wet newspaper.

"Mr. Broussard," she says.

"Call me Aaron."

"I didn't mean to sound hard-nosed."

"I didn't tell you the whole story. My daughter got herself to the ER. The hospital called the cops on their own. Latour showed up again. I felt the back of my daughter's head. It felt like a softball. I told him that by anyone's measure, this was felony assault. He blew it off. That's what happened. I don't hold it against him. Everybody has to stack his own time."

"Where'd you learn that expression?"

"Who cares? Y'all have a wire inside Ginny Stokes's congregation, don't you?"

The skin on her face shrinks. "Shut up," she whispers. I start to speak anyway, but she takes my hand and digs her nails into the palm. She speaks with her head down. "He reads lips. What you said could get someone killed."

The mustached man says something to his two friends. They turn around and look at us. I look directly at them, then pick up the check.

"What are you about to do?"

"Pay the check, then go to the men's room."

"If you go to their table, you and I are done."

I start to get up.

"Let me say something," she says. "Then make your choice."

It doesn't take her long. She says the loss of her niece is like the loss of the child she was never able to have. The daily acceptance of that loss is the reason she is drawn to me, and for that reason alone she will consider me a kindred spirit forever, and she doesn't care what others think of our being together.

When she finishes, I look down at my plate.

"You're just going to sit there?" she says.

My Stetson is crown-down on the table. I take a bite of a

french fry and wipe my mouth with a paper napkin and flip my Stetson on my head. "Let's take a ride."

"What for?"

"Call it the wild side of life."

Her mouth opens. "If you're saying what I think, you're the most disappointing man I've ever had the misfortune to meet."

"My taste buds are back. I once ate twelve Buster Bars. I'm going to go for thirteen. There's a Dairy Queen on Higgins."

"You don't really intend to do that, do you, Mr. Broussard?"

"Aaron."

The three men get up and walk past our table. The detective named Latour walks within three feet of my shoulder. I can see the pistol clipped on his belt, his flat stomach, the silk shirt and gold tie clip he wears, the black hair on the backs of his wrists, and smell the cigarette smoke in his clothes and the fried food he has eaten and the hint of deodorant under his arms. I lift my eyes to his. He looks right through me. It's obvious he has no idea who I am and probably no knowledge of Fannie Mae's death. Spotted Horse sees the look on my face. "What are you thinking about?"

"My daughter said to give you her best."

She takes a breath and holds it and then lets it out slowly. Her eyes are sleepy, as though she's drifting away.

"Do I sound strange?" I ask.

"You're a good man." She touches my ankle with the toe of her shoe. "Good people are the ones who get hurt the most. Don't let the world I live in suck you into its maw."

Ten minutes later we walk outside into the sun-spangled coolness of the day. The mountains are etched sharply against a flawless blue sky that arches from one horizon to the other. One hundred yards away are the water tower and the original buildings of old Fort Missoula, where Black bicycle troops were stationed to help dispossess the Indians of the lands they had owned for over ten thousand years. The story of the fort is one of exploitation and the deliberate division of oppressed people, and I try not to dwell upon it. But I cannot help it, just as I cannot help thinking about my ancestors who fought for the South at Shiloh and Gettysburg. Spotted Horse follows me to the Dairy Queen and shares one Buster Bar with me at a cold plank table under a tree that has no leaves. It's not a very romantic setting, but it's a special moment just the same, and when she asks what I'm thinking about, I lie and tell her nothing because her words to me about kindred spirits are in a category you hide in a secret place, maybe a magical pool where one day, when the world is too much with you late and soon, you dip your hand into a source of strength that becomes your light, your sword, and your shield, and after that moment you join a pantheon that's for the ages.

Chapter Eighteen

At FOUR-TWENTY A.M. a shock hits the house and almost knocks me out of my bed. The moon is up and I can see snow flying parallel to the ground. Then something hits the house again, shaking snow off the roof, sending a load straight down past my window, thudding like lead when it hits the flower bed and wheelbarrow and coiled garden hose that has frozen as solid as concrete from the water I left in it.

I go downstairs and look through the back kitchen window. A little girl in a thin lavender dress without a coat or hat or shoes is looking back at me from the center of the yard, her blond ringlets touching her shoulders, her short, puffed, lace sleeves exposing most of her arms. The prints of her bare feet on the lawn lead back to the chicken house, which is built onto the side of the barn. I pull a coat off a peg in the mud-room and go down the back steps into the windstorm.

"What's your name, little girl?" I ask.

Mary, she says.

"Are you lost?"

No.

"What are you doing here?"

Looking for Fannie Mae. I can't find her.

"How do you know my daughter, Miss Mary?"

She saw me playing with the animals and showed me how to make their shapes with my hands in front of a lamp. Want to see?

"What were you doing in the chicken house?"

Playing. Can I come in your house?

"If you'll let me take your picture. Otherwise no one will believe you've been here."

She looks sideways and seems to frown.

"Did I make you mad?" I ask.

I don't like being dead. Where is Fannie Mae?

"She comes and goes. Can I do something for you?"

I saw you shooting at a soldier.

"He was killing the Indians, Mary. Little children."

Don't talk bad about the soldiers.

"Let me go in the house and find a coat for you."

I don't care about coats. Fannie Mae was supposed to wait for me. Then she ran off. I don't like that.

"That doesn't sound like Fannie Mae," I say.

You think you're smart? Listen to this: "Mary, Mary, quite contrary, how does your garden grow? With silver bells and cockleshells and pretty maids all in a row."

"I'm cold, Mary. Come inside with me. I bet you're hungry."

Did you hear the poem or not? The silver bells are thumbscrews. The cockleshells put the squeeze on the prisoner's private parts. The queen of England used those things on the people she hated.

"You shouldn't talk about things like that."

Aunt Ruby has to release the Old People.

"I'm not sure you're her niece, little girl."

You better watch how you talk. Watch this.

She stands on the tips of her toes in the frozen grass and stretches her arms toward the sky and speaks in a language I cannot understand. The snow in the air and the snow on the ground begin to swirl, forming a funnel that peels the remaining ice and snow off the roof and scoops up the topsoil and the bricks that border the flower beds and spins all of it cyclonically, along with the frozen garden hose that is now as supple as a snake and straightening like a whip. Mary snatches the hose from the funnel and points the nozzle at the carpet of frozen green grass and uses it like a welder's torch and burns the date July 4, 2012, into the sod.

Then she's gone and the funnel disappears and everything inside it clatters to the ground. There is no sound other than the door to the chicken house squeaking in the wind. I cross the lawn, the grass like spikes under my shoes, and go inside the chicken house. The walls and floor are splattered with blood and feathers and wings torn from the chickens' dead bodies. The stench is unbearable, its rankness far more stringent and feral than that of blood and feces alone. The only odor I remember like it came from body bags on a six-by that was blown off the road by a land mine south of the Thirty-eighth Parallel and left in a ravine for a week in ninety-degree heat. But even that doesn't quite describe it. I think of a brothel area in a town on the Gulf Coast where I lived many years ago, and I think about the ditch behind the cribs where the whores emptied their buckets in the early-morning hours, and I think about the stink rising from that ditch as well as the smoke from the sugar refinery and the raw garbage burning in the trash barrels behind the cribs and the occasional sheets and tick mattresses that would be stacked on the fires and the salty smell like rotten fish that seemed to live in the soil. The stench of all these things would flatten in the wind and hang in a gray cloud over the shacks of Black people, then seep into the white part of town, at which time the sheriff would send inmates from the parish prison with cans of kerosene to set the ditch aflame.

I pull my coat over my nose and back out of the chicken house and clear my throat and spit, then go in my house and open a bottle of mouthwash and gargle with it and spit it in the sink. My armpits are looped with sweat. I left the chicken house door open, and now feathers are blowing in the yard and a fox is standing in the doorway with a chicken's head in its mouth. I do not want to accept what has happened in the last fifteen minutes. Nor do I wish to tell anyone about it. I lie down on the couch, shivering under a blanket, and watch the dawn crawl over the mountains. I refuse to close my eyes until the sun has driven the darkness from my house and my land and my trees and my animals and I am sufficiently safe to let sleep have its way.

One hour later, I wake in an embryonic ball, my arms clasped around my head, wondering where my daughter has gone.

Chapter Nineteen

Aᴛ ᴏɴᴇ ɪɴ the afternoon I call Spotted Horse on her cell phone and tell her about the little girl in my backyard. "What's the significance of July 4, 2012?" I ask.

"That's the day my niece was kidnapped at the powwow in Arlee. She went to get some fry bread. She was found in a garbage dump the next day."

"You think the little girl in my backyard is your niece?"

"Maybe physically."

"The little girl had blond hair."

"My sister married a white man. Both of them died in a car accident, and I took over Mary." I heard her blow into the receiver. "My little Mary."

"Miss Ruby, I think I smelled sulfur in the chicken house."

"Maybe you did. I think the little girl you saw was Eugene Baker."

"What does Baker want from me?"

"Your soul," she says.

"Why me?"

"He doesn't like you. Can you do me a favor?"

"Sure."

"Don't call me 'Miss' anymore."

"I won't." Then I say it again before I can stop. "Miss Ruby, can I say something personal?"

"Go ahead."

"I think you've had enough grief without the likes of me around."

"I'll make the decision about that," she replies. "We have a bond, Aaron Broussard. Certain kinds of loss are forever. Not many people understand that."

I believe those are the saddest words I have ever heard. I have another question for her, one that has confounded me since I saw the piece of notebook paper on the cellar floor, but I cannot bring myself to ask her now.

I WAIT UNTIL FIVE in the afternoon before I call again. "Ruby?" I say.

"We're making progress," she says.

"The little girl's visit brings back a question that has more to do with John Culpepper and Sister Ginny than it does with the little girl. Why is it that Culpepper could read the note I picked up on your cellar floor, but McNally could not?"

"I think the note was written by an evil spirit. Evil spirits do not have dominion over one another. Only good people are vulnerable to them. People like Baker and McNally are blind to each other's iniquity; only good people are caught by their snares. I thought I already explained that. Actually, that's how it works most of the time in the world of the living."

"Okay, I buy John Culpepper as a decent enough person in spite of his background with the Klan. But what about Jeremiah? He's always been a pretty good fellow."

"I'm not so sure about that," she says.

"Can you get rid of the mashed potatoes?"

"There's a rumor. He got it on with a confidential informant when he was with the Drug Enforcement Administration."

"I never heard that. Also, that's not the equivalent of original sin."

"I think he's also a screw-down, marry-up kind of guy. Put it this way. He cut a wide swath through the res."

"That's not the Jeremiah I know."

"Because you want people to be what they're not."

"Hope to see you later, Ruby."

"*Hope* to?"

"Yeah."

"What's that mean?" she says.

"It means I don't want to talk about my friends behind their back."

There's a pause. "I'm having a hard time handling what you just said."

"Sorry, I didn't get much sleep last night. I wanted to tell you about the little girl, and I did. Goodbye." I hang up as softly as I can.

The sun is already setting and I have no idea where Fannie Mae has gone. The Bitterroot River has taken on the dark green undulating luminescence of a river that could have flowed through ancient Avalon when the world was new and filled with romance, although we think of the Middle Ages as a time of darkness and ignorance. Those who believe that know little about it and usually have no problem with the mass slaughters of the twentieth century. I can almost hear Merlin's blessing of his people at Stonehenge or young Arthur rasping Excalibur free from the magical stone or the Maid Marian and Robin of Locksley and his Merry Men roasting a boar on a spit while the poor and the abandoned dance and play their dulcimers and flutes and fiddles inside the glorious green-gold glow of Sherwood Forest. Who needs drugs and booze?

The phone rings, breaking my reverie.

"Hello."

"I'll hate myself for making this call," Ruby says. "What you said to me was abusive and self-righteous. I'm really disappointed in you, sir. You don't know how much that hurt. I hope you have a good life."

So much for romantic dreams out of medieval times. I want to put my head on a butcher block.

Chapter Twenty

THE NEXT DAY is Thursday. I put on a mask—not because of the virus but so I can endure the stench of the chicken house and chop a hole in the ground with a mattock and bury the feathers and entrails and frozen bodies and smashed eggs of my poultry, then scrub the wood floors and walls with Clorox and Ajax. But no matter how long I scrub or mop, I can't get rid of the smell. I light two lanterns and set them on the floor in hopes of cauterizing the air. Then I feel a presence standing behind me in the doorway, and I turn and see a figure backlit by the sun and wearing a Felix the Cat T-shirt and an Easter straw hat with plastic flowers on it.

"Hi, Fannie," I say. "I was worried about you."

What's that smell?

"A little girl named Mary was here. She said she's Ruby Spotted Horse's niece. She said you taught her how to make shadows on the walls that look like animals."

I don't know her, Pops.

"I didn't think so. Where did you go?"

To ask for an extension.

"What was the answer?"

Rules are rules. There're billions of people out there.

"You were clean and sober. It's not fair."

Neither is death. I wasn't ready. I was supposed to promote your new book. That's why I was allowed to hang around. Now you've gotten yourself in a mess.

"Talk to someone."

Stick with Short Stuff. She can do anything I could.

"I just offended her."

What am I going to do with you, Pops?

She's beginning to fade into the light as though molecularly dissolving into pollen.

"Don't go away, Fannie Mae. Come back. I can't take this."

I don't want to scare you, but there're creatures following me. I don't know who they are. I don't think they're supposed to be here. They're frightening to look at. There's a pause, then her voice changes when she says, *Oh, Daddy. Oh, Daddy. Oh, Daddy.*

She only called me Daddy when she was afraid. She starts to cry. Her words crackle like static in an electric storm. She breaks apart in the wind like a thunderclap and is sucked away, the remnant of her voice fading into the chirping of a tiny bird abandoned in the nest.

I TRY TO PRETEND I've created a fantasy. But I know better. I go into Lolo and order lunch at a sandwich shop but can't swallow my food. "You feeling sickly, Mr. Broussard?" the waitress says. She's shy and young and is embarrassed by her question.

"I look a little gray?" I ask.

"No, sir. I just wanted to say I'm real sorry about your loss."

"Thank you. But I'm okay. Just pack it up for me, will you?"

"Yes, sir," she says. "I think there's a boy been looking through the window at you."

I turn around but see no one outside the window.

"He's gone now," she says.

She packs up my sandwich, and I go outside and look up and down the highway. The submarine sandwich feels warm and heavy and greasy through the tightly wrapped sack cupped in my hand, and I throw it in the trash can. Then I see Jack Wetzel walking toward a biker bar at the intersection where Highway 12 commences westward over Lolo Pass into Idaho. I get in my pickup and drive to the bar and park and go through the door. I can hear pool balls clacking and a jukebox playing, and I smell my old enemy, alcohol of any kind, which hangs on the edge of my sleep or whenever the sun turns into a sliver of black carbon and slides off the edge of the earth.

Wetzel is not there. Two bikers in jean vests are playing nine-ball. The bartender looks at me. His body is truncated, his face bearded, his earlobes hung with gold rings, his forearms wrapped with hair and leather wristbands. "What will it be, my man?" he says.

"My man?"

"What are you having, sir?"

"Nothing. What happened to that kid who came in here?"

"There was no kid in here."

"Don't tell me that," I say.

He balls a dry cloth in his hand and idly rubs a spot on the bar. The pool players have rested the butt ends of their pool cues on the floor. Their bodies are thin and motionless, bent like bananas, framed like carrion birds against the glow of the jukebox.

"You guys see that kid who came in here?" I say.

Neither of them responds.

"Time for you to travel, bub," the bartender says.

"Give me a Collins with cherries and orange or lime slices in it. And cut the 'bub' shit."

"I can see it's gonna be one of those days," he says. "A young guy came in here, used the restroom, and left. Maybe that was your guy, maybe not. Now get the fuck out of here."

The darkest days and nights of my life have been connected with alcohol. Its effect on me involves the instant release of the gargoyles I've kept closed up in the subconscious since I was a little boy. The room is beginning to spin, then it warps out of shape as though it is made of reddish-black licorice. The two pool shooters look at me like pallbearers. I hear someone pick up a phone and punch in three numbers.

I stare into the bartender's face.

"What's with you, man?" he asks.

"You are. With me, I mean. In my thoughts."

"What are you talking about?" he says.

"I was thinking about killing you."

"You were *what*?"

"I'll leave. I'm sorry for having bothered y'all."

I walk out the door onto the wide gallery that fronts the building. I feel as though I'm walking with buckets on my feet, and I have to grasp the railing before I fall down. Jack Wetzel is standing on the shoulder of Highway 12, trying to thumb a ride with one of the truckers shifting down for the long grind up Lolo Pass.

"Hold up there, kid," I yell.

A diesel truck boomed down with ponderosa has pulled to the side, the driver shoving open the passenger door for Wetzel to get in.

I start running as best as I can for a man my age. "Jack!" I yell. "It's Aaron Broussard! I'm the only friend you've got, kid!"

He hesitates, then gets up into the cab and pulls the door shut behind him. The truck swings back on the road, blowing a black cloud of nitrogen oxide in my face.

I FEEL MY GEARS starting to strip. I cannot deal with the image of my daughter being pursued by monsters on the other side of the veil. When I return home, I occupy myself in whatever fashion I can to keep those images out of my head. I finally connect with a graduate student at the university who says he will tutor John Culpepper's son for fifteen dollars an hour. I tell him to ask for only seven and I'll add eight to it, but he should say nothing to Mr. Culpepper about our agreement.

"They're poor people?" he says. "Because if they are, I can go down on the price a little bit, Mr. Broussard."

"Nope, leave the price right where it is."

"You're a kind man."

"I just threatened to kill a man in a saloon in Lolo," I reply.

"You've got a great sense of humor, too."

I make it to five o'clock without buying a bottle of Scotch and drive to Ruby Spotted Horse's house on the res. I have no idea whether she will be home or not. If it's the latter, I'm going to stay there anyway and either sleep in my truck or break into her house and see what is in the back of her cellar.

It's cold when I arrive, the magpies pecking the pumpkin rinds in the adjacent field, the few leaves on her maple trees lit by the sun's last yellowish-red effort. Her cruiser is parked in the yard. Although the house was built much later, it reminds me of seventeenth-century Pilgrim homes, put together by shipwrights, the design angular and utilitarian, the once-silvery wood blackened from grass fires, the windows little more than gun loops, sacrificing light for the containment of heat, and perhaps because of the late-sun-orange smoke billowing from the two chimneys.

I knock hard on the front door with my fist. Ruby opens

the door, a sandwich in one hand. "I told you about coming here without calling."

"Would you have given me permission?"

"No."

"I saw Fannie Mae. She said she's being pursued by creatures she called frightening."

"Have you been drinking? Because that's what you look like."

"I thought about it. But I didn't. May I come in?"

She rubs the heel of her hand in her eye sockets. "I'm really tired. I've got an awful lot to deal with."

"I understand."

"Where do you plan on going right now?"

"Back home."

She nods as though in agreement with me. But she is not in agreement with me. I think she is very angry. "What did your daughter say when she left you?"

"I don't know. She broke into hundreds of gold particles. Then she and her voice were sucked away."

Her sandwich is dripping on the rug. She seems to have nowhere to put it nor words that will take care of the problem I've brought her.

"You said you have a lot to deal with," I say. "Can I help?"

"I don't think we're very good for each other, Aaron."

"You have someone else to lean on? McNally, your ex, your colleagues? I don't see them here."

"Yeah," she says.

"Yeah what?"

"Yeah, maybe you can help," she replies. "How does it feel to be so fucked up you can understand someone like me?"

She offers to fix a sandwich for me. "I don't eat meat anymore," I say.

She gets a box of doughnuts out of the icebox and sets it in front of me on the kitchen table, then sits across from me and resumes eating her sandwich, her eyes empty. Her tabby cat, Maxwell Gato, sits on the table alongside us.

"The only other person I've seen allow pets on the table was my daughter," I say.

"Most pets have better hygiene than human beings," she replies. "At least Maxwell Gato does." She picks him up, kisses his head, and sets him back down.

"What kind of trouble are you having?"

"My ex is filing suit for half the house. He's also telling people I'm crazy and I'm mixed up with an old man, namely you, and talking out of school."

"I don't get that last part."

"Ray has told my superiors I've given you information about a major investigation into drug trafficking. I can lose my job."

"You made a slip, but I didn't repeat it, so your ex is lying."

"When did I make a slip?"

"You asked me about my visit to Virginia Stokes. I figured somebody carrying a wire told you."

"You figured wrong," she says. "I patrol that area. I saw your truck parked by Stokes's church. Forget it. Ray is out to get me. He lies and lies until his lies become the truth. I've never known anyone like him. He's the most selfish human being I have ever known."

"I think something or someone much bigger than your former husband is on your mind."

"Okay, here it comes," she says. "I'm one of the Guardians. I signed up for life. The only way I can get out of my situation is to find a replacement."

"Me?"

"You fit the profile. A loner, an idealist looking for a cross, a guy who hates the Herd."

"I'm not signing up. Put that down as DOA and FTS."

"What is FTS?"

"You'll figure it out."

"Aaron, you have every sign of a man experiencing a nervous breakdown. Except it's not a nervous breakdown. Everything you and I have seen is real. In fact, it's even worse than real. Your daughter has become prey to spirits like Eugene Baker. Notice I'm talking in the plural. Would you like to see who is behind the stones at the back of my cellar?"

No, I would not. But I've already gone across a line and entered an unseen world in which my daughter has disappeared and may be in the hands of predators.

"Answer me," she says. "Are you willing to look at what's down there? Because if you look, you will never be the same. Tell me now."

Chapter Twenty-One

Five years ago Ruby set up a wireless security camera in front of the entrance to the tunnel at the back of the cellar. The tunnel had been breached six times, through guile or someone piercing a piece of crumbling rock and slithering a serpentine finger through the hole onto the petroglyphs that covered the keystones. Ruby did not know how many of the Old People escaped, but each instance was followed by bizarre crimes in the Pacific Northwest that remain unsolved.

We go into her living room, where she turns on the fifty-inch television and uses the security-camera app to pull up a video, the images blurred and fixed in place. The light from the ancient fixture in the ceiling is muted; the room smells faintly of dust and old wallpaper, in essence, the past. "You ready?" she says.

"Sure," I lie.

"You got it," she says. She picks up Maxwell Gato and puts him outside. "You want the sound on?"

"Why would I not want the sound?"

"Ask me that three minutes from now."

She starts the video. The landscape on the screen seems

infinite, dotted with burned cities, backdropped by a red sky from the horizon to the heavens. The earth is scorched and the roads threaded with lines of refugees and ox-drawn wagons that have wooden wheels and starved horses half-dead in their harnesses and donkeys and mules who are being beaten with whips. But the screen does not limit itself to one historical period. Roman soldiers plow salt in the ruins of Carthage; Vikings set fire to merchant ships whose sails are painted with the star and crescent moon of Islam; English soldiers called "the goddamns" are executed by Joan of Arc's soldiers after they have surrendered; the Imperial Japanese use blindfolded Chinese peasants roped to wood stakes for bayonet practice; and on a distant hill, three figures are nailed on crosses against a red sky.

The images are kaleidoscopic, the severity of their visuality an assault on the sensibilities, the kind of material that television producers incongruously warn their viewers not to watch. If the images possess a theme, it's very simple: The present is no different from the past, and in some ways it is worse. The most haunting images are the flash-burned shadow of a child on the wall of a roofless house at Hiroshima; a Jewish mother leading her three children to a crematorium; and a white mob descending on the Black district in Tulsa, Oklahoma, murdering many and burning out ten thousand, the fires smoldering and the stench clinging for days.

But I quickly discover I do not possess sufficient moral authority to judge others. An event of sixty-seven years ago appears in the lower-right corner, then the images expand until they cover the entire screen.

"I don't know how that got there," Ruby says.

"It's all right."

"No, I'm going to turn this off," she says.

"Leave it."

It's night on the screen, the monsoon season just beginning. Thirteen other soldiers and I are up to our ankles in an irrigation canal on the edge of a rice paddy. The rain is clicking on my poncho and steel pot and blowing in my face. A Chinese probe is coming toward us inside the fog. They move slowly, spaced apart, their burp guns slung from their necks. A trip flare pops and drifts over the paddy, hissing with smoke and a brilliant incandescence. The Chinese freeze and turn into stick figures, looking at the ground so their faces don't reflect the light of the flare. Someone down the line coughs, then a Chinese soldier clanks a potato masher on his helmet to ignite the fuse and flings it into the canal. It blows water and mud into the air but hurts no one. Regardless, everyone opens up, a thirty-caliber streaking tracers across the paddy. A Chinese soldier carrying a captured American flamethrower on his back lights us up, arching intermediate bursts of liquid flame into the canal, boiling the water and turning our medic into a blackened cipher.

In my peep sight, I catch the soldier with the flamethrower and burn the whole clip. Even though I'm looking through iron sights and the stock is jerking against my shoulder, I can see his face clearly. He's no older than I am. Though three rounds hit his tanks, they don't explode; they leak before fully igniting. The Chinese soldier struggles to get the canvas straps off his shoulders, then is enveloped in flame and runs blindly through the paddy, his mouth open, his pain so intense it absorbs his screams before they can leave his throat.

"Fucking A, Broussard!" the sergeant yells. "Fucking A! Now let's kick some ass!"

I see myself smiling on the screen. Ruby turns off the television. "That's enough," she says.

I look at the floor. My hands are gripped under my thighs.

"You okay?" she says.

"Yes," I say. I stare at the darkness of the television screen. I see my reflection, but I'm not sure it's me. My face looks twisted, like those of the gargoyles who live in my sleep.

"I'm going to bring Maxwell Gato back in," she says.

"You don't let him watch TV?"

"He's afraid of the set," she says.

But I'm not thinking about the cat. I lean forward, a pain like a shard of glass in my stomach. It passes, but instead of feeling relief, I want to drink, and I mean drink: Scotch and soda, vodka with Collins mix and cherries and orange slices, Jack Daniel's with a Heineken back, buckets of Champale, and the real deal when you want to cook your head, absinthe distilled from wormwood.

Ruby comes back into the room with Maxwell Gato cradled in her arms. "What are you thinking about?" she asks.

I rub my nose with the back of my hand. "Nothing."

"I worry about you."

"Don't."

She puts Maxwell Gato on the coffee table and sits down next to me on the couch. "We have a lot in common," she says.

"We're loners?"

"I'm not like other people. Neither are you. Why should we pretend?"

"I'm old, Miss Ruby. You're young and beautiful."

"What does it take for you to stop using the word 'Miss'?"

"Search me."

She stands up and looks at me a long time. "Is there something wrong with me?" she asks. "You think I'm immoral?"

"No, ma'am."

I don't know what to say. I can't quite tell her how I feel. "How about some ice cream?" she asks. "Would you like that?"

"That would be fine."

"You're a strange man."

"Could I use your bathroom, please?"

"It's just off the dining room," she says. "Yes, you can certainly use it. Please."

She walks away, her back stiff with either hostility or dismay. The bathroom door has a milk-glass knob on it, probably one made in the 1890s. I go inside and turn the key in the lock. The floor is made of wood that has never been painted and for years has probably been cleaned with a wire brush and bleach and vinegar. The ceiling is plated with stamped tin; the bathtub has claw feet and a long streak of orange on the porcelain under the faucet. The simplicity of the room and its resistance to time is comforting in a way I can't adequately explain. Perhaps simply because it's far from the canal near the Thirty-eighth Parallel. Or maybe because it reminds me of Yoakum, Texas, when I stayed with my grandfather at the end of the Great Depression and woke in the morning to birdsong and the smell of smokehouse meat. Damn the century in which I was born. Would that I could return to the natural world, one of flowers and fruit that could be picked from the tree, one in which the gift of life was gift enough.

But what does this really mean? The truth is, I can't look at my reflection because I fear I will see the face of an eighteen-year-old who laughed after he incinerated a peasant who probably wanted nothing more from life than a few more bowls of rice for his family. Somehow the callousness I showed in the canal is linked to my inability to find Fannie Mae, as though the absence of goodness in my deeds has empowered my enemies and left me in their sway. I sit on the side of the tub, my angst so great that I see myself loading the M1 again, and this time I tuck the muzzle under my chin.

Then I realize something is wrong, something whose potential is worse than the footage I watched on the television screen.

I go into the kitchen. There are three bowls of ice cream on the table. Ruby has waited for me, but Maxwell Gato has started in on his two scoops of vanilla, his tail straight up, his pink seat pointed at me.

"That scene in Korea is not how it happened," I say.

"I don't understand," Ruby says.

"I took no pride in killing the Chinese soldier who carried the flamethrower. The sergeant was KIA the previous week. I remember him well. His name was Geissler. He was a good fellow from St. Louis. He was not in that canal. Somebody is trying to put my head in a vise."

"You're accusing me of doing something like that?"

"No, it's the nature of evil. It makes you resent yourself. It fills you with guilt. It steals the sunlight from your life."

"So what am I supposed to do with the video?"

"Destroy it."

"You think that's going to get rid of what's under my house?"

"No, but we don't have to let it ruin our lives," I reply.

"You said 'we.'"

"I guess I did. Would you stand up, please?"

"What for?" she asks.

"Just stand up."

She gets up slowly. I put my arms around and press her body against mine, my chin resting on the top of her head. "You're a really nice lady, Miss Ruby."

"Thank you," she says.

I pull her tighter. She steps on top of my shoes. I can feel my heart beating against her cheek, her fingernails seeking purchase in my back. I pick her up on my chest and bury my face in her neck and want to stay there forever.

Chapter Twenty-Two

Two days later, on Saturday morning, I see a boy in laced new work boots and starched and ironed navy blue strap overalls over a pressed denim shirt, with a fresh haircut, walk up my drive and mount the steps and knock on my door. He wears neither a hat nor a coat and seems so frail in stature that a hard wind could blow him down the road. He's looking over his shoulder and does not see me when I approach the door. "What do you want, Jack?" I say through the glass.

"Need to talk," he says, turning toward me with neither fear nor anger but a deadness in his eyes that doesn't go with his years.

"I tried to stop you on the highway, but you climbed into the cab of a log truck. That was rude."

"I had some people after me."

I wait for him to continue, but he doesn't. I unlock the door and step outside. His skin has a translucent bleached look, his tats and his veins like faded print on parchment. "Say it," I tell him.

"You pissed at something?"

"Yeah, I gave you a break when you came to my house to

either rob or kill me. Now your brother is dead, and the cops are probably looking for you. I don't want you dragging your problems on my gallery."

"On your what?"

"Get out of here," I reply.

"You said I was stand-up and had moxie."

"What about it?"

"Nobody else ever said that to me."

"So?"

"I need a job. Anything. I want to start over."

"What about the cops?"

"Unless you file charges, they don't have anything on me. Plus I'm not a big ripple in anybody's life."

"That's not what I'm talking about. Your brother was torn apart. I think the cops have a few questions for you."

"My brother tried to slam a gram, then went crazy and climbed between two boxcars while they were moving."

"I was told you set fire to your home when you were twelve."

"I was cooking my father's dinner while he was balling a woman he brought home from a truck stop. I burned his food, so he slapped me all over the kitchen and threw me out. He must have left the burner on. But I didn't do it."

I wonder how much of his story is a lie and how much is true, and more importantly, I wonder if he knows the difference.

When I don't speak, he gazes down the slope, his expression whimsical, narcissistic, the kind of kid who feeds on thoughts about the importance of his own mortality. Then he looks at me again. His eyes are flat, impenetrable, like watermelon seeds. "You think I'm some kind of monster?"

"If you work for me, it's hit-it-and-git-it all day long, and no profanity while you're on the property."

"You didn't answer my question."

"Yeah," I say. "I didn't."

"Why?"

"Because you shouldn't have asked it."

His face clouds as he looks at the river and the undulation of the waves in the mid-current and the tangle of cool green-yellow light sealed under it. His face is fine-boned, his skull probably as fragile as an eggshell. "I didn't have much of an upbringing. But I learned early that manners and morality aren't the same thing."

"Where you staying?"

"At the Poverello," he says.

"You need a few dollars until you can make a payday?"

"Yes, sir, I sure could."

I hand him a twenty-dollar bill, but I don't quite let go of it. "You wouldn't jump me over the hurdles, would you, Jack?"

"I don't know what that means, sir," he replies.

"That means you wouldn't play a trick on me, would you?"

"No, sir."

I release the double sawbuck and shut the door and softly slip the bolt.

MY CHARITABLE ACT, if that's what it was, brings me no peace. I don't know where Fannie Mae has gone, nor how to get her back. I drive to the cemetery and place flowers on her grave and speak to her through the ground. The wind is cold, the mountains blue in the distance, the birch tree above her grave denuded of its leaves, the white bark cracked with brown and black rings around the trunk and limbs. I squat down by the bronze plaque on the grave and run my fingers over the letters in her name.

"You've got to give me a sign, kid," I say. "Your old man is about to lose it."

A little boy is running through the cemetery, flying a kite with the American flag emblazoned on it. He almost runs me down. His father grabs him by the hand and apologizes.

"That's all right," I say, squinting up at him. "It's a fine day for kites."

They walk away together, the father resting his hand on the little boy's shoulder. Then I go down on one knee and say a prayer, ignoring the moisture and rich black soil in the rolls of sod and grass that have not mended the work of the gravedigger's steel bucket. I belong to a house church, but I don't pray in public except when I come here; if I did not pray here, I might smash my fists against any surface I can find.

Two shadows, one long, one short, fall across the plaque.

"Sorry to bother you again," the father of the kite flyer says. "Is that Tacoma yours?"

"Yes, sir, it is."

"You left your engine running."

I stand up and brush off my knee, then feel in my pocket. "Must be somebody else's vehicle. I have my keys."

He points at my truck. "That black pickup?" he says. "It's running, whether it's yours or not."

"Thank you," I say.

I wait until they're gone, then walk to the truck. The tailpipe is vibrating, the engine idling. As soon as I unlock the door, the engine dies. There is no key in the ignition. I look back at the grave. A solitary robin is standing on the plaque. The robin looks at me, then lifts into the air, circles once over my pickup, and flies away.

———————

THAT NIGHT, AFTER I fall asleep on the couch with a quilt over my head, I hear a clanking sound in the fireplace. I pull the quilt off my head and sit up. Fannie Mae is sitting in a straight-back chair by the hearth, jabbing at a burnt log with a fire poker. Her skin is lit by a watery yellow nimbus shaped like a candle flame, except it gives no heat and is flickering like a lightbulb on the verge of shorting out. She gives up on the fire and drops the poker in the ash.

Sorry I couldn't get back to you sooner, she says. *I had some trouble with a couple of guys.*

"Major Baker was one of them?"

Yep, and some who are a hundred times worse.

"Who are they?"

World-class assholes.

"Why are they allowed to bother you?"

They're not. It's me that's going against the rules.

"Because you're looking after me?"

Somebody has to. What were you doing with Short Stuff?

"Forget about me. Who were the people chasing you?"

They belong in hell. That's not a figure of speech. That's where they escaped from.

"Do you want me with you? I can do the footwork."

Don't you dare think like that. That's what they want. They fear your goodness.

"I doubt that."

She doesn't answer.

"You sound tired."

I am. It's you who has the power. That's what you don't understand, Pops. It's the living who have to keep these assholes locked up.

"You have to stay with me, Fannie Mae. That's been my prayer since you died. That you'll always be with me."

I love you, Pops. You're such a good dad. You don't know how much I miss you. But at a certain time you have to say farewell.

"I will not do that. Never. Not in this world, not in the next. Where are you going?"

I get up from the couch and walk toward her. The nimbus is jittering, her dimensions shrinking, her face dissolving, her mouth moving without sound, perhaps in protest. Then she's gone and the room spins so violently that I fall sideways and the floor comes up and hits me like a fist. I lie inches from the fireplace, the smell of ash and carbon in my nostrils, my right arm twitching, my mouth drooling on the hearth, my eyes sightless, as though they have been picked from the sockets.

It's called hysterical blindness. I call it another night in Gethsemane, a garden you never want to visit.

THE MANAGER OF the Poverello, our local homeless shelter, dropped off Jack Wetzel on Monday at eight a.m., and the two of us went to work cleaning the barn and then running a plumber's snake through a stopped-up sewer line and then splitting firewood. I have no doubt he's a good worker. It's noon now, and so far Jack hasn't taken a break except to use the bathroom. I go inside and look at a manuscript I can't finish or even think about, drop it in a drawer, and watch Jack through the window. It's obvious he takes pleasure in a skill he has just learned. My firewood is stacked in the open air against an outside wall of the barn under a roof supported by poles. Jack balances a segment of ponderosa on the block, tamps a wedge even with the grain, and raises the maul high above his head and splits the wood cleanly and to its base. I go back outside. "You're getting to be a pro," I say.

"Thank you," he replies.

"You never split firewood before?"

"No, sir." He pulls off the work gloves I lent him earlier and touches a blister on his palm.

"Maybe lay off the maul for a while," I say.

"It don't hurt."

"Lay off it just the same. Want to go to lunch with me at Fiesta en Jalisco?"

"I brought a sack lunch from the Poverello."

"Well, it looks like you do real fine work, Jack."

"I appreciate you giving me a chance, Mr. Broussard. I know I say the wrong things to people sometimes," he says. "I mean talking like a smart-ass."

"Don't worry about it. I'll be back later. Can you hold things down?"

"Yes, sir," he replies. "Want me to clean that chicken house?"

"It could use it."

I DRIVE MY AVALON to a Mexican restaurant on Brooks in Missoula and look in the rearview mirror as I turn into the parking lot. A red Ford F-150 is tight on my bumper, close enough that I dare not touch the brake. I go on through the lot and park in back. The driver of the Ford beats me to the entrance of the restaurant. "How's it hanging, slick?" she says.

"How are you, Sister Ginny?" I reply.

She's wearing camouflage pants and a nylon vest and her red cap, her gold-dyed hair stuffed inside it. "I'd like a little chat with you."

"About what?"

"Business and money. I'll buy you lunch."

"That kind of conversation at the table goes against my raising, Miss Ginny."

"Maybe at your house sometime?"

We're blocking the entrance, the people behind us too polite to push us out of the way. "That would be fine, Sister."

We go inside and she sits down across from me in a booth, making a big whooshing sound when her rump hits the vinyl. Her eyes go all over the young woman who waits on us. A man passes our table and tries to say hello to her. She mouths *fuck off* and gives him a glare even after he's gone.

"Who was that?" I ask.

"Some shit-bird with a broom up his ass."

"What did he do?"

"Said the warranty on my running boards wasn't any good because I ran over a rock," she replies. "You have anything to do with the music in your movies?"

"Writers have no influence in Hollywood."

"That doesn't make sense. Without a writer, you don't have a script, right?"

"That's right. That's why we're not liked."

"I used to sing with a country band. I've written a couple of songs with John Culpepper. Maybe you can pass them on to somebody?"

"I'm not supposed to look at uncopyrighted material."

Her eyes are the color you see inside an oyster shell. "You can get sued for plagiarism down the track?"

"It's called proof of access," I say.

She looks sideways out the window and bites a tortilla chip. "The Jews run Hollywood?"

"No."

"That's what I've always heard."

I prepare for the dreary two-thousand-year-old lies that never seem to die. But I'm wrong.

"What kind of money does it take to make a movie?" she asks.

"It depends. The key is usually OPM."

"What's that?"

"Other people's money."

She crunches the tortilla chip between her molars. "I can put up seven figures. What if me and you got together?"

"Thanks for the offer, Miss Ginny. I write books and stay out of trouble."

"It's Sister Ginny. I don't like that cutesy *Gone with the Wind* rhetoric. It's like none of those people ever passed gas. I mean get a fucking life." Both her hands rest like bear paws on the edge of the table. "So no-way-Ray on the movie, huh?"

"I thought we agreed not to talk business."

She begins drumming her fingers, then accelerates the rhythm and increases the volume. I look around to see if anyone is watching. She picks up the menu and pretends to read it. "You eat here a lot?" she asks.

"Yeah, the owners are friends of mine."

"It's good?"

"Yeah, they're from Guadalajara."

Her eyes wander around the room. I'm convinced there is nothing behind them except moths flying inside an empty closet. Then she tears the menu neatly in half and rolls the halves into a cone and places the cone in her waterglass.

"What I'd like to do is produce your book about the Texas Ranger who gets captured by Pancho Villa. We could shoot it down in Monterrey. You got the action and I got the traction, Jackson. Think it over."

On her way to the door, she juts out her elbow and knocks the man from the truck agency into the glass counter.

Chapter Twenty-Three

WEDNESDAY MORNING JEREMIAH McNally turns on my dirt lane in a sheriff's department cruiser and parks in front of the house. Another plainclothes is with him. The two of them get out and begin walking up the incline. The second man is Joe Latour, the sheriff's deputy who responded to the 911 dispatch when Fannie Mae was beaten and ended up in the ER. He's wearing a tweed sport coat and a knit necktie. He studies the house, the trees, the weathervane on my roof, the horses in the pasture. I'm on the veranda before he and Jeremiah can make the steps.

"That's far enough unless you have a warrant," I say.

"Dial it down, Aaron," Jeremiah says.

"You want me to call my attorney?"

"We're not here to bother you, Mr. Broussard," Latour says. He has a hardcore-gravel New England accent. "We talked to Jack Wetzel at the Poverello. We wanted to warn you about something."

"No, that is not the reason you are here," I say. "You want to connect me with some guns that were dropped in the parcel chute at the post office. I'll make it easy for you. I'm the person who dropped them there. Where I got them and how I got them is my business. If dropping guns in a post office receptacle is a crime, I have not heard of it."

"Yeah, you're probably right," he says.

"Mr. Latour. I've made my peace with you—"

"It's Detective Latour."

"No, sir, it's Mr. Latour. You're not welcome here, sir."

"I'm sorry you feel that way."

"What the hell is this about, Jeremiah?" I say.

He takes a four-by-five color photograph out of his coat pocket and hands it to me. "You ever see this guy?"

The photo is a close-up of a stout, late-middle-aged, perverse-looking man at a carnival, probably at twilight; behind him, in contrast, a Ferris wheel is printed against the sky, and the red buttes on the rim of a desert have the soft glow of rubies. The man has silver hair combed straight back and a face that looks like it doesn't work right, as though the motors in it are in conflict with one another. One eye is either half-lidded or sunken deeper than the other. He's wearing a black suit scrolled with sequins and a turquoise shirt wrinkled with light and a necktie painted with a rearing horse.

"No, I've never seen this man," I say.

"You seemed to dwell on his picture, though," Latour says.

I crimp my mouth and don't reply.

"That's Jimmie Kale," he says. "Also known as Jimmie the Digger."

Nor do I show any acknowledgment of his statement.

"Joe is talking to you, Aaron," Jeremiah says.

"I know no one by the name of Kale," I reply.

"We think he brought a huge shipment of meth to Montana," Jeremiah says. "Maybe it got buried and him with it. Or maybe he did the burying. After he shot five or six guys. He's been known to bury people alive."

"There's another thing you need to be aware of, Mr. Broussard," Latour says. "Jimmie Kale is the single most important drug source on the res. The Indians hate this guy. He ruins their children and destroys their families. We want to give the Indians all the help we can."

"What does this have to do with me?" I ask Jeremiah.

But Latour answers. "We think Jack Wetzel may have been at the burial of the meth, or the money they got for the meth, and maybe the five or six guys who got a bulldozer load of dirt in their faces."

I hear Jack crank up the chainsaw and touch it to a log in the barn. "I think you're after the wrong kid."

"Yeah, he's a ball of sunshine," Latour says.

"I've got a deadline with my editor," I say to Jeremiah. "I'd better get on it."

"Aaron, I want to say something in front of you and Joe," he replies. "I've given a lot of thought to these fantasies Ruby Spotted Horse is trying to shop around."

"They're not fantasies," I say.

"For whatever reason, she's jerking both of us around, and you're buying into it, like those hot coals you dug up and put in my hands. That was some trash you burned and buried. Same thing goes with these rumors about monsters on the res. Clayton Wetzel fell under a boxcar. The waitress was getting it on with a couple of psycho Nazi bikers who thought she was a snitch, so they chain-dragged her and dumped her body under a bridge. That's not just me talking, it's the pathologist and a couple of feds."

"You've got the bikers in custody?"

"We're not there yet," he says.

"I think you're full of it, Jeremiah," I say. "Shame on you."

"You're a hard man to talk to, Mr. Broussard," Latour says.

I look him full in the face. "You didn't kill my daughter,

Mr. Latour. But you didn't help her, either. I think there was gloat in your eyes when you left the ER. Why, I don't know. Maybe my daughter threw the first punch, but that would be out of character for her. I hope you have a good life, and I have nothing else to say."

THAT NIGHT I HAVE a visitor in my bedroom. I knew he would come. I don't know if I believe in destiny, but I do believe we make bad choices that occur in a split second—say, a glance at a face in the crowd, a bump against someone in an elevator—and find ourselves in the company of people who can suck the life out of us. The average person does not do well when he or she falls under the sway of the benighted, or what I call the descendants of Cain. Maybe the metaphor I borrow is excessive. But the creature who has just appeared in my bedroom in the middle of the night is not one whose physiognomy can be easily explained.

His radiance is as bright as the fire in front of a smithy's bellows. The suppuration on his skin glistens like glue. His blue uniform is torn and streaked with ash, stinking of cordite and feces and the raw smell of blood, his epaulettes caked with mud, the scabbard of his sword dinged from battle.

But I don't fear him, and that's because I have never known a bully who was not a coward. I sit on the side of my bed, my bare feet on the floor, and look at him indifferently. "Back again?" I say.

What do you mean, "again"?

"You showed up here in the guise of Ruby Spotted Horse's niece. Pretty cheap way to behave for a United States army officer, don't you think?"

I'm here to speak to you as one gentleman to another.

"Sorry, I'm not keen on the way you do business, Major Baker. You know, the mass murder of indigenous people and that sort of thing?"

I can bring your daughter back to you. I can give you powers you cannot imagine.

"If you have any power, why is your name synonymous with nineteenth-century genocidal scum?"

I was carrying out the orders passed down by others.

"That was Adolf Eichmann's defense."

Who?

"What do you want from me, Major?"

It is not I who asks anything of you, sir. It is for others far greater in historical importance than I. Look about you. The Second American Revolution has begun. Join us.

"You stay away from my little girl, you piece of shit."

How dare you!

I pick up a straight-back chair and throw it at him. It bounces harmlessly off the wall. The major disappears with the ease and rapidity of someone stepping through a black curtain that subsumes and folds around him and leaves no trace of his former presence.

I get dressed and go downstairs and build a fire in the fireplace, but I cannot get the coldness out of the house. I put on a wool jacket and gloves and double-lined trousers and an overcoat and still cannot get warm. I drive to a truck stop in Lolo and drink coffee until dawn, the snow spitting against the windows, the glass vibrating from the tractor-trailers grinding up Lolo Pass. I want to believe in the normal world, one that is governed by reason and humanity. I want to believe that the Major Bakers of the world are anomalies, that the sun will rise in the east and light the snow blowing from the trees on the mountaintops and drive the shadows from the hearts of good men and women everywhere, undaunted, the green republic just over the next hill.

THAT SAME DAY Jack Wetzel shows up at work right on time, but with a mouse under his eye and booze on his breath. I bring him into the kitchen and tell him to sit down at the table while I get him a sweet roll and a glass of chocolate milk. He sits with his hands clapped between his thighs, his cap pulled down tight on his head. "It's cold in here," he says.

"The issue is showing up for work still drunk."

"I ain't drunk."

"Yes, you are. And on top of it, you were in a fight."

"Me and Leigh Culpepper got into it with some guys. Over a girl. It was dumb." He blows his nose in a handkerchief.

"You know Leigh Culpepper?"

"We hang out sometimes. Why?"

"I'll drive you back to the Poverello and we'll start over tomorrow."

"I got here on time."

"There were some cops here yesterday, Jack."

"About me?"

"You ever hear of a man named Jimmie Kale? Or Jimmie the Digger?"

His eyes have become sleepy, as though he's a couple of quarts down. "I don't know."

"Don't know what?"

"I don't know anything. Leigh copped a little acid last night. I had a bad trip. Leigh's got a big commitment to it."

"This man sells meth and buries people alive. At least that's what the cops say."

"That's just a story on the res. The cops probably want you to make a movie out of it." He stares me in the face. "Hey, come on, Mr. Broussard, I had a slip. I can work. I like it here. I don't want to go nowhere else."

I put the chocolate milk back in the icebox and wrap the sweet roll in a paper towel and put it in his hand. "You can't run machinery with booze in your system, Jack. I'll take you back to the Pov now. If this happens again, we're done."

He tilts up his face. "It ain't right the way you're treating me."

I pick him up by one arm and walk him to my truck. He feels as light and delicate as a crippled bird, stripped of the strength and willpower that he exhibited while splitting firewood. The sun is hardly over the mountain and his day is already mortgaged. I open the passenger door on my pickup and help him inside. "Where'd you get the acid?"

"Leigh Culpepper. He kept pestering me and finally I took it."

I close his door, then get behind the wheel and start the engine. "You know what the hard road is?"

"Chain-ganging or something."

"It's also a metaphor for a way of life. When you're thirty, you'll look fifty."

"I got no plans on being thirty," he replies.

WHEN I RETURN HOME, I call the tutor I hired to help Leigh Culpepper at the vocational college. "How's Leigh doing?" I ask.

"Real good, Mr. Broussard. He's a nice young guy."

"No problems of any kind?"

"He wants to please his father. They belong to a church down in the valley. Fundamentalist and racial stuff, I think. Not good. Anything wrong?"

"Nope. Thanks for your help. Send me a bill whenever you want."

AT 10:45 A.M. I call Ruby Spotted Horse on her cell phone. "Can I come out to your place this evening?"

"This is my day off," she says. "You can come out now."

I pull into her yard one hour and fifteen minutes later. At this juncture I need to make a confession, one that is a bit personal and involves a lie of omission and the penchant of a man from a bygone era. On my last visit to Ruby's house, I picked her up on my chest and buried my face in her neck and swung her around, but I did not feel it proper or honorable to take advantage of her loneliness or her willingness to be charitable to a grieving elderly man.

She has obviously seen me through her front window and is waiting at the door before I can knock. She is wearing a loose yellow dress that could have come from any American decade, the kind of dress the girl next door used to wear, or the girl at your church picnic, or the girl you took in your convertible to the drive-in restaurant.

"Hey," I say.

"Hey, yourself," she says. "I fixed a lunch."

"Let's talk first." We go inside, and I put my arm across her shoulders and walk her to the couch and ease her down on the cushions, then sit beside her. "That's a lovely dress."

"Will you stop acting so weird?"

"I had a visit last night from Major Baker."

"It wasn't a dream?"

"No, he wants to enlist me in his cause." She starts to speak. "Listen to me, Ruby. This is about us, not about Baker. I was thinking about how he came into my life. It was through you."

Her face starts to drain.

"No, no, listen. We met by chance. A 911 call. There's a reason for our meeting. You're one of the Guardians, and it's obvious that one way or another I may take on the same role.

In fact, I may not have a choice. My daughter is being harassed by Baker and probably by people worse than he. What I am saying is I'd really like to spend a lot of time with you. But you have to make an informed choice. Elderly people can be a burden. It's not coincidental that large numbers of people in this country are indifferent to the rate of virus contagion in our old-age facilities."

"I already told you, Aaron. We're not like other people."

"People will call you a gold digger. Some of your colleagues will make cracks behind your back. Others will grin at each other when we walk by."

"Fuck them."

"That's one way of looking at it," I say.

"Good. We've got that out of the way. Let's eat. Do you mind if Maxwell Gato joins us?"

AFTER WE FINISH, she picks up the cat and puts him outside. He hangs in her hands like a sloth. The snow is blowing sideways, and dust is swirling out of the pumpkin field. But my conscience still bothers me. I feel uncomfortable, too easily self-convinced that I've been forthcoming and protective and honest about the price she will have to pay in a relationship with a man my age. The United States prides itself on the freedom of the individual, but we are still a Puritan nation and obsessed with sex. Also, small towns are small towns, on the res or in Missoula, which right-wingers here call "the People's Republic."

"What do you want to do?" she asks. We're in the middle of the kitchen. She puts one hand on her hip, causing the yellow dress to become lopsided.

"You don't have a video of *Shane* or *Red River*, do you?"

"No."

"*Red River* is John Wayne's best film. Montgomery Clift is great in it, too."

"Would you please tell me what you want to do?"

"I don't know."

"I'm going to kick you in the shins."

"Do you have some blankets?" I ask.

"What do we need blankets for?"

"Emergencies. This is Montana. Put on a warm coat. Maybe a fur hat."

"Are you having a psychotic break?"

"Could be. Let's go."

"Where?"

"Out there." I point through the glass at the Missions. "Better bring Maxwell Gato back inside in case we're gone for a while."

She chews on her lip, her body ten inches from mine. She smells like flowers, even though I don't think she uses perfume. Her dress looks like it's made from crepe paper. My face is burning, my throat dry.

"I'll be back down in a few minutes," she says. "You're really nuts, Aaron."

WE DRIVE DEEP into the Mission Mountains. It's difficult to describe their magnitude. The peaks are seldom visible because of their altitude. From a distance the forests resemble lichen on the slopes. Rocks as big as five-story houses lie in streambeds. One wheel hooking over the road's edge could send us fifteen hundred feet straight down. The air is not only cold but rarified and feels like a razor blade sucked into your lungs. The hunters and trappers are gone with the season, like primeval people whose claim on the land amounts to a scratch on a pebble.

The road was cut by a bulldozer decades ago and is littered with slag and splintered pieces of dead ponderosa that have fallen from above. We go through a dip, then ascend through a cloud thick with ice crystals and pop out on a vista that makes you dizzy. Down below is a lake that resembles a blue teardrop among evergreen forests that roll over the hills as far as the eye can see. I shift into low and we begin a descent akin to an elevator that has snapped its cables. Rocks are banging under the fenders, the brakes squealing, the tires thudding in the potholes because my springs and shock absorbers are shot. We go through a washout, the frame slamming the road so hard the glove box springs open, scattering road maps and junk all over Ruby's lap. Then the road levels out, and in the distance we can see a meadow that slants down to the lakeshore. There are no boats or cabins or machinery of any kind on the lake. Even the Forest Service signs have been broken off and ground to pieces by winter avalanches. A mother bear and her two cubs, one black, the other rust-colored, are chugging up the hillside from the lake. They look as small as chipmunks when they enter the forest. I roll down the window and realize I'm soaking with sweat. I let the truck coast through the meadow all the way to the lakeshore, the grass whispering under the truck's frame.

"I never knew this was here," Ruby says. "How did you find it?"

"I got lost on a backpack hike and ran into an elderly Indian man in the middle of nowhere. He was wearing buckskin. He walked out of the trees and gave me some smoked venison and told me about the lake and then disappeared."

"Who was he?" she says.

"I think he was a spirit. I think the natural world is full of spirits."

We get out of the truck and walk down to the water. The surface of the lake looks to be dented with raindrops. But these are not raindrops. The cutthroat are feeding, their backs gently roiling the surface, their gills painted with fire. The sun is bright overhead, the slopes around us forming a great green bowl, one that may have boiled with lava millions of years ago.

"Why did you bring us here?" Ruby asks.

"I want to make a pact with you. This place is the one where we make our bond. If a day comes when one cannot find the other, this is where we go and wait for the other, no matter how long it takes. No exceptions allowed."

She's wearing a long wool coat over her yellow dress, with a black kerchief tied under her chin. "I've never had anyone say something like that to me," she says.

"So what do you say?"

She looks at the lake. "It's actually blue. Not green-blue but blue."

"The bad road keeps most people out. I've never taken anyone else here."

But she has not answered my question. She hugs me and presses the side of her head against my chest.

"You okay?" I ask.

"I think so."

"Want to build a fire and make a tent? I have an air mattress, and I filled up Maxwell Gato's bowl. I've got some cans of beans we can put in the fire."

"I'd really like that," she says. "I really would."

She tightens her arms around my back. I can feel her breath inside my shirt.

Chapter Twenty-Four

THE NEXT DAY, as I'm about to leave the Lolo post office, John Fenimore Culpepper taps one knuckle on my truck window. He's wearing a mask emblazoned with the American flag. I roll down the window. As most of us have learned in our virus culture, it is hard to read the intentions or state of mind of a fellow American when the lower half of the face is covered.

"Yes, sir?" I say.

"Can I have a talk with you? Out under the tree?"

I cut the engine. "Sure. What's going on?"

We walk into the shade of a tree by a drop box. "I want to thank you for getting that tutor for my boy," he says.

"It was no trouble, Mr. Culpepper."

"My boy likes the campus and the instructors they got out there, and he says the kids ain't bad, either. But the tutor has made all the difference, I mean with Leigh's special needs and such."

I want to change the subject because I do not want him to know I'm subsidizing the tutor. But my general discomfort with John Culpepper is for reasons far more serious. Jack

Wetzel told me that Culpepper's son gave him LSD. Maybe Jack was lying, maybe not; however, there was no reason for him to lie. My other problem is I believe Culpepper is more victim than perpetrator. I think he's carrying a wire for at least one law enforcement agency. If so, he's doing it for money, or he's terrified at the prospect of confinement.

"Maybe someday I can play you a few tunes or do some house repairs for you," he says. "I was a right good carpenter before me and John Barleycorn fell off the roof, know what I mean?"

"Sir, I don't want to intrude in your personal life."

I have barely gotten the words out of my mouth when I see Fannie Mae by my truck, waving her hands for me to shut up.

"Go ahead," Culpepper says. His face looks carved from wood, his gray eyes no more readable than a pair of Life Savers.

"I think you've got yourself in a nest of hornets, and if they don't sting you to death, the cops will."

"Run that last part by me again."

"Were you in a war?" I ask.

"No."

"In a war a significant number of people are considered expendable. Eventually Sister Ginny and her cohorts will go down. Don't take their fall. Don't be one of the expendables."

His eyes are frozen, his mask puffing in and out with his breath. "Where'd you get your information?"

"Nowhere. It's a surmise on my part."

"A what?"

"A feeling."

"My wife has pancreatic cancer. She'll be dead in another year. Then it'll be just me and my boy. I cain't go to prison. Leigh gets in trouble when I'm not around. You hearing me, Mr. Broussard?"

"Yes, sir."

"Thirty years ago I fired a gun from a car into a colored church. I killed a little boy. I see him every night in my sleep. That's why I got out of the Klan."

I look away from him. The image he has created is one of the worst I have ever dealt with.

"Sister Ginny says I been baptized in the blood and I don't have to worry about going to hell," he says. "What's your opinion?"

"I don't have that kind of knowledge."

"You don't understand what I'm saying, do you?"

"Understand what?"

"I'm already in hell. I ain't got no way out. It waits for me every night and day. That's what hell is really about." He crosses the post office driveway and walks through Fannie Mae and out the other side as though she's not there.

FANNIE MAE COMES to see me that afternoon, right after I've woken from a nap on the couch. Jack Wetzel showed up sober this morning and is replacing the clips on my back fence. The television is on, and the president of the United States is advocating that his followers liberate the state of Michigan. Fannie Mae sits down on the far end of the couch and picks up my feet and drops them on her knees.

"Where have you been?" I say.

I overheard your conversation with the cops about Jimmie Kale, so I asked around.

"Forget Kale or whoever he is. Why did you disappear?"

Because I don't have much time left before I need to move on, and in the meantime I have to protect you from yourself. That includes your relationship with Short Stuff.

"That's none of your concern, and don't call her that."

I'm in charge, Pops, so put the cork in it.

She has been saying this since she was five years old. "Ruby is different, Fannie."

No, she's not, but no matter. Live and let live. Jimmie Kale used to be a country singer in West Texas until he got run out of the state for messing with underaged girls.

"People don't get run out of the state for moral turpitude."

He was probably doing some hits on the border for the Mexico City cartel. Anyway, he went to Albuquerque and hooked up with the meth culture. The stories about his burying people alive are true. There're other stories that are worse.

"I don't know if I want to hear this."

You got to get yourself out of this, Pops. That includes Short Stuff. Look, I like her, but a younger woman is a younger woman.

"I feel like checking out."

What? Her voice fades, even though the word she just spoke contains only one syllable.

"I don't feel like living anymore. It isn't that I want to die; I just don't want to live."

Now is not the time to hang it up. This is the time to stand up.

"Has Major Baker tried to hurt you?"

The guy to watch is Kale. He buried some transporters up to their necks in Coahuila and decapitated them with a road grader.

"No more, Fannie Mae. I think you're starting to feed on this."

She looks at my feet. *You have holes in your socks.*

"Who cares?"

There's one other thing about Jimmie Kale. Some people say he's already dead but doesn't know it. Did you hear me? He's dead and killing people.

"No more about Kale."

I try to warn you, but you never listen. You think of others but don't think of yourself, and that hurts them all the more.

She lifts my feet and places them on the floor. I know what's coming next. "Don't leave. We can find a way to change the past. To go back to the first inning."

Got to boogie, Pops. Tell Jack Wetzel I'll rip him a new one if he lets you down.

Then there's a tinkle of wind chimes and she dissolves into thousands of molecules like the shimmer in champagne. The television is still on. I have not touched the remote. But the channel is no longer CNN. Instead I'm watching the History Channel and panzer tanks destroying the Warsaw ghetto. A little boy in short pants and a dress coat and a white dress shirt is surrendering to SS officers with his hands in the air. His face is tight with fear. I do not know what any of this means. But for some reason I cannot get John Culpepper and the child he murdered out of my mind, nor can I believe I stood inches away from him, breathing the same air, basically speaking the same regional dialect, as he told me he sent a bullet blindly into a church building where a poor Black family dressed in their best clothes would hear a bullet *pock* through the glass or splinter a board and see their child killed by a shooter who would never be punished and whom they would not recognize if they ever saw him on a street.

I feel I have not only become a witness to his crime but have been incorporated into it.

I GET UP FROM the couch and walk down to the pasture to see how Jack Wetzel is doing with his work. His canvas bag of tools is lying on the ground by one of the steel stakes on the back fence, but he's nowhere around. The job I've assigned him is not a difficult one. He only needs to tamp down the stakes and replace the clips the deer have popped loose running through the fence. I want to believe that Jack has a chance, but I know the odds are against him. Every time I look at him, I feel there is someone hiding inside him that even he cannot deal with.

I start walking down the fence, the pine needles blowing out of the trees. Behind a desiccated shed, I see Jack inside a pool of dark shade with three of my horses. He's feeding them apples he has cubed with a pocketknife and set in his palm so the horses will not bite his fingers. He grins when he sees me. "I was just taking a little break," he says.

"That's fine. Where'd you learn how to feed horses their treats?"

"At the juvenile farm in New Mexico. Mr. Broussard, I still can't tell you how sorry I am for showing up drunk. I don't know what got into me."

"Yesterday's box score. Does Leigh Culpepper have a problem with LSD?"

"I don't want to be a snitch, Mr. B."

"I talked with his father earlier today. I didn't mention anything about you or Leigh or hallucinogens. But my silence bothers me."

He feeds the last of the apples to the horses and wipes his hands on his jeans. "You look kind of tired, Mr. B. Is anything wrong?" While he's talking, he stretches a crick out of his neck.

That's it, right there, the mark of every sociopath, the invasive comment, the secret gleam in the eye, the test of the envelope.

"You lost your father in a fire, Jack. What happened to your mother?"

"She's probably on her back somewhere."

"Rough way to talk."

"You got to excuse me for it. My upbringing wasn't the best. I better get on it, Mr. B."

He starts walking toward his bag of tools, then stops and turns around. "Oh, there's some shingles ripped off the chicken house. If you got some spares, I'm right good at roofing."

TWO DAYS HAVE gone by and it's now Monday evening. At 7:45 p.m. Jeremiah calls me. "Hey, Aaron," he says.

"Jeremiah, how you doin'?"

"I wanted to apologize. I know you've had a lot of stress, and you sure don't need me piling it on."

"Don't worry about it. The issue is about events you and I have seen or heard in one way or another. There is no scientific explanation for them. To dismiss them is a mistake."

"This is how I see it, Aaron: one man's religion, another man's superstition. That said, something unusual is happening, I just don't know what."

"You sound like you're already cutting bait," I reply.

"I'm in trouble, Aaron. Remember Betty Wolcott, the German gal who waited on us at the café when the Black Lives Matter demonstration was going on? I went out with her a couple of times. Now she's been missing four days. I'm being questioned. Along with Jimmie Kale. He was hitting on a nineteen-year-old Asian girl in the kitchen."

"You're a suspect because you went out with the victim twice? That doesn't sound right."

"I made a mistake with a confidential informant when I was at the DEA."

"I know about that. Fooling around with a CI isn't the equivalent of homicide."

"She was found dead in her garage with the car running.

The tox scan showed high levels of downers and alcohol in her system, so it went down as a suicide or just an accident. But some people didn't buy it."

"Why?"

"She had bruises from a fall at an ice-skating rink. I know that's where she got them because I was with her. But I couldn't find any witnesses."

"Do you have a lead on Kale?" I say.

"You know Ray Bronson, Ruby Spotted Horse's ex, right?"

"Yes."

"He was seen in a cabin on the Jocko with Kale."

Take note of the passive voice. "You're sure?" I say.

"God, I hate this," he says.

"Hate what?"

"Telling you how dumb I am. I'm sure because I saw them there. I was in one of the cabins. With a gal from the res."

"I appreciate the information, Jeremiah."

"I feel rotten, Aaron. You probably think I'm a sex addict."

"You're just human, brother. I have to run. I'll talk to you later."

I ease the phone receiver into the cradle and send up a quiet prayer of thanks for all my gifts, particularly the years spent with Fannie Mae and the knowledge that I don't have to live in guilt and fear.

Chapter Twenty-Five

THE NEXT DAY, in the late evening, a waxed purple Cadillac convertible with fins and chromed wheels and blue-dot tail-lights and a starched-white top drives slowly up my lane, passes the house, then stops and backs up the lane and into the driveway and all the way to the lawn. The driver cuts the lights but remains in the car. I click on the outside light and step outside. I can hear the heat ticking under the Caddy's hood.

"Who's that?" I say.

The driver rolls down the window and flicks a cigarette onto the lawn. Then he gets out and closes the door, which means he has fixed his interior lights so he cannot be illuminated when he enters and exits the car.

"I need to know who you are, partner," I say.

There's a mauve glow on the river and the meadowland beyond, enough to silhouette the driver but not enough to reveal his features.

"You want me to call 911?" I say.

He fires up another cigarette, the lighter's flame as warm and soft as a candle's. "I'm looking for a young fella," he says. "Jack Wetzel is the name. I'd like to tell you I got a barrel of money for him, but truth is, I ain't got dick except a message from his mother. Can I come up without getting shot?"

The accent is five-star peckerwood, like a bobby pin twanging. He walks into my outside light without waiting for an answer. He's wearing shined needle-nose oxblood boots, a dull-white suit with a vest that has the color and design of a sliced pomegranate, and the most beautiful black John B. Stetson hat I have ever seen. His cigarette is of foreign make and gold-tipped. He takes it from his mouth and blows a smoke ring. "Where's Jack at?"

"Jack who?"

"Jack Wetzel. My nephew."

"He's not here."

His eyes are not symmetrical and his facial skin is like tallow and seems to knot and unknot itself. "Know where he went?"

"I couldn't say."

"Can I use your bathroom?"

"The plumbing is stopped up."

"You don't have a shitter in back?" His face is solemn. Then he starts laughing. "Just kidding. Hang on." He walks to the flower bed and unzips and urinates into the shadows. Then zips up and whistles. "Wow, I must have had a quart backed up. I tried not to hit your rosebushes."

"You're Jimmie Kale," I reply. "A couple of cops told me you might be around. You were a country musician up in the Texas Panhandle."

"Goddamn, son. You did your homework. Now, about Jack—"

"With respect, Mr. Kale, I can't give out information about other people. I also have to get back to work."

"I was hoping you'd h'ep me find him. I've had three or

four people tell me he's working for you. Is he staying with you or in town?"

"I think you bear Jack ill will."

"That's the silliest thing I've ever heard."

"This is about meth, Mr. Kale. I'm not fond of people who make or sell it. Neither are the Indians."

He tries to see past me, his face knotting. "Who the hell is that? Why's she giving me that look?"

I glance behind me. "What are you talking about?"

"The woman in your doorway."

"What woman?"

"The squaw. Right yonder."

I open the screen and stick my arm inside the door and click the overhead light off and on three times. "I'm the only person here."

Half his face seems to soften, as though it's beginning to melt and he has no control over it. "She's gone now, but what I seen was a short little bitch in white buckskin with dark hair and a knife in her hand."

"I'm afraid you didn't."

"She's got knockers and deep-set eyes. She looked me up and down, like I was trash. I won't abide that. Get her out here."

"I don't know what to tell you, partner."

He's breathing through his nose. But I am probably more disturbed than he is, particularly after his description of the Indian woman.

"Okay, I ain't gonna press it," he says. "Tell Jack I'm at the DoubleTree."

"No, sir, I will not give him any message at all."

"You've got yourself an attitudinal problem, Mr. Broussard. You're too damn snooty for your britches."

"The Indian woman you saw?"

His eyes fill with expectation. "She was there, wasn't she?"

"You were probably looking at your worst nightmare, Mr. Kale." I glance at his Caddy. "I love your wheels. Those were the days, weren't they?"

He stares at me, his mouth open, waiting for me to continue. But I don't.

I CALL RUBY AND tell her what just happened.

"I'd get rid of Jack Wetzel," she says.

"I can't do that. I have to ask a question, Ruby. It's about the Indian woman in the doorway."

"You mean was it me?"

"*Was* it?"

"I took a nap this evening. That's all I can tell you. I'm not holding back on you. I don't have control over my life anymore."

"The Indian woman was holding a knife."

"Maybe there's another answer here. Maybe Kale fried his circuits with his own product," she says. "My advice, if he comes after you or Wetzel, is to cap him. This is still Montana."

"I had a talk with John Culpepper. He told me he killed a Black child when he was in the Klan."

"He confessed that to *you*?"

"He's full of guilt. But I think he's going to get himself killed."

"Leave him alone, Aaron."

"You know what happens doing discovery. A witness for the prosecution can end up on a meat hook."

"Culpepper rolled the dice a long time ago," she says.

I KNOW MY RELATIONSHIP with Jack Wetzel seems excessively charitable. But few people realize how the system works. The children of rich people do not go to juvie. Nor do they end up in shithole county jails where they get turned out and passed around. In a mainline joint they either get an "old man" or they're cannibalized. I do not want to describe the details, because there are certain kinds of knowledge that leave a stone in your heart, and the sexual subculture in a prison is one of them.

The inhumanity in a prison is not planned. It's inherent in the institution, feral in nature, sweaty, often depraved, and cruel to the bone. At age eighteen I was in a lockdown unit fifteen feet from the death cell in a Louisiana prison. My only possessions were my clothes, a tin cup, a tin plate, and a spoon. The food cart came into the bull run at 0700, grits and black coffee and one slice of white bread. At noon the cart returned with spaghetti or rice and gravy and again one slice of bread. There was no supper, but the trusties let us load up with leftovers from the noon meal that later we heated on a community stinger.

These things, however, are of small relevance. The inhumanity I witnessed was an execution fifteen feet from the lockdown unit in which I was confined. Back then, in Louisiana, the electric chair traveled from parish to parish. Two big generators on the back of a truck were brought to the jail by the executioner, and the rubber-encased power cables were roped through a barred window on the third floor and attached to the electric chair, whose nickname was Gruesome Gertie. That evening an electrical storm swept across the wetlands; the booms of thunder and sheets of rain slapping against the jail were deafening, augmented by the generators kicking to life, spinning with a whine and gaining speed until the centrifugal roar was louder than the storm.

I wanted the generators to drown out the sounds from what was called the death cell, the minister reading from his Bible, the condemned man whispering an apology, the strained creak of the leather when the first jolt hit him, his body vibrating against the oak frame of the chair, the metal cap on his head smoking and starting to rattle.

The rain had stopped. The sky was an ink wash, the willows and cypress and gum trees along the Calcasieu River half-submerged in the whitish-green blanket of lichen lifting and dropping with the tide. There was no glass in our windows and I waited in the silence for the cool sweetness of the storm to bloom inside the jail. Instead, our home in lockdown was visited by only one odor, like someone ironing damp clothes in an airless room on a summer day, the iron just hot enough to scorch.

So today when I see a kid like Jack Wetzel or Leigh Culpepper, I try to put a bandage on a hole in the dike. It's like prayer. What's to lose?

I CALL THE POVERELLO and someone puts Jack Wetzel on the line.

"Jimmie Kale was just at my house," I tell him. "Looking for you."

"Oh, shit," he says.

"I'll make it short. He'll find you at the Pov. I'm going to make arrangements for you in a motel in Bonner. I don't want you to come to work for a couple of days because he'll probably cruise the house. You copy?"

"Yes, sir."

"Why's he after you, Jack?"

"I muled his meth. I know his operation."

"Good try. A guy like Kale doesn't risk a homicide beef over the testimony of a drug transporter, partner."

"Maybe I know where some bodies are buried."

"You saw the bodies go into the ground?"

"I didn't say that."

"Jack, it's wake-up time. I'm the only friend you have."

"Mr. Broussard, Jimmie the Digger isn't human. People in Albuquerque are scared shitless of him. I ain't gonna talk about him to anyone, not you or anyone else. If you don't like it, I'll take my chances on my own."

"Did Kale kill your brother?"

"No."

"Who did?"

"We were standing by the railroad track on the res, like behind the nightclub. Then a guy came out of the fog with these other guys behind him. Clayton told me to run. I said I wasn't going without him. They ripped him into pieces, his arms and legs and head, and I started running. I ran and ran until I fell down, then I got up and ran again."

"Who were these guys, Jack?"

"They looked like they were in Civil War uniforms. They smelled like shit. I mean like for real, the way human shit smells."

"Who was giving the orders?"

"The first guy to come out of the fog. He had those things on his shoulders."

"Epaulettes?"

"Yeah, that's it. He had on a sword and pistol, too. He looked like he'd been in a fire."

"I'm going to call my friend at the motel now, then I'll call you back. Jack?"

"Yes, sir?"

"You ought to be a writer. Think about it."

I call my friend in Bonner, an old logging town eight miles from Missoula on the Blackfoot River, and make an arrangement for Jack at the motel. The Blackfoot Valley is the site of the book and the movie *A River Runs Through It*. On the confluence of the Clark Fork and Blackfoot rivers is a legendary saloon named the Milltown Bar, Café, and Laundromat. It was once visited by Ernest Hemingway on his way to Ketchum, Idaho, where he took his life. A millworker at the bar looked at him and said, "Guess who thinks he's Ernest Hemingway."

Papa replied, "That's because I'm Ernest Hemingway," and bought the house a round.

True story, the kind that gives me an excuse to smile on a dark night.

Chapter Twenty-Six

Do you ever have this feeling about your time on earth? It's the second inning, then the fifth and the top of the eighth, and you look at the scoreboard and the angle of the sun and feel the chill in the air, and you wonder where your life has gone.

I have that feeling now. Jack Wetzel's description of Major Eugene Baker and the murder of Jack's brother was more than stark. It was proof that Baker had the power to commit crimes in the present and not simply re-create them in the form of an apparition.

In his career he was obviously an implementer of Manifest Destiny. He asked me to join his cause without describing what it was, but I have no doubt he wants to continue his war against indigenous people under a black flag and, for whatever reason, wanted me on board. So far he has not tried to hurt me physically. Why, I don't know. My guess is he doesn't have many arrows in his quiver. I think he is probably an emblematic character, one if given flesh and blood again would wage war against the third world in search and control of natural resources.

I mentioned Ernest Hemingway. Many years ago in Miami

I was friends with his brother Leicester and the crime writer Charles Willeford. Leicester was at the Hürtgen Forest during the Battle of the Bulge; Charles was at Arnhem and at night took his tank through German lines and piled twenty-three grunts on it and brought them home. Both Charles and Leicester were at the liberation of Dachau, as was my first cousin Weldon Holland, and not one of them would talk about the experience, except for one statement made by Weldon: "The inmates wanted to touch and hold us. They wouldn't let go."

I believe all three men represented what is best in us. Now, on a quiet evening when I hear a coyote howl behind my house or a whirring sound like a windup clock about to strike the hour, I wonder if my time has come and if I have done enough to justify my span on earth. I wonder, as Robert Frost once said, if my sacrifice is acceptable in the sight of the Creator. I wonder if I have made a difference.

Why do I brood in this fashion? I'll tell you. Maybe we have already entered the time of Major Eugene Baker and those like him. Maybe we're about to see the horses in the Book of John up close and personal, their chests heaving, their breaths hot, their mouths and necks lathered, thundering across a ruined world peopled with skeletons. But the darkest hour is not in the prophecy of a Hebrew evangelist who lived two thousand years ago; it's in the soul. That's why I sit here shaking in the dark, the way you shake when the malarial mosquito has its way, wondering if my legs will fail me, as the Yankee soldiers must have wondered at Marye's Heights when they slipped on their own gore and asked that this bitter cup be taken from their lips. Is it now my turn?

It's four-twenty the next morning. I have stared at the ceiling since midnight. The moon is full, marbled with shadows that look like a bruise. A V-shaped flock of geese headed south interdicts the light between the moon and my window, then makes a turn and descends into the yard. In seconds a figure dressed like a late-nineteenth-century dandy comes through the wall and sits at the foot of my bed. His mustache is waxed and pointy on the ends, like a villain's in a silent movie, his eyes as shiny and black as oil. *Top of the morning to you,* he says.

"I thought you'd be along," I reply.

His eyes twinkle. He takes a long drink from a dark green bottle, then balances it on his thigh and wipes his mouth with his hand. *Now, how would you be knowing my goings and comings?*

"I suspect you're a rake at heart?"

I let my boys have a stop-off with the girls in Wallace, Idaho. I don't do that sort of thing myself. They're good boys, actually, considering the severe orders given them by General Sheridan.

"I know who you're working for, Major."

I doubt that.

"The same people T. E. Lawrence warned us about."

I don't know the fellow.

"The issue is energy. Humps like yourself do the scut work."

I know your daughter's secrets. I know the men in her life. A sorry bunch, if you ask me.

"A few were no good. But at least they didn't murder women and children."

That old saw about extractive industries. I rode a horse. You own and drive a motorized vehicle. Which of us has used up more of the earth's resources?

"I've seen your work, sir. There is no cruelty, no form of atrocity, that isn't attached to your name."

Yes, and believe it or not, it pains me. I get no rest, no sleep. It's not an easy go, sir.

"Why haven't you tried to do me physical injury?"

He offers me the bottle, but I shake my head.

You like to play rounders?

"Baseball?"

My lads and I are good at it. Be among us, Mr. Broussard. You were a soldier. Enjoy the tankard of ale, the kiss of a fair maid, the rumble of the caissons, the thrill of the charge, and the ring of the sabers.

"You tore up Clayton Wetzel, Jack Wetzel's brother?"

It was his time to go. He didn't like that.

"Why him and not me, Major?"

Because you're a Goody Two-shoes.

"I wish you wouldn't insult me in my own house."

You're what they call a bleeding heart, sir. War can be grand.

"This is what I think, Major. You have power to hurt only the afflicted. You're part of a disease. War is your cathedral, death and suffering your paramours, and failure your legacy. In other words, you're a bloody fucking sod in a charnel house."

He gets up from the bed and toasts me with the bottle. *Grandly said, sir. You're right, I live in the Book of Revelation. You sleep in a clean bed among the angels. You try to help young ruffians who will probably end up with the likes of me. But praise me just a little, will you, sir? I tried. It wasn't easy to serve under men who burned and laid waste from Atlanta to the sea.*

"You fought under a black flag, just like Quantrill, Major. Take your shame somewhere else."

You've hurt me deeply. But so be it. The major drains the bottle, then drops it, letting it roll across the floor. He walks through the wall, and a second later there is a clapping of wings and he rises with the geese and flies away, silhouetting against the moon. I push myself off the bed, the room tilting, my gyroscope gone. I pick up the bottle by the neck. The glass is thick and handblown, moist and sticky to the touch, the major's handprint like the webbed smear of a transitional creature from an earlier time.

THREE DAYS HAVE passed. An Indian boy was throwing stones in the Flathead River when he saw an object stuck on the limb of a downed cottonwood close to the opposite bank. The object was large, asymmetrical, puffed, bobbing in the tangle of branches, colorful rags streaming in the riffle. A magpie was perched above it on one of the tree branches. The boy threw another stone and the magpie flew away. It was evening and the sky was bone-white and empty, the hills brown, the wind raw. The boy picked up a piece of driftwood and jumped from one boulder to the next until he could grab one branch of the tree and poke the object. Before he could make contact, he slipped and fell into the current and was swept into the cottonwood and a woman's body that had probably been pinned for days under the surface.

Her long hair was dull red with streaks of blond. She was submerged faceup, her hair undulating with the current, her eyes blue and doll-like, her mouth open, as though she had been startled, maybe by an innocuous source. The river pressed the boy against her, her arms floating unrestrained and flaccid and curling around him. He began thrashing, swinging his arms in front of him, screaming for help. But he had pulled her loose from the tree, and her weight and the entanglement of the tree branches were about to take him under. That was when he realized he had become witness to the creation of a flaw in the world that should not have been there, a monstrous deed he would be afraid to report, a deed no one would want to hear about.

He was revolted by her body and hit her with his fists and crawled across her and tried to shove her away from him. But her body bobbed along with him until the two of them struck a sandbar and he felt his feet touch the gravelly bottom of the river. He stared down at her face as he rose from the water. Her eyes would not leave his, as if she were begging him to undo her fate.

"I'm sorry," he said. "I didn't mean to hit you."

Then he felt like a fool for the inadequacy of his words. And for his inability to look at the rest of her body. The stonelike immobility of her eyes, the bluish discoloration of her skin, the hair twisted around her throat were permanently stamped in his memory; but those were not the images that caused him to vomit in the water. She had been eviscerated. When his parents found him, he could not stop sobbing.

THE READER OF this account might wonder why I would write in such arguably offensive detail about the Indian boy's traumatization. The question is a valid one. My answer: Evil is real. It is not an abstraction. The little boy will carry a reel of film inside his head until his death, and over the years few people will understand the haunted look that will swim into his eyes without apparent cause. What are its origins? I don't know. A serpent in a tree? Maybe the La Brea Tar Pits? That's not the issue. The real question is its level of intensity, its constant growth and replication, the incredible power it gives to political simpletons and street people alike.

Brigands, confidence men, Robin Hood, Blackbeard, Moll Cutpurse, Cattle Annie and Little Britches, William Clarke Quantrill, Belle Starr, the Daltons, jolly madams the size of blimps, the James-Younger Gang, the Rose of the Cimarron,

Billy the Kid, all morph into folk myth and thread in and out of our history and literature. But individually or collectively, few of them could compete in terms of damage with their modern descendants. Why? If there was ever a war against drugs, we lost it years ago. One man like Jimmie Kale can destroy an entire community. Or a state. The metastasizing of the addiction doesn't sleep; it spreads twenty-four hours a day. And most of Kale's products, in particular meth, are a surefire ticket to psychological and moral insanity.

There are some who would not consider the little boy on the Flathead River a crime victim. But he is, and he will remember the dark handiwork of a stranger or strangers every time he hears the singing of water.

A week after the discovery of the missing waitress, I receive a call from Jeremiah McNally. It's a call I do not want to take.

"I wonder if you can help me out," he says.

How about that as a conversation starter? "What can I do for you, partner?"

"The coroner says Betty Wolcott died from blunt trauma, maybe done with a tire iron. I think they're going to stick it to me."

"I thought you said Jimmie Kale might be a suspect."

"Not like I am."

"Will you please spit it out."

"The coroner thinks Betty was pregnant."

"So?"

"She was," he replies. "She told me a few days before she went missing. I told her I would pay for the adoption or whatever else she wanted to do. She told me to fuck off."

"I'm sorry to hear all this, Jeremiah. I don't know how I can change anything."

"You know what's inside a guy like Kale. He did it. I know

he did. Jimmie the Digger isn't just a criminal. He's evil incarnate. And nobody I work with gets it."

"You've got some good cops there," I said.

"Oh yeah? Try this. Jimmie Kale cruised your house. With one of our guys trailing him. Did somebody bother to inform you a creep with the morals of Richard Ramirez was looking in your windows?"

"Kale is lots of things, but not a voyeur."

"Kale was at the Pov looking for Jack Wetzel. He played a few tunes on his guitar for the residents. They gave him a big hand. Starting to get the picture? You're shit and Kale is a great guy and I'm about to get a two-by-four with nails in it kicked up my ass."

"What about Betty Wolcott?" I ask.

"I'm not following you."

"I'm sorry to say this, but it seems most of your concern is about yourself."

The phone goes silent.

"Did you hear me?" I ask.

"I told you about the medical report. She was beaten to death with a tire iron or something like it. How do you think I feel?"

"Why are you so sure Kale did it?"

"Because it's either a guy like him or these monsters you and Spotted Horse believe in."

"I see."

"You're angry?" he asks.

"No."

"I've said the wrong things?"

"Jack Wetzel has disappeared from the motel where I arranged for him to stay. If I learn anything about him or Kale, I'll call you. Take it easy, partner. The night is darkest just before the dawn."

"Where'd you get that crap?"

On Pork Chop Hill, I think. But I keep my history to myself and quietly hang up.

I HOOK A FRESH haybale from the top of the stack and drag it to the barn door and pop the string and feed the horses. I love the grassy smell on the horses' breath, their nuzzles when they think I have treats for them, their physical disclaimers when they've been up to mischief, such as downloading in the barn, jerking loose the electric cord on the tank warmer, scratching their rump on the fence rails and getting their tail caught between the rails and the posts.

I give each of them alfalfa nuggets or apple and berry cubes for their treats. Another of their favorites is pulped sugar beets. Friends say I spoil them. I tell my friends the horses don't feel that way at all.

Snow is blowing like chicken feathers in the sunlight. The water in my tanks comes from wells and is always ice-cold and smells like water probably smelled on the first day of creation. The horses let the wild turkeys and the whitetails share the tanks with them. They pretend they're frightened and let the yearlings chase them around the pasture.

While having these thoughts as I walk down the slope, I see a familiar Ford truck turn into my drive. It's Sister Ginny. I go around the side of the house to head her off before she can reach the veranda. Too late. She's hammering on the front door with such force that the side of the house is vibrating.

She sees me when I round the corner. "Why don't you get a doorbell?"

"I don't have many visitors."

"You got a nice house here. Show me the inside while we talk."

"Beg your pardon?"

She's wearing a straw cowboy hat and a long coat with a fur collar and a pink dress that sticks out from the bottom of the coat. "You got earplugs on?"

I put on a mask. "You mind wearing one of these?"

"Fuck no," she says, and takes one from her pocket and puts it on.

"Please come in," I say.

She goes inside before I can get out of the way.

"You're thunder and lightning, Sister Ginny."

"How'd you like to get your mouth washed out?"

I close the door behind us. Before I can speak, she goes to my gun cabinet and begins naming every gun in the rack.

"That's impressive," I say.

She takes off her hat and scratches her hair. Her hair is as yellow as paint. "I got a lot on my mind. You got a snack, a candy bar, something like that?"

"I suspect I do. Let's—"

"You don't know if you have food in your pantry or fridge?"

"How about we dial it down, Sister?"

"Were you ever in a monastery? Because that's the way you act."

"How about this? I'll fix us a snack, and you sit down and shut up."

She screws a finger in one ear and looks at it. "I guess that's direct enough. All right, we'll do it your way."

She sits at the breakfast table, her eyes going up and down my body as though she's examining a side of beef in a meat locker. I know I will have to ventilate and sterilize the entire first floor of the house. "Did you think over the possibility of us making a movie?" she asks.

"With all respect, Sister, you might have good ideas for an adaptation, but I'm not good at it. I'm a novelist."

"William Faulkner didn't write the script for *The Big Sleep*? Mario Puzo didn't write the adaptation for *The Godfather*? Tell me that's not the best movie ever made."

"You're right."

"So I'm the problem?" she says.

I'm pulling food from the icebox now and I don't want to face her. Nor do I wish to hurt her.

"Want me to shove you inside that box?" she says.

I put the food on the drainboard. "I think you're probably a talented lady, Sister Ginny. I admire anyone who can write screenplays. For me, it was like packing an elephant in a phone booth."

"See, that last sentence is a pretty good line." She stands up and takes off her coat. "It's hot in here. Got anything to drink?"

"No," I reply. "You want whole wheat or sourdough?"

"Whatever you got." She sits back down, her eyes taking me apart again. "You think I'm gonna hurt your reputation, maybe embarrass you in front of your Hollywood friends?"

"I don't think that at all."

Her mouth is a tight line, her chest rising and falling. I see Fannie Mae on the other side of the kitchen.

I look back at Sister Ginny. "What's bothering you, ma'am? And don't say it's me."

"I think about what it might have been like."

"If you'd been dealt a different hand?"

"Yeah," she replies. Then she repeats herself. "Yeah, that pretty much says it."

"It's never too late."

"Stuff your bromides up your nose." She glances over her shoulder. "What are you looking at?"

"Nothing."

"You and me could have some fun."

I begin slicing a roll of sourdough.

"Maybe rip some butt," she says. "Show those fuckers in Hollywood how to make a movie."

"Sister, that kind of rhetoric is for punks and douchebags. The real gladiators are the people who weigh ninety pounds soaking wet."

She gets up and straightens her shoulders and stares out the back window. "What do you really think of me?"

"You were not abused as a child, but you were abandoned by a father you loved. His departure was probably without explanation. Your childhood ended on the day he left. However, you became a survivor. Many of the men at your church are sexual fascists. They know you're not the wrath of God, but they believe you can call it down on their enemies. Secretly you hate these guys."

She continues to stare out the window. The hills and fields are dark, and the moon is rising high above them. "You got a fine place here."

"Yes, it is."

She looks up into my face. "Last chance."

"For what?"

"Getting it on."

"It would be a great honor, Ginny. But you deserve a much better man than I."

"Good try."

"I'm being straight with you. I can't deal with my daughter's death. It's like I have a cannonball in my chest. Fannie Mae is standing behind you, just five feet away. I can see and talk with her, but I can't join her if it's by my own hand. In so doing, I will lose my soul."

Her eyes have the mixed coloration and intensity of agate. "How'd you know all that about my father? Don't lie."

"Because you're flat hell on wheels, Miss Ginny. And I said 'Miss Ginny,' whether you like cutesy *Gone with the Wind* rhetoric or not."

She picks up her coat and straw hat and taps me on the chest with the flat of her fist before I can distance myself from her. "See you around, Buster Brown. I'm not done with you."

Chapter Twenty-Seven

FANNIE MAE SITS down across from me, wearing a short black wool coat that has brass buttons and green cactuses and red flowers sewn on it, and stovepipe Mexican boots and dark trousers with purple stripes in them. But she doesn't speak.

"Did I do something wrong?" I ask.

I don't think you understand what's going on, Pops.

"Don't start."

Why do you think all these people keep drifting in and out of your life?

"You got me."

They can't fix their problems. They want to touch your hand or maybe even your bare foot and be set free. Somebody before your time had the same problem.

"That's foolish."

You're stuck, Pops. Better get yourself some sandals.

"I was afraid you had gone away. Maybe for good."

I'm here, aren't I?

"I went to the cemetery."

Stay out of that place. It's a real drag. Remember that ghoul from the church who tried to sell us a plot in Wichita? You said you had made mistakes in your life, but nothing to war-rant spending eternity in Kansas with the dust and tumble-weeds bouncing across your grave. You remember what the guy said?

"No."

"I take it you're not from this area."

"What are we going to do?" I ask.

Like you used to tell me when I was little: "Ease up on the batter, little guy."

"Why are you dressed like that?"

I was down on the border again. Jimmie the Digger has given a lot of money to refugee programs. You think he's buy-ing his own constituency?

"Probably."

I found out something else: Sister Ginny used to sing and play keyboard and mandolin for him. You're not going to like this, Pops. I think both of them want the same thing from you.

"I know what's coming. Turn off the faucet."

You remember all those segregationist assholes out of the fifties and sixties. Every one of those bastards grew up in the Baptist or Assemblies of God Church, and all of them were scared shitless at the prospect of going to hell. That's why every one of them made public apologies.

"You're wrong about people seeking me out, Fannie Mae."

You know your biggest flaw, Pops? You don't believe the people who say you were a good dad. Anyway, I'm awful tired right now. May I sleep on your couch?

"Are you sick?"

At heart I am. Sometimes we carry it across the Divide. It doesn't seem fair, does it? I wish I hadn't fucked up.

I'VE LOST TRACK of the seasons and cannot make distinctions between All Saints' Day and Thanksgiving and Christmas and New Year's and ceremonial carved pumpkins and Saturnalian eggnog and fruitcake and the day when, with Forest Service permission, Fannie Mae and I would drive up Lolo Pass into the national forest and cut down a huge dark-green Douglas fir, the snow shuddering on the branches with each stroke of the saw.

I feel drunk and lose my balance, although my last drink was forty-three years ago. My dreams are filled with monsters from night to dawn. I hear voices constantly, but they are not Fannie Mae's or the voices of anyone I know. They are accusatory, strident, profane, and vulgar. My thoughts are lascivious and sometimes violent. The worst time is at twilight. If I lie down, the inside of my eyelids turns into a movie screen the color and texture of pink rose petals. I see my best friend, Saber Bledsoe, running with me through a slit trench, our chests heaving, our boots splashing, our canteens and bandoliers and ammo cans and a thirty-caliber rattling, a 105 round arching out of its trajectory with a sound like the Creator unzipping the sky.

I use any surrogate I can to remove the venomous presences inside my head. I split wood, comb out the horses' tails and treat their feet, replace the brooder lamps in the chicken house with panel warmers, install a better security system in the house, and hire a wrangler friend to help with my chores and keep me company. But reason and coherence have departed from my life. I've lost contact with Jack Wetzel; for all I know, Jimmie Kale has found him and, for whatever motivation, put him through the tortures of the damned. I go out to dinner with Ruby Spotted Horse and pretend that people are not looking at us. I wonder about questions of morality and how they apply to the angst of an elderly and lonely man and his attraction to an attractive and brave and intelligent young woman. I also fear the day that Fannie Mae will leave me. At four-twenty every morning I wake and have no idea where or who I am.

It's Saturday and raining in the hills and snowing higher up. I put on a slicker and an Australian campaign hat and feed the chickens and walk among the horses and give them their treats. During the winter in Montana we have chinooks that come upon us unexpectedly, huge gusts of warm air that blow from the southwest and drive the temperature up to seventy degrees. Today is one of those days. The horses play in the flurries and roll in the mud wallows. Wild turkeys rim the stock tanks and peck at their feathers, and now that hunting season is over, the deer and elk drift down from the mountains and are at peace with the world, as though no one has tried recently to kill them.

I know little of theology, but I believe the big cathedral is the one I'm standing in. That's why I'm so disturbed when I see Jimmie Kale's Cadillac come up my lane. I go through the back door, stop at the gun cabinet, and go out the front before he can exit his vehicle. He rolls down the window. "You look like you're fixing to wet your pants," he says.

"Off my property, Mr. Kale."

He pushes open the car door and gets out. He's dressed western, wearing the same type of black Stetson I have, his coat open, his stomach squeezing against a silver-and-gold buckle the size of a heliograph. "Pull your stiff one-eye out of the light socket, son," he says. "I'm here on a peaceful mission."

"Mr. Kale, if you call me 'son' again, I will knock you down."

"Go ahead. Then you'll never find out why I'm here. That don't sound too smart."

"I'm not interested in your message. Write that on your forehead. Or text yourself. Or stick a note up your cheeks."

"This is about Ray Bronson, the ex of that little gal you been squiring around town. What's her name? Spotted Heifer?"

The pistol I took from my gun cabinet and stuck behind my belt is my grandfather's .45 single-action Peacemaker. It's a heavy gun, with six fat bullets in the cylinder, and has sharp angles and is pressing painfully into my spine.

"Bronson thinks he's still got his brand on her. He says he's gonna hang you upside down and cut off your toes. Half-breeds sometimes combine the worst of both races. That's Ray Bronson. Thought you ought to know."

"Here's my problem with that, Mr. Kale: I heard he was your friend."

"Call me Jimmie. Everybody does. I bought a couple of pieces of land from Bronson. Which is what I want to do with you." He gazes admiringly at the house. "Name your price."

"For my ranch?"

"No, your grease trap. Have you had your hearing checked recently? I'll give you two million. Cash money or any way you want it." He raises a hand before I can speak. "I know you're a rich man, but I can make you a lot richer. I know you got meadowland up Lolo Pass. I'll take that, too. Top dollar. Know why? Because Ted Turner ain't nobody's fool. That ole boy has got himself over a hunnert and fifty thousand acres of Montana land, which translates into the best land in the U.S. of A."

"I'll say good evening to you, Mr. Kale."

"You got a gun stuck in your belt, don't you?"

"Yes, sir, I do."

"You ever shoot anybody with it?"

I work the Peacemaker out of my belt and let it hang from my right hand, my fingers outside the trigger guard. "No."

"But you've shot people?"

"I can't remember."

He puts a piece of ball gum in his mouth and crunches it with his molars. "You've probably heard a lot of tales about me. But tales is all they are."

"Have you seen Jack Wetzel?"

"I have not seen the little shit."

"Goodbye, Mr. Kale."

"Boy, you're a hard-nosed son of a bitch."

I start to walk away.

"Hold on," he says.

"What?"

"You're from Texas?"

"Texas and Louisiana."

"Your middle name is Holland?"

"That's correct."

"Your family ain't from around Yoakum and Victoria, are they?"

"They are."

He looks sideways, then back at me; he huffs air out his nose. "You related to Sam Morgan Holland, the preacher and gunman who was pastor at the New Hebron Baptist Church?"

"He was my great-grandfather."

"I declare."

"What are you trying to say?"

"He killed my great-grandfather over a whore named the Cimarron Rose."

"She wasn't a whore. So watch your damn mouth, Kale."

He bows to me, opening his palms as though in supplication. "My mama always taught me not to get above my raising. Thank you for taking me down a notch, kind sir. You are a true gentleman of the Old South. Didn't your ancestor kill a bunch of Indians in Oklahoma?"

"They were comancheros."

"Have you explained that to Miss Spotted Turtle?" He glances at the Peacemaker. "Don't shoot yourself in the foot. Let the church roll on, boy, and remember, a family that prays together, stays together."

Then he drives away, his radio blaring out Little Jimmy Dickens's recording of "May the Bird of Paradise Fly Up Your Nose."

I EXPERIENCE TWO KINDS of blackout that aren't chemically induced. The first is not harmful. I cannot remember writing what is written in my books. When I look back at the printed pages, it is as though someone else wrote them. Hemingway and Faulkner spoke of having the same experience, so I have never worried about my obvious neurological flaw. The second kind of blackout is a different matter. I step into a hole in my memory bank that operates like a cocoon and leaves me with no memory of my actions or events that have occurred outside my skin, sometimes for as long as two days. Neurologists and psychologists have been of no value. One analyst, a nice man at LSU, said my history was consistent with multiple personality disorder.

But this is the way I feel about it today: What's the big deal? We all get to the same barn.

WE'RE IN THE New Year now. The pandemic is still with us, but Ruby Spotted Horse and I got our vaccines and we have a new president and the days are longer and there are buds on my apple trees. Most importantly, Fannie Mae has stayed with me. I'm one of those who like to believe that the passage of time will heal all wounds. Unfortunately, that is not always true. The murders of Clayton Wetzel and the two waitresses remain unsolved, and a night does not pass without Major Baker and his colleagues leaving a hint of their presence—ball lightning inside the woods above my house, a U.S. Army cavalry spur jutting from the dirt in the pasture, .45-70 shells of the kind used in the trapdoor Springfields of the era, a finger bone that could have belonged to a child.

I had hoped to make a change in Jack Wetzel's life, but I have heard nothing from him, and none of his friends at the Poverello have any knowledge of him, either. I can only pray that he has not become a victim inside Montana's transient subculture. We have to remember that Montana was the home of the Unabomber. Because of its size and small population and lack of regulation or widespread law enforcement, it is also the sheltering place of psychopaths on the drift, child murderers, neo-Nazis, self-declared militiamen, meth heads, gun fanatics, and people who are off the grid and so crazy there is no category for their neuroses, although they are not here in great number.

Sound like an exaggeration? Our sister state is Idaho.

The kid I hoped to help the most has turned out to be the biggest disappointment. Leigh Culpepper made good grades at the vocational college and was liked by his instructors. The tutor I subsidized not only helped him with his textbooks but introduced him to the Missoula City Library and had him reading *Huckleberry Finn* and *The Hunters* by James Salter.

Then something went wrong. Leigh missed classes without explanation, then two days ago got into a shoving match in a campus restroom and mimicked an instructor's stutter in front of the class.

I asked the tutor about Leigh and drugs.

"He told me he had spells. I asked him if he'd been smoking any weed. He said no. I asked him about the harder stuff. He wouldn't answer."

At noon today I called his father and left a message. It's now ten after three. My front windows are open, and my veranda is flooded with sunshine, and baskets of petunias hang from the eaves, and the Bitterroot River is high and slate green and running fast through the cattails.

The phone rings. I look at the caller ID and don't want to pick up. Then I take a breath and put the receiver to my ear. "Thanks for returning my call, Mr. Culpepper."

"Is this about Leigh?"

"Yes, sir."

"The college expelled him. I don't know how it happened. Leigh was doing so good at everything."

"What do you think the problem is?"

"A couple of times lately he came in drunk."

"Just drunk?"

"Or maybe hopped up."

"Know a kid named Jack Wetzel?"

"Kind of a rodent-lookin' kid? Yeah, he was hanging around awhile. You think he has something to do with Leigh drinking or drugging?"

"Jack Wetzel is a troubled young man, Mr. Culpepper."

He waits for me to continue. Now is the moment I have to make the choice: Do I inform on Jack and Leigh or walk away? A man like Culpepper could have many reactions. The world in which he grew up was one of superstition, fear, violence, misogyny, racism, lynching, and medical practices that are literally out of the Dark Ages.

"Jack told me Leigh gave him LSD," I say.

I can hear Culpepper breathing against the receiver.

"Mr. Culpepper?"

"He said my boy's a drug dealer?"

"No, sir, he didn't say that."

"Then what was he saying?" he says, his voice taking on an edge.

"He said Leigh was heavy into it. But Jack is not always honest. Maybe Jack was giving hallucinogens to Leigh."

"Why didn't you tell me what was going on?"

"I try to stay out of other people's business."

"You're talking about the kind of drugs Charlie Manson used to make killers out of those kids in California. You're telling me my boy is like them kind of people. That's hard to take."

"Jack and Leigh aren't Manson and Leary. Kids make mistakes, Mr. Culpepper. Don't judge them too harshly."

"Mr. Broussard, if I catch somebody giving my boy LSD, they ain't gonna be around long enough to judge."

"What if your boy was the giver?"

"I'd hate to say. I really would."

I cannot see his expression through the phone, but his tone creates an image I remember from my days as a reporter in a southern state: firelight flickering on the faces of white-robed men staring up at a burning cross, their humanity and ability to reason given over to a sick ethos invented for them by others.

Chapter Twenty-Eight

THE NEXT DAY I stop at the delicatessen inside Harvest Foods, Lolo's only grocery store. Working people are eating an early lunch at the tables; the day is bright and last night's snow is melting on the roof, and spring and a cheery note are in the air when Jeremiah McNally grabs my arm roughly from behind. "I got to talk to you," he says. "Now."

I pull his hand loose. "Don't bend my threads, Fred," I say, and try to smile.

He smells of nicotine and alcohol; there's a razor nick inside the dimple on his chin. He's obviously wired. "Don't let me down, Aaron."

I push my cart to an empty table in the corner and sit down. "What's going on, partner?"

He sits down across from me, his eyes sweeping the other tables and the deli counter. "I'm going down for that situation in the Flathead River."

"The murder of the waitress?"

"Yeah, Betty Wolcott. Guess who's making the case on me? Joe Latour, the guy who wouldn't let your injured daughter in his cruiser."

"Lower your voice."

"I'm going down for the whole bounce, Aaron. I could ride the needle."

"Stop it. What's their evidence?"

"My DNA is all over her apartment and her car and on her body or in her body and I don't know where else." His gaze slides off my face.

"Is there something you're leaving out?"

"No."

"How about the waitress who was found under the bridge at St. Ignatius? They got you for that, too?"

"Yeah, they might try. You think that's funny?"

"I'm trying to help you, partner."

"Well, you're not," he says. He gets up and goes to the beer cooler and returns with a six-pack, one can torn loose and already open in his hand. He chugs from it and sets it down on the table.

"You're testing the envelope, Jeremiah."

He pulls out his badge holder and opens it on the table. "They can live with it."

"What can I do for you?"

"You can be my friend. Tell those assholes what's going on."

"I'm not sure what you mean."

"Tell them about the spirits locked up in Ruby Spotted Horse's cellar. The Indians you saw that guy Baker kill behind your house."

"You've become a believer in the preternatural, and you want me to proselytize Latour for you?"

"I can't follow what you're saying."

There's no point in speaking to him. He's obviously gone over a line and won't be coming back for a while. He burps under his breath and takes another hit from the beer. The manager is headed for our table. I ease the beer can out of Jeremiah's hand and place it on the floor.

"You don't believe me, do you?" he says.

"DNA on the body of the victim doesn't add up to a homicide charge."

"It's all political. BLM are running cops through the wringer. So cops hang one of their own out to dry. That's me, a jockstrap on the wash line."

"I'm sorry this is happening to you, Jeremiah."

Many years ago I learned that we discover the best and worst in people when they're under duress. I think that principle has certainly borne out with my pitiful friend. I wish I had not been witness to it. I take his car keys and drive him to my home and keep him there until he's sober. He weeps in shame before he drives himself home.

AT FOUR P.M. the same day I park by the courthouse and walk through the front entrance of the sheriff's department and go straight to Joe Latour's office. His door is half open; he's at his desk and looks at me over his horn-rims when I tap on the jamb. A framed photograph on the wall shows him in police uniform, shaking hands with George W. Bush.

"What's up, Mr. Broussard?" he says.

"Need to talk to you about Jeremiah McNally."

"In regard to what?"

There are a dozen possible answers to his question, almost all of them intrusive and self-destructive. "I have information that may help in the investigation of the Wolcott murder."

He closes a folder on his desk blotter. "Pull up a chair."

"Thank you."

Then Fannie Mae walks through the wall and sits on a file

cabinet behind him. She's wearing snow boots with her jeans tucked inside them, a dark blue Union Army kepi, a Bugs Bunny T-shirt, and a navy peacoat. She gives me a double thumbs-up.

Latour studies my face, then looks behind him. "Something wrong?"

"No, not at all."

"So what's the information?" he says.

"Jeremiah says he's going down for the Betty Wolcott homicide. I think y'all are going in the wrong direction."

"How did you come to this profound conclusion?"

"I believe supernatural forces are involved. Not with just the Wolcott woman but in the deaths of Clayton Wetzel and the waitress up at Ronan, Irene Barr. I think the man who did these things was Major Eugene Baker. The same man responsible for the Baker Massacre on the Marias River."

"Glad you brought that info in. I'll let everyone know. Anything else?"

"Do you really believe someone like Jeremiah McNally would cut the entrails out of a woman's body, a woman he dated?"

"That applies to anyone. But someone did it." He looks at a clock on the wall. "Thanks for coming in."

"You're making the case on the basis of his DNA?"

"Know what?" he replies. "I don't think you're here about McNally. I think you've still got resentment about the way you think your daughter was treated."

"It's the opposite, Detective. I'm here in spite of the way you treated her and your failure to check the security cameras outside the nightclub. Then you all didn't go after the assailants for nine weeks. Aside from her physical pain, do you have any idea how much she suffered emotionally? Does any of this register with you at all, sir?"

"It's not a perfect system," he says.

"I'll give you directions to Fannie Mae's grave. Maybe you can tell her that."

"All right, so fuck me."

I look at Fannie Mae. Her expression is serene, almost beatific, as she goes into a sequence of Italian sign language, beginning with the gripped-biceps, curled-up forearm, and clenched-fist symbol for shove it up your ass, followed by double bones that simply mean fuck you twice, asshole, followed by double horns that can mean eat shit or you're a cuckold, followed by the flip-off on the chin that translates into blow me, beat it, or here's the sweat off my genitalia.

Latour follows my line of sight. "What are you grinning about, Mr. Broussard? Because whatever it is, I don't think it's funny."

"Please accept my apology."

"I'll share some information with you. The media doesn't have it yet, but everyone else does. Betty Wolcott died of blunt trauma, not, thank God, of the evisceration. The tire jack in the trunk of McNally's car was covered with her blood and hair, and so were the bottoms of his shoes that he threw into a Dumpster. He fooled me like he fooled you. He had porn and sex toys in his apartment. He's a sad, sick man who ruined his career."

"I don't buy it."

"That's your choice. I have work to do."

I get up to go. I've accomplished nothing. He has already gone back to his paperwork. I start out the door. Then he flips his ballpoint end over end into the wastebasket with a clang. "Hold on," he says. "If I were you, I'd see a counselor. I'm not being sarcastic. I think you have some serious psychological issues."

"I love the word 'issues.' It covers everything. Illiterate people can't get enough of it."

I start to go a second time. But I should have known that Fannie Mae wouldn't leave the fray without charging full blast into enemy lines. She pulls the framed photo of Latour and the president off the wall and sails it through the glass in his office door, scattering shards that look like broken ice on the hallway floor.

I can see Fannie Mae; obviously Latour cannot. He sits wide-eyed and openmouthed in his chair, his arms crossed over his head, as though the building is crashing down upon him.

"That's my little girl at work, Mr. Latour," I say. "Does that kid rock or not?"

IT'S WEDNESDAY NIGHT. Ruby and I decide to attend an outdoor showing of *Shane* behind the Roxy Theater on Higgins. The viewing area is lined with folding chairs between the back wall of the theater and the rear of the Episcopalian church. There are lighted apartments on the second story of the theater and more apartments in the alley that runs along the side of the church. I mention such detail for a reason. Humping your pack up Golgotha can leave you wondering. But as I look at my surroundings now, I'm reminded of the ivy-covered brick bungalow on the cul-de-sac street in Houston where I was born, and the centuries-old live oaks at the end of the block, and the flowers that bloomed in pots and gardens at every brick house on the street.

I think also of the years we lived in New Iberia and New Orleans, and the way the morning smelled of ponded water and stone stained with lichen and jasmine and four-o'clocks and the fecund odor of fish roe in the bayou and bruised mint in the courtyards and the open-air markets in the French Quarter, the crates of fruit and shrimp and fish and crabs stacked on the sidewalks. And the most poignant image of all, the one that defined the existential and ephemeral and heart-breaking imprint on our souls, one we could neither quarrel with nor of our own volition choose to reject: an orange moon in late autumn above an ocean of sugarcane swirling in the wind, the stalks hammered with streaks of purple and gold, clacking like broomsticks, the smoke from the sugar refineries electrified with floodlights, all of it as transient as an ancient fish working its way out of the sea and onto the sand.

Just before the movie starts, Ruby takes my hand. "I bet you're thinking of your childhood."

"How did you know?"

"Because you treat a movie theater like you're in a church in 1945."

"That's what a good theater is," I reply.

George Stevens's 1953 movie is one I learn from no matter how many times I see it. The primeval backdrop of the Grand Tetons represents the first day of Creation, and on it we see a wandering light-bearer played by Alan Ladd and a gunman named Jack Wilson played by Jack Palance, but at the center of the story is eight-year-old Joey Starrett, the one whose eyes we see through, the one who learns courage and humanity and honor not just from his struggling sodbuster parents but from Shane, a man with no past and no last name and who, in the last scene, is absorbed by the mountains he came from. It's the most religious film I have ever seen, although the film contains no reference to religion.

About halfway through the story, Jack Wilson, evil incarnate, appears in the tiny godforsaken settlement on which the sodbusters are all dependent. I have to use the restroom. I work my way between the chairs and the back of the theater, then see a man and a woman and a boy emerging from the alley next to the church. They pull chairs off a stack and snap them into a sitting position and clang them on the asphalt while talking to one another. The man lights a cigarette. The flame illuminates his face. It's Jimmie Kale.

I go into the theater, then try to return to my seat without drawing the attention of Kale and his companions. I sit back down and pick up Ruby's hand and hold it in mine. Why hold her hand? I don't know. Is there a tuning fork inside us that warns about the presence of evil or at least its product? I think there is. Someone's fingers slide over my shoulder and squeeze. I turn around and see the face of the one person I truly hoped I would never see in the company of Kale or Ginny Stokes. His face seems older, his head sharper in its angularity, an avaricious intensity in his eyes. "How you doin', Mr. B.?" he says.

"How are you, Jack?" I reply.

"Long time, no see."

"Yes," I say, my eyes straight ahead.

"I'm working for Mr. Jimmie."

"Yeah," I say, nodding.

"You doin' okay?"

Those around us are beginning to get irritable.

"I'll talk to you later, Jack."

"Yeah, sure. I just wanted to say hello. I had to get out of town for a while."

I lean forward so I can no longer see him on the perimeter of my vision. I hear him knock into a chair as he rejoins Kale and Sister Ginny. In the last scene of the film, Shane tells Joey there's no living with a killing and no going back on one and that Joey must return home and grow up to be strong and straight. As Joey runs toward the mountains calling for Shane to come back, there is a plaintive echo in his voice that's like the guttering flame of a votive candle, so delicate in its flickering that the audience is afraid to breathe upon it. I glance over my shoulder. The chairs occupied by Kale, Ginny Stokes, and Jack are empty, a bag of popcorn left on one, popcorn and butter trickling on the asphalt.

Chapter Twenty-Nine

GOOD RIDDANCE, I TELL myself the following day. But I should have known better.

It's noon now, the sky like an inverted blue ceramic bowl. I hear the sputtering engine of an airplane above the house, then see a shadow rippling across the backyard and the barn and the pasture. Out on the back steps, I see a red-white-and-blue two-seater biplane that banks violently and almost collides with the mountain. The pilot straightens out and comes back toward the pasture but is losing altitude, gunning the engine, the wings tilting. He and the figure in the rear seat are wearing goggles and leather aviator helmets and white scarfs trailing from their necks. The horses are panicked and running from one end of the pasture to the other. The plane scrapes the top of a ponderosa, dips suddenly, and bounces off the ground once, then twice, ripping off one side of the wings on a tree and crashing through a wire fence before coming to a stop, the propeller stubbed into the dirt, the tail painted with the Stars and Stripes, sticking up in the air.

The pilot unstraps himself and drops to the ground and pulls off his goggles.

Guess who? "You got to let me borrow your shitter this time," he says, unbuttoning his overalls and shoving them down his hips. "I dumped a whole load in my jockeys." He steps out of his overalls one leg at a time. "Come look if you don't believe me."

"I accept your word, Mr. Kale," I reply.

Jack Wetzel gets out of his seat and walks toward me, pulling off his goggles. "Sorry we busted your back fence, Mr. B. I'll round up the horses."

"No, you won't," I said.

"Sir?"

"You have some explaining to do, Jack."

"Don't be fussing at him, Mr. Broussard," Kale says. "The boy's been doing the best he can."

"You keep your own counsel, Kale," I say. "I've had it with y'all. There's a hose in the backyard. But that's as far on my property as you're going to get."

Kale picks up his overalls, his legs bare, his jockey underwear, as he said, soiled. "You're a Holland, all right," he says. "Cain't wait to clear the holster."

"What are you after, Kale? Why do you keep coming around?"

"Business. Goodwill. Montana is like Colorado was seventy-five years ago. There's a fortune to be made."

"I wouldn't do business with you if you had a retroactive patent on the wheel. That said, get on your cell phone and bring a flatbed and a crew out here and get this junk out of my pasture. I'll fix the fence myself."

"I was gonna ask you to have dinner with me and Sister Ginny."

"Are you serious?"

"You he'ped her boy. She feels obliged."

"Her boy?"

"That's right. Jack is her son. You brought a family back together."

"Jack and his brother told me they didn't know her."

"Well, now you know," he says.

"Is that true, Jack?"

"Yes, sir."

"I don't care if y'all are lying or not," I reply. "I wish you the best of everything, Jack. One last note: Get away from Kale. He's evil from his hairline to the balls of his feet."

I start to walk away.

"That's all you gonna say, Mr. Broussard?" Jack asks.

"You remember what Shane said to Joey in the movie last night? 'You have to be strong and straight.'"

"We left before the ending," he says.

"Why?" I ask.

Jack looks silently at Kale.

"We left because that movie stinks," Kale says. "With his shirt off, Alan Ladd looks like a Hollywood faggot."

I walk down the pasture and step through a rail fence and go inside the tack room and put together a half-dozen leads and halters and begin rounding up my horses. I guess my attitude toward Jack seems unforgiving. Secretly, I want him to follow me to the tack room, to denounce Kale, to apologize for the lies he has told me, or maybe to ask questions about George Stevens's great film. But there are times when the lights of pity and charity have no influence upon evil, and we have to let it go for what it is.

After I catch up the horses and do a temporary repair on the fence with a battery-powered corral kit, I call Ruby and ask her to meet me for a Mexican dinner at Fiesta en Jalisco on Brooks. But the last words of Shane and Joey still echo in my head. I wish I had been kinder to Jack. I look out the back door at the place on the grass where Kale washed himself. The hose is neatly coiled and detached from the faucet so it won't freeze up at night and break a pipe inside the wall. Jimmie Kale would not have those kinds of concerns.

JUST BEFORE I LEAVE to join Ruby, I look through the living room window and see Fannie Mae idly throwing rocks in the river. Before I can go outside, she appears beside me, a smooth rectangular stone in her hand.

"Trying to give me a coronary?" I say.

Here, feel this.

I touch the stone, then jerk my hand away. "It's hot," I say.

It's part of a tomahawk. See the groove?

"Why is it hot?"

It's from the massacre. It's a sign, Pops. Our war is with Eugene Baker. You've got the blues over this Wetzel kid. He'll take you down with the ship.

She walks to the gun cabinet, her reflection wobbling in the glass. I join her reflection and look at her looking at me. *You might have to do things you don't want to,* she says.

"With guns?"

Yep.

"Can you get me out of this?

There's a lot of worry on this side of the veil, Pops. The neocolonial fuckheads who've been running things since the Spanish-American War are trying to turn the Big Blue Marble into a necropolis.

"Don't use that kind of language. What's the matter with you?"

Listen to the dead. I want to stay with you, but I've been with you extra-long, or at least that's what the others are saying.

"Who are the others?"

People who died before their parents. Losing a child is the worst thing that can happen to a human being. That's why we're allowed to stay with you for a while. But only for a while. I've used up my extensions.

"I don't know if I'm going to make it without you. I've been taking Prozac."

Is it working?

"If you're crazy, how can you tell when you're well? Did Baker kill the waitresses or Clayton Wetzel?"

Hard to say. But that's not the issue. Your enemies know your weakness, Pops. That's not good.

"What is my weakness?"

You believe in your fellow man.

Her reflection disappears from the glass. But that's not what bothers me. My reflection disappears also.

I CAN'T CONCENTRATE AT dinner with Ruby. "What's the matter?" she asks.

I have told her many times about my relationship with Fannie Mae. Oddly, I don't know if she is convinced of its reality, perhaps because it pales in comparison to the panoramic display of historical violence and misery sealed inside her cellar.

"I have a bad feeling," I say. "It's like an ulcer or a cancer in the stomach. It dries out my mouth and takes away my breath, and then I feel a piece of wire tightening itself around my head, cutting off the blood to my brain."

Ruby doesn't speak. Outside, the sky is black, the street streaked with rain and the lights of cars. "It's a foolish way to be," I say. "But that's the way I felt when I experienced my first combat. I couldn't catch my breath. I felt like my skin was coming off. My teeth were chattering."

"You want to go?" she says.

"No."

"Can I do something?"

"The real problem is a warning given me by my daughter."

"That someone is going to hurt you?"

"No, the real problem is I may have to kill somebody." My hands are clenching and opening on top of the table. I can feel the waitstaff and people in the other booths looking in our direction. "My father was furious when I joined the army. He swore no one in our family would ever take a human life again."

"Then take no more," she says.

I stare at her blankly, then pinch my mouth with my hand and nod as though I have either said too much or said something shameful. "Yes, that's the answer, isn't it? I said the same thing to Jack Wetzel. You can't undo a killing. And you can't live with it, either."

There's sadness in her eyes. I completely forgot she shot and killed the rapist and murderer of two children. There was no mistake about her intention, either; she capped him four or five times from a short distance.

I try to change the subject. "Did you know A. B. Guthrie?"

"Who?"

"Bud Guthrie. He wrote the adaptation of *Shane*. He lived up in Choteau."

"No, I didn't know him."

"He was a great writer," I say. "*The Way West* and *The Big Sky* are two of the best novels in American literature. Academics will forgive any sin except commercial success. Over a twenty-seven-year period I taught in four universities and one community college and never heard his name mentioned."

She looks wanly out the window at the car lights in the rain; she has probably gone to a place inside her head for the rest of the evening. It's my fault. Participating in the mortality of others leaves a stain you don't easily rinse from your soul. That's why Fannie Mae advised me to listen to the dead. They have far more wisdom than the living.

But there is a macabre element in this. In one way or another, many of us have contributed to the membership of the dead. I have. So has Ruby. So have Jack Wetzel and John Culpepper and Ginny Stokes and perhaps Jeremiah McNally. So has the drunk speeding through an intersection, never seeing the crash in his rearview mirror. So do the right-to-life supporters who approve of the bombing of innocent civilians in foreign countries, and so do the politicians who love wars but never go to them.

I quit hunting when I realized why I did it. I was the giver of death rather than its recipient. Now I feel at peace with those whose voices are stopped with dust, whose anger has been taken from them, who have silently forgiven us for committing a theft that is unforgivable, just as Shane said. But the sword is not easily beaten into a plowshare. It's a great challenge and not easily borne. Hence the Holland curse. We wrote our history in blood.

FIVE DAYS LATER I receive a phone call from John Culpepper. "I don't want to pester you, Mr. Broussard, but my boy went off three days ago, and I thought you might know where he's at."

"No, sir, I'm afraid I don't."

"I think he went off with the Wetzel boy. You ain't seen him?"

"Last week."

"He didn't say nothing about Leigh?"

"No, sir."

"Nine bikers at Sister Ginny's church got arrested for transporting meth. They think I'm the one snitched."

"I don't want to get involved in this, Mr. Culpepper."

"This is all happening because of the little boy I killed. The Bible says it. The sin is unto the seventh generation."

"That's a symbolic statement, sir."

"I'm gonna get whoever give my boy the LSD. That was the sweetest boy in the world till them goddamn people come here with their dope and their homosexual marriages and all the rest of it."

How do you address a mindset like this? You don't. I try to console myself. "Them goddamn people" is a collective term, so maybe he won't single out Jack Wetzel. But my self-consolation is of little value. I fear for Jack's life.

"How about we have a cold drink on my veranda, Mr. Culpepper?"

"It's all coming to an end."

"What's coming to an end?"

"Everything. The world. It's in the Bible."

"Sir, don't do this."

The line goes dead.

THAT EVENING THE lead story on the local six o'clock news is the attempted suicide and arrest of Jeremiah McNally. The charge is homicide. The camera shows two plainclothes detectives walking him from his apartment to an unmarked car, an overcoat draped over the handcuffs on his wrists. His face is unshaved, as though half of it is patinaed with metal filings. Neighbors called 911 when they smelled gas leaking around the newspaper he had wadded under his apartment door. I start to turn off the TV but stop when I see a face in the crowd I would not expect to be there.

I have finally bought a smartphone, and I call Ruby's cell phone. She answers in her cruiser. The connection is bad, and she keeps fading in and out. "Where are you?" I say.

"North of Evaro Hill. By the casino. The sky's black. We've got a mean one coming."

"McNally was on the evening news. He's under arrest for the murder of the waitress. It looks like he tried to kill himself."

"How?"

"He turned on the oven."

"He went out on a gurney?"

"He walked out in cuffs."

"When suicides pull the plug, they pull the plug."

"You're not a McNally fan?"

"I think he's a fraud."

"Ray Bronson was in the crowd."

The connection is breaking up again. "Repeat," she says.

"Your ex, Ray Bronson, was there. Why would he be there?"

"Ray doesn't do anything that isn't about Ray. What's your twenty?"

"I'm home."

"We've got some spot fires breaking out below Lolo Peak. I may see you later. You okay?"

"Sure. Why wouldn't I be?"

"It's like you said at Fiesta: I think the shit is about to hit the fan. But I don't know why. How's the weather at your place?"

"Quiet."

"Get ready. The wind is ripping up trees along the Jocko. Gotta go. Out."

Chapter Thirty

I WALK OUT ON the veranda. The air is unseasonally warm, the early leaves of the cottonwoods barely puffing, the barometer dropping, a few rain rings dimpling the fast-running smoothness of the river. The sun is setting beyond Lolo Peak, but that is not why the light is fading. Montana and Louisiana share many similarities. The light doesn't die in the evening or before a storm. It's sucked into the earth, and almost immediately the trees become still and the leaves turn a darker green and the fish begin softly rolling under the surface of the lakes and waterways, disappearing with no sound, leaving not so much as a wrinkle. It happens in minutes. The air is clean and the blackness of the clouds and the trees of lightning pulsing inside them pose no threat, offer no warning, and instead are a testimony to the continuity of creation.

And it's all free.

I go back inside and hope that Fannie Mae will join me. She always loved thunderstorms, even as a little girl, when we lived in the Florida Keys. She loved the waterspouts even more when, on a blazing-hot day, one would drop from a single roiling black cloud into the ocean and turn into a wobbling tube of spun glass. You never forget those moments, do you? *Why did you have to die, Fannie Mae? Why? Why? Why?* Those words beat in my head like the drumming of a taskmaster on an ancient prison ship filled with convicts at the oars. To my mind, the greatest suffering depicted in the entire Bible is that of Jesus' mother at his crucifixion. I don't know how anyone could bear it.

These thoughts give me no rest and tempt me into a dark place where the sword seems a far more appropriate symbol of justice than prayer beads or beneficence purchased at the expense of those who are gone and have no one to speak for them.

I open windows all over the house and fix a fried-egg sandwich and put it and a scoop each of potato salad and dirty rice and a slice of pecan pie on a tray with a glass of iced tea and sit down on the back steps and try to look at all the great gifts of the world.

The wind is up, blowing pine needles from the roof and feathers from the door of the chicken house. It's a grand storm-tormented evening, the kind that somehow restores your faith and allows you to prove that insularity and freedom from fear are one and the same and that God is a friend and not a bearer of wrath and destruction.

I pick up my dishes and turn around so I can open the door. Then I hear an object whip past me, like someone trying to spit something off his tongue. But it does more than pass by my ear. It slices the skin, the kind of cut that stings right away. I drop the dishes and press my hand to my ear and then look at it. There is a star of blood in the center of my palm, as though it fell from an eyedropper. An arrow with a steel head, one as thin and sharp as a razor, is embedded in the wall of the washhouse attached to the house, the feathered shaft still quivering.

The yard and the pasture are empty. Whoever shot at me was far away. I can hear thunder beginning to crackle in the clouds and the horses nickering in the pasture, probably wondering if I will put them away for the night, which I always do in violent weather lest they be hit by falling trees. I go back in the house, dress my ear with some iodine, put on a slicker and my beat-up Stetson, drop the Peacemaker in my right-hand pocket, and walk down to the tack room. Why do I not dial 911 with my newly purchased smartphone? The adherents of Eugene Baker threw down the glove, not I.

I LEAVE THE ARROW in the washhouse wall and wait an hour before I call John Fenimore Culpepper. I cut to it as soon as he picks up. "How you doin', Mr. Culpepper? A short time ago somebody shot a hunter's arrow at me. He fired from a good distance but was able to clip my ear. That means he has a powerful arm and a good eye. You know anything about this?"

"You accusing Leigh?"

"Did he return home? Has he contacted you? I saw his archery setup when I visited your house."

"If somebody shot an arrow at you, Leigh didn't have nothing to do with it. His bow and quiver was stolen."

"When?"

"It was that Wetzel boy. Leigh sticks up for him, but I know it was him. He probably sold it for dope."

"I dimed your son, Mr. Culpepper. I think he has reason to resent me."

"You did what?"

"I told you he was using acid. I informed on him."

"Leigh don't go after people. It don't matter what they do."

How about painting a swastika on a stranger's barn? I think. But I do not say it. "I didn't call the cops. That doesn't mean Jack Wetzel or Leigh gets a free pass. It means the opposite. Are you reading me on this, sir?"

"If you're threatening my son, you'll have me at your door in the next fifteen minutes."

"Sorry to hear you talk like that, Mr. Culpepper," I reply. "I thought better of you."

I break the connection and look out the front window. The storm clouds up Lolo Pass are as black as soot. Ruby's cruiser turns into the driveway, headlights on, windshield peppered with rain. She runs up the flagstone path to the veranda, her campaign hat on, her face uplifted and shiny, lit by the porch light, full of expectation.

I TELL RUBY WHAT has happened.

"You should get a couple of security people out here," she says.

"Nope. Waste of time. Silly. End of discussion."

"You don't know the whole situation," she says. She has taken off her hat and is wiping the rain out of her hair. "I know a couple of feds working on the res who say McNally is a degenerate gambler and into Jimmie the Digger for large amounts of money. They say my ex is a hump for him, too."

"McNally told me he had seen them together."

"Anyway, my ex is a dingleberry and has finally found his place in the universe. The feds told me they dug up a site that Kale had used for years. There were three sets of human bones in it but no money or stash."

"So it's true about Kale killing numerous people?"

"Ray's terrified," she says. "Actually, I feel sorry for him. He called me on my cell a little while ago. He wants me to help him get into the witness protection program. I told him he had to have something worth selling. He started crying. He says the people at the site on the res were buried alive."

"It's not what I want to believe, but I think Jack Wetzel was there."

"You think Wetzel shot at you?"

"Hard to say. Jack is duplicitous and wants money. Leigh Culpepper wants the approval of his father. I took that away from him."

We're standing by the gun cabinet. I can see our reflections, as I did with Fannie Mae. Ruby presses herself against me, her cheek flat against my heart. "You're a good guy, Aaron."

"So are you."

"I'd like to go up to Alberta and just keep going on all the way to the Northwest Territories. Just you and me."

"That sounds like a fine idea," I reply.

"I'm tired of pandemics and sleazy politicians and stupid people who refuse to put on a mask. I'm tired of greed and wars and people ruining the planet. I'd like to go where people have never been and stay there the rest of my life."

"'One generation passeth away, and another generation cometh, but the earth abideth forever.'"

"Where's that from?" she asks.

"Ecclesiastes 1:4. I've been stealing plots from the Bible for sixty years."

She's not listening. Her body is close to mine, her eyes shut, her chest rising and falling, the top of her head under my chin. When I try to move, she tightens her arms around me. We stay like that for a long time. I close my eyes and almost fall asleep while standing up. When I open my eyes, my reflection has disappeared from the glass, although Ruby's remains. This time I'm not afraid. I even wonder if I would be better off on the far side of the veil.

THE LANDLINE RINGS on the kitchen counter. I pick it up hesitantly. This is not a night I want to hear any more about the problems of others. "Hello?"

"Well, how you doin', Buster Brown?" Sister Ginny says. "I saw a cruiser parked in front of your house. You putting the blocks to Pocahontas?" She pauses. "That's what I thought. Mr. Broussard, you are the dumbest white man I have ever met. Jimmie Kale is gonna split you up the middle, pour salt in your insides, and tack you on a fence post, like they do crows down in Texas. Are you listening?"

"Not really," I reply. "I'll be hanging up now."

"Listen up: My son almost pinned your head to a wall. Yeah, Jack is my son. Don't worry, I slapped the little shit upside the head till he thought he was a girl. Anyway, he wants to apologize."

"It's been great speaking with you," I say. "I'll be toggling off now. You know, putting the blocks to people and that sort of thing."

"Jack stole the bow from John Culpepper's house. As we speak, I'm making him return it. Jack holds you in high regard. Give him a chance."

"Where is Leigh?" I ask.

"Living up in a cave or some shit. I think the kid has scrambled his own brains."

"Tell Jack to give me a call."

"You'll talk to him?"

"Yes, ma'am."

"Listen, Aaron, don't throw away this opportunity." She has never used my first name. "Go in with me and you'll have more money than you ever dreamed of. All of your books will be on cable television. You got the manners and the talent, and I know how to kick ass. In comparison, what you got now is dick."

"Why were you with Kale at the Roxy?"

"He's a walking bank with as many friends as a pot of goat piss on a radiator."

I can't believe I'm having this conversation. "Go easy with the Culpepper family, Sister."

"I'm supposed to be afraid of people who think the earth is six thousand years old?"

"A man already in hell doesn't have a lot to lose. Thanks for your offer. You should think about scriptwriting. You're one for the ages."

There's a beat. "You mean that?"

"Straight up."

I HANG UP AND turn around. Ruby is standing right behind me, looking at a text message. "Jesus Christ," she says.

"What is it?"

"Jeremiah McNally was in a holding cell. Nobody took his belt. He hanged himself. This time he went all the way."

I have to sit down. Like the loss of a child, the suicide of a friend or family member is one you never get over. I know because it runs in the Holland family. The person who commits it blights the life of every person around him. I have a hard time forgiving those who leave such an unjust burden for others to carry. Ruby looks sick.

"This is no one's fault," I say.

"I called him a fraud."

"Don't butt into this, Ruby."

She widens her eyes and blows out her breath. "Okay, you're right."

But I'm not doing too well myself. I liked Jeremiah, and it's hard to accept the darkness that obviously lived inside him.

"What's the deal with Stokes?" Ruby says.

"I'm not sure. She's trying to act like a mother, but she's a consummate liar also."

There's a flash of lightning in the trees up the hill, followed by a boom of thunder that rattles the dishware in the cabinets. Inside the trees, a Douglas fir is ablaze from base to top, illuminating a circle of men in blue uniforms and kepis and slouch hats, all of them armed with pistols or .45-70 carbines. A figure I can't make out is encircled by several enlisted men. The rain drenches the fire, and the soldiers disappear as though zipped up in a black bag.

"Your face is white," Ruby says.

"Sister Ginny is going to make a move. Using her son or Jimmie Kale."

"How do you know?"

"Major Baker is here. He's a parasite. Evil can only function if it has a host. That's why he's come in our midst."

"What did you see up there?"

"Baker's men are holding someone captive."

She looks at me, then at the bottle of Prozac on the kitchen counter, then back at me, blinking. "Who?"

I can't think or speak. I feel weak all over. "I don't know. I couldn't see well. They were too far away."

"A man or a woman?"

My heart is beating as loudly as a conga drum in my ears, the rancid stench of fear rising from my armpits. "The light was too dim," I say. "There were too many people among the trees. It could have been anyone."

I pray I did not see Fannie Mae.

Chapter Thirty-One

Rᴜʙʏ ɪꜱ ʜᴇᴀᴅᴇᴅ up Lolo Pass, where a fire has burned down a church and jumped the highway and is climbing up the side of Lolo Peak. The rain that should have impeded the flames has been undone by the velocity of the wind. Crown fires, the kind that leap across the canopy of the forest, cannot be out-run by people on foot. The years 2020 and early 2021 have produced record droughts. I think we're in for it.

I get a sleeping bag from the closet and open it up like a blanket, lie down on the couch with a pillow under my head and Grandfather's Peacemaker under the pillow, and pull the sleeping bag up to my chin. Why choose the heavy single-action revolver for self-protection rather than weapons in my possession that are far more sophisticated? The Peacemaker is part of the man and the times in which he carried it as a Texas Ranger and town marshal. From Reconstruction to the Dust Bowl, Grandfather went up against some of the most danger-ous gunfighters in Texas, including Harvey Logan, a member of the Hole-in-the-Wall Gang.

In early 1934 Bonnie Parker and Clyde Barrow and Ray-mond Hamilton and his girlfriend camped on Grandfather's ranch during a dust storm so thick the dust piled to the bottom of the windmill blades; Grandfather had to nail wet burlap over the windows. My cousin Weldon Holland fell in love with Bonnie and said she was nothing like the woman smoking a cigar with her foot on the bumper of a stolen car. I loved the stories that Weldon and Grandfather told me, and I ached to have been born in that era.

Grandfather did not abide complexity. When asked the secret of his survival in over a dozen gun duels, he said, "Take your time and don't miss." He had no formal education but owned a set of encyclopedias he read from cover to cover over the course of his life. He and Weldon put a wreath on Bonnie's grave. Grandfather's axiom was "Love the Lord and love the world and don't let anybody tell you one is exclusive of the other."

So that's why I pick up Grandfather's Peacemaker. I feel its weight and heft and coldness and know that I'm carrying a tradition that has few equals. It's a pretty good way to feel. Or at least that's what I tell myself.

The rain is coming down steadily, snow sliding down the windows, electricity veining in the clouds. I do not want to think about the apparition of Major Baker and his men and their captive in the trees. In fact, I tell myself the sun will rise in the morning, the fires will die in the mountains, the fish will leap in the streams, and the earth will in some way be mended.

It's after midnight now. I know that somehow I missed something about the logic of Ginny Stokes's statement regarding Jack Wetzel's theft of the bow and quiver and her directive for its return. Yes, under reasonable circumstances Jack should have gone to the Culpepper home and apologized. But Leigh is not at the home. He is probably somewhere up one of the creeks in the Bitterroot Mountains. Jack Wetzel, a drug mule who hates and fears authority, will have to deal on his own with John Culpepper, a former Klansman who for thirty years has probably sought out a scapegoat or a villain he could punish for the Black child he murdered in Alabama.

I sit on the side of my couch and rub my face. The sky is still black and the rain still falling, like a curtain protecting me from the world. I want to fix a sandwich and a glass of milk and go back to sleep. I despise the idea of what I have to do.

I go in the kitchen and turn on the light and call John Culpepper. Perhaps fifteen rings go by. My conscience is almost home free and I start to hang up. Then I hear him clearing his throat. "Who the hell is this?"

"I'm sorry to call so late, Mr. Culpepper. It's about your boy and Jack Wetzel."

"Time for you to mind your own business, Mr. Broussard."

"Sir, this is very important. If you'll give me a minute or two—"

"What I'll give you is hell. Don't ring my phone and don't darken my door. I cain't tell you how I strongly I feel about this."

"Yes, sir," I say. "I shouldn't have called. I won't do it again."

He hangs up.

I CANNOT BE CERTAIN of the events that followed. Perhaps that is the way of most tragedies. It's grand to think of our denouement in terms of a five-act Elizabethan drama, but it seems that happenstance often holds more sway than the rules of Aristotle's *Poetics*. Age cheats us in a peculiar fashion; it does not come with wisdom. I wanted to undo my youthful mistakes by reforming Jack Wetzel and helping Leigh Culpepper and his father lead lives that education and poverty had denied them. My best efforts came to nothing. However, I'll let the reader judge. Perhaps indeed the weights on the scale get balanced and in the fifth act a semblance of catharsis and order is imposed upon the players and we continue our lives and do our best until the day comes when we have to go either gentle or raging into that good night. I suspect the real issue is how we conduct ourselves when the ironies of fate seem more than the soul can bear.

The television and newspaper accounts about John Culpepper and Leigh and Jack were fragmented and probably made little sense to an outside observer. But someone with any knowledge of the damaged lives they had been dealt would understand how a kingdom can be lost for want of a nail.

Jack or his mother had bought a gas-guzzler, but Leigh had no money for a vehicle and had run away from home and encamped in an overhang up in the Bitterroots. Pretending to follow his mother's order, Jack put the bow and quiver of arrows in the backseat of the gas-guzzler and drove toward the Culpepper house. Once out of sight, he switched direction and headed south for Blodgett Canyon, west of Hamilton, and walked two miles soaking wet into the wilderness to wake his friend in an overhang and ask him to deliver the quiver and bow to John Culpepper, whose wrath he feared.

Just before sunrise, Leigh dropped Jack at a truck stop and drove to his home on the back road not far from my ranch. Evidently John Culpepper had seen the gas-guzzler on several occasions and had never seen anyone other than Jack drive it.

The weapon he used was probably under his bed and already loaded. It was an AR-15, the civilian equivalent of the M-16, but unlike the latter, it never jammed. When the sheriff's deputies arrived, Culpepper was hardly intelligible. The AR-15 was in a puddle of water in the middle of the yard. Culpepper's wife, who was screaming on the porch, had raked her husband's face with her fingernails and had to be sedated and taken away in an ambulance.

Culpepper told the deputies he heard a vehicle with a broken muffler coming up the back road, then saw it turn into the yard, its headlights on high beam, the windshield wipers slashing across the glass. The driver cut the engine and headlights and stepped into the yard, then removed an archer's bow from the backseat. Culpepper added that he was sure Wetzel was there to do bodily harm to his family.

The driver was wearing a hooded raincoat. The bow was in his left hand, as though he were about to nock an arrow on the string. Culpepper raised the AR-15 and began firing. He said he did not remember how many times he pulled the trigger. A deputy picked up nine spent cartridges from the porch and flower bed. At least three rounds struck the driver. The driver was identified as Leigh Beauvoir Culpepper. He died in the ambulance en route to the hospital in Missoula, just as the sun was rising above Mount Sentinel, at the bottom of which was the vocational college Leigh Culpepper had attended.

John Culpepper was taken to jail for his own protection, according to a Ravalli County Sheriff's Department press release, then allowed to return home with his wife three hours later.

AT TWO-FIFTEEN P.M. the same day, I get another call from Ginny Stokes. "You've heard all about it?" she says.

"The shooting?"

"What do you think? Has Jack contacted you?"

"Why would he call me?"

"He's in trouble. I'm the one who forced him into the situation. That mean I'm the stink on shit."

Through the window I can see Lolo Peak and columns of smoke in the rain. "If Jack calls, what do you want me to tell him?"

"To get out of town."

"He didn't do anything wrong," I reply.

"Culpepper will blame him for everything that's happened. He'll probably blame you and me, too."

"Goodbye, Sister."

"Don't hang up on me. I'll come over there and rip your ass out of its socket."

I hang up and call my wrangler friend who watches the house, and arm the security system and put on my old Stetson and canvas coat and drop Grandfather's Peacemaker in the right pocket, and leave the house before Sister Ginny can call back or block my driveway.

I DO NOT KNOW where Jimmie the Digger lives. But his kind is not hard to find. Wherever the dependent and vulnerable are, wherever there is corruption or cops on a pad or a government that inculcates in the electorate vices like lotteries and casinos and a shuck like the harmlessness of weed, Jimmie the Digger will be there, too.

I drive up Evaro Hill and onto the res and stop at the nightclub close by the spot where Clayton Wetzel's body was torn into pieces. The same bartender is there, wearing pigtails and a silver-and-gold rodeo rider's belt buckle. There are few people in the bar. "Me again," I say.

He leans on his arms, his chest the size of a rain barrel. "How you doin', Mr. Broussard. What can I serve you?"

"Know a character named Jimmie Kale? Aka Jimmie the Digger. Has an adenoidal accent, kind of like a parrot or Willie Nelson."

"Do I know him personally? No, I don't."

"But you know who he is?"

"Yeah." He looks at the tops of his hands.

"You don't feel comfortable talking about him?"

"I don't need guys like that coming around."

"I understand," I say.

"It's meth and opioids. They're all over the place. It's not just the kids. It's the whole family. Custer would love it."

"Where can I find Kale?"

"I hear he's got a fuck pad up the Jocko. You'll see some cottages by the bridge. Take a right and keep going up the river."

"Can I buy you a drink?"

He puts a toothpick in his mouth and rolls it across his teeth. "Me and some others run a program for teenage addicts. When you've got time, you might make a contribution."

"Maybe so."

He flips the toothpick into the trash can. "About Kale? Watch yourself, Mr. Broussard. I've heard stories about him I don't want to think about."

I HEAD UP THE highway. The Jocko Valley is feed-grower country, and the fields are sodden and green and smoky from the rain and the spot fires ignited by lightning. The highway dips down to a bridge on the far side of the river. I turn and pass some rental cottages under birch trees and drive up a slope toward the Mission Mountains.

I have no plan, at least no conscious one. However, I know in one way or another I've already cast the die. I cannot continue to live the way I have lived since my daughter's death. Psychoneurotic anxiety and agitated depression coupled with an ideational personality produce a combination that is like being boiled alive.

In part I know that the choice is not entirely mine. Major Eugene Baker is back in town and obviously for a reason. Jeremiah McNally has committed suicide; Leigh Culpepper has been shot to death by his father; and John Culpepper, after shooting his son multiple times, claiming self-defense and misidentification of the victim, has been released by the authorities. In the center of all these events are people like Jimmie Kale, spreading an addiction that is arguably genocidal.

I rumble across a bridge and see a white cottage with a green alpine metal roof and flowers planted in a line of coffee cans on the front porch. Kale's Caddy is parked in the dirt drive, brown maple leaves pasted like spiders on the starched-white top. The wind is out of the north, swirling off the Missions, the sun buried like a dull silver coin in the clouds, some of the flower cans rolling back and forth on the porch.

My black Stetson is blown off my head as soon as I step out of my car. It bounces end over end into the Jocko. I beat on the door and make as much noise as I can. Kale opens the door in a purple suit and shined cowboy boots and a black shirt with tiny pink roses printed on it. "You trying to tear my house down?" he says.

"See the news?"

"No, and I'm not interested, either."

"John Culpepper shot and killed his son by mistake. He mistook him in the dark for Jack Wetzel. I thought Jack might be headed your way. He doesn't have many friends right now."

"Number one, I don't know John Culpepper from monkey jism. Number two, Jack Wetzel is a walking promotion for the pro-choice movement, and number three, who told you where I live?" Over his shoulder I can see a tall young Indian woman in the kitchen. She is wearing tight shorts and cowboy boots that look brand-new and a T-shirt that reads "Love It or Give It Back."

Kale follows my line of vision. "*What?*" he says.

"I'd call you white trash, Kale, but you don't make the bar. You're a disease, like the Black Plague in the fourteenth century. You know the children's rhyme 'Ring around the rosie . . . all fall down'? The roses were the black sores that spread all over people's bodies when the plague passed through their town. That's you, Kale. You come to town and people die, and in the meantime you get your ashes hauled wherever you can."

The woman in the kitchen had been cooking eggs and sausages, stirring them with a spatula. But now the spatula is barely moving as she listens to our conversation.

Kale looks over his shoulder again, then back at me. "People got a false impression of me. I've done a lot of good around here. Things maybe you don't know about." He waits for me to reply. But I don't. "Why you looking at me like that?" he says.

"I heard you were cruel to animals."

"Then you heard wrong." His eyes follow my right hand. "What are you doin'?"

"I think you help people like Eugene Baker and Phil Sheridan and John Chivington."

"I don't know anything about these people. You got some kind of brain tumor?"

"Sheridan said, 'The only good Indian I ever saw was dead.' Chivington said, 'Nits make lice.' You have any firearms here?"

"What if I do?" he replies.

"I'm glad you feel that way. I'll be outside a few minutes. Some people believe you're already dead. I think that might be true."

"I think you're fucking out of your mind. If I didn't have company—"

"I'm glad you mentioned the lady in the kitchen. I think she should leave."

The Indian woman turns off the burners on the stove as though in slow motion and, in the same fashion, picks up the skillet with a hot pad and takes it and the spatula to the sink and rinses them with cold water, then turns off the faucet and stares out the window at the rain misting on the meadows.

"Miss, did you hear me?" I say.

"Yes," she answers.

"None of this is your fault."

She nods, then puts on her coat and goes out the back door. I look at Kale. "I'll be outside," I say.

I go out on the porch and pull the Peacemaker from my pocket and aim at the Cadillac's grille with both hands, arms extended straight out. I fire into the grille with the first round and put the second round through the hood and the firewall and dashboard. Then I hear Kale behind me. I turn just as he swings a baseball bat across my back, knocking me sideways off the porch into the mist, Grandfather's Peacemaker flying from my hand.

"You thought I was some kind of douchebag out of one of your fucking books? You were gonna ruin my car, run off my gash, get me to beg, make me your punk?"

I try to stand, but he swings the bat into my arm and flattens me in the mud, then kicks me in the back of the head. "You didn't answer me."

"Bugger off, Kale."

He gnarls the tip of the bat into my neck and keeps his foot on my chest. "How do you want it? I can start with your shins. They break like sticks. Or I can take your head off with one swack. Your choice."

My head is swimming, as though something has pulled loose inside it. He kicks me in the face. "Want some more?"

"You know your problem, Kale? You're you. That won't ever change. You were unwanted in the womb. When you're in the ground, no one will take the time to piss on your grave. How does it feel?"

Chapter Thirty-Two

I KNOW I'M ABOUT to buy it. I think of the teardrop lake high up in the Missions where Ruby and I made our troth. I know it waits for me and eventually for her and maybe for Fannie Mae as well. I believe the world to be a cathedral shaped by a divine hand, and if this is true, I should fear death no more than I should fear returning to the home of my birth. As William Shakespeare said in *Henry IV*, "we owe God a death and let it go which way it will he that dies this year is quit for the next."

I wait for the blow that will shatter my skull and brain like a flowerpot. But it doesn't happen. Kale is still clenching the bat, except in a defensive position, staring at the fog puffing off the Jocko. "What's goin' on here?" he says.

The fog thickens and rolls closer to the cottage. It's steel gray, like curds of smoke from an industrial incinerator. Then a huge reddish-orange glow blooms inside it, and I see the major and his troopers and Fannie Mae gathered together, firelight flickering on their faces. All of the soldiers are in dress blues. The major has pulled his sword from its scabbard and is resting the blade on his shoulder.

Got yourself in a fix, Mr. Broussard?

"What are you doing with my daughter?"

Spoils of war?

"My ass," I say.

How about a trade? I give you back your daughter and take this lovely bag of garbage off your hands.

"That's it?"

Then you come along, too. We'll make a frolic.

Jimmie Kale's expression is like a bowl of porridge. "Deal me out," he says.

I can see Fannie Mae clearly now. She mouths her words slowly. *It's a scam, Pops. Tell him to eat shit.*

"Your record is a bit disturbing, Major," I say. "I don't think negotiations with you are a good idea."

Have I ever lied to you?

"Not to my knowledge. But your pretense as a soldier simply carrying out orders doesn't wash."

You don't think the Rebs were cruel? Sending the slaves to the auction block after Lee took Chambersburg, Jeb Stuart rounding them up outside Washington?

"Those were despicable acts," I reply.

Let's put things a little closer to home. You didn't see your F-86s mow down Korean peasants trying to flee the bombing of their cities?

"Yes, I did."

You liked that, did you?

"You make your case, Major, but you're still the bloody instrument of an iniquitous cause."

He thrusts his sword angrily back into the scabbard. *What should I do with you, sir?*

"Whatever you wish. My guess is you don't have any power over me. Nor do you have power over my daughter."

Fannie Mae smiles.

I'm vexed, Mr. Broussard. I've treated you with dignity and respect.

"You're no different from Kale, Major. You have spread misery and death among innocent people. You forced them into freezing water and burned their tepees and blankets and clothes and food. Few, if any, ever visited more pain on the Blackfeet."

His jaw is clenched, his face twitching as though each of my words is pricking his skin. *I'll be back. I promise a resolution of this. In the meantime I'll put into abeyance your troubles with this pitiful peckerwood. I will also ensure your daughter's safety.*

"No," I say. "You must release her, Major. She doesn't belong with you."

Mr. Broussard, it's you who's the problem. Your daughter extended her stay far beyond the time usually allotted for those in her situation. Pardon me for saying this, but you're not the good father you think you are.

With the flick of a salute, the fog closes around him and his men and Fannie Mae, then recedes into a horizontal vortex two hundred yards up the Jocko. The baseball bat held by Kale is ripped from his hands by an invisible force and sails like a helicopter blade over the roofs of the cottages down below.

I pick up Grandfather's pistol and wipe off the mud. Kale is in a stupor, hardly able to walk. "Check yourself into counseling and tell the therapist what happened today," I say. "I bet he'll get a laugh out of it."

Then I get in my car and drive home, wondering if I will ever see my little girl again.

———

IT'S LATE THURSDAY afternoon. The rain has been unrelenting. High winds have knocked down power lines all across the county. The fires on the res and up Lolo Pass have put Ruby on double shifts. I have screwed candles in bottle necks and placed them in saucers and lit them in the living room and kitchen. The room is alive with shadows, all of them somehow threatening. The beating I took from Kale has left its mark. My ribs and right arm and my back ache; a bruise the color of an eggplant has spread across my forehead and the bridge of my nose. I sit in front of the fireplace and wait, my loaded M1 propped against the couch, Grandfather's pistol on the footstool.

For what or whom do I wait? My enemies. I know that's a broad statement, and perhaps once again I'm being grandiose. But I know they will come, in the same way a soldier digging a hole with his e-tool knows he has entered into a contract he cannot rescind. Though the hole in the earth may be protective in intention, it is also a grave, and the soldier knows this, knows it is not natural, but accepts with each thrust into the dirt the commitment he has made to his country and to his enemy, one who will validate *his* side of the contract as soon as the opportunity presents itself.

Previously I mentioned the bugles the Chinese blew in the hills to keep us awake. I welcomed them. If they wanted us awake, chances were they would not attack. Of course, sometimes they mixed up the signals to keep us confused. But silence on the firing line at night can be like fingernails screeching on a blackboard.

As the sun dies, I dial Ruby's cell phone and leave another message. It's my third. Her husband is a weak and angry man; he is also an addict and, I suspect, controlled by Jimmie Kale, and I fear what he may do to her. My call goes immediately to voicemail.

By seven p.m. the sky is completely dark, the candles guttering when the wind steals under the doors. I am certain my visitors will call upon me before sunrise. Am I prescient? Not at all. The enemies I have described to you are of a particularly predictable kind. At some point in their lives they turned off the light in their souls. From then on they stopped keeping score. But each knows when his time is up. They form symbiotic relationships with their own ilk and seek a host that is already purulent. You've met them, either individually or as a group. Tell me, when you looked into their eyes, did your blood freeze, did your throat go dry? It's a frightening moment.

Other than Ruby, the array of people who have come to my house from the vandalization of my barn door to the present had a self-serving reason. However, I don't know what it is. Perhaps it's simply greed or celebriphilia. Perhaps I'm simply an adverb in their lives.

The swastika on my barn was the childish exercise of xenophobes. The attempted break-in of my house by Jack and Clayton Wetzel was obviously more complex and contradictory in purpose. I'm sure they were the same pair caught on surveillance cameras burglarizing small businesses in Lolo. They seem to have the standards of petty thieves. Except their weapons were sophisticated and murderous in capability and automatically exposed them to far more time in prison should they be caught.

The Wetzels told me they only wanted to steal food. Just as Jimmie Kale only wanted to buy my ranch. Just as Ginny Stokes only wanted to be the film producer of my books. But I remember a particular detail now that seemed unimportant at the time. When I knocked the Wetzels around with a broom in the barn, they had hay and chicken manure smeared all over their clothes. But did they acquire it before I took them into the barn or afterward? I can't remember. I put another log on the fire and wonder who else might be outside, perhaps parked by the river, perhaps walking through the puddles in the side yard. Ray Bronson? Ginny Stokes? Jack Wetzel? Jimmie the Digger? Sister Ginny's badass bikers? Or John Fenimore Culpepper?

I feel myself drifting off to sleep. Do you have those moments when you surrender your worries and let go of the earth and float away to a place where the stars look like a highway of crushed ice? It's a safe place, in all probability the womb, surrounded by the humming of your mother's blood, a cloak that is invulnerable. That's where I find myself now.

I feel the warmth of the fireplace in my sleep and a song playing on a radio. The song is "Dear One," sung by Larry Finnegan. It was released in '61, but it was really a memorial to the previous decade. In it, the mailman comes to the singer's door, as one might deliver a draft notice. But the mailman gives the singer the last letter his girlfriend will ever write to him. She has given her heart to another, but the singer accepts what she has done and does not condemn her for it. The sense of loss in the song is enormous. But the loss is not about the girl; it's about an era.

I wake up suddenly and expect the song to disappear in the cold and mundane reality of the room. Instead it continues to play; in fact, the driving beat of the song rises in volume. The logs in the fireplace have turned to ash, the candles I lit now piles of beaded wax. The back door is open and the rain is blowing inside the house. I get up from the chair and put on my coat and pick up Grandfather's pistol from the footstool. A red Ford truck is parked in front, high beams tunneling through the rain, radio blaring, windshield wipers slapping time.

I open the front door, squinting, trying to see past the glare of the headlights. The driver's door opens, and the little blond girl who called herself Mary is standing in the rain, smiling.

"I'll shoot you," I say.

No you won't, she says. *You're a fraidy-cat.*

I cock the Peacemaker and fire. The bullet blows out the glass in the driver's door. She laughs in my face and disappears.

Now I remember exactly where she was standing in the backyard. In front of the chicken house after its interior had been destroyed and the chickens torn apart and the floor and walls soaked with a stench I associated with a ditch in Louisiana where the whores poured out their waste buckets. The same place Jack Wetzel wanted to put new shingles on.

Ginny Stokes called me dumb? That was kind.

"Dear One" is still blaring through the speakers in the Ford. The passenger door opens and a man gets out. A leather belt is cinched around his throat and hangs on his chest like a necktie. *They fucked us, Aaron,* he says. *Can you get us out of this?*

It's Jeremiah McNally, named for a prophet and now wearing a symbol that could have been the top half of a shepherd's hook. "How can I do that?" I ask.

Let the Old People go.

"From Ruby's cellar?"

It's only right. They've paid for their bad deeds. You're a kind man. Don't stop being who you are.

"Are you really Jeremiah?"

Sure as you're talking to me.

"You eviscerated the waitress?"

Only after she was dead. I wanted to hook up her passing with the murders on the res. We'd had a flat, and she wouldn't shut up while I was changing the tire, just kept talking about her pregnancy, and finally I got up and hit her. Don't look at me like that. Nice woman, but my ears were throbbing.

"You hit her with the jack?"

I wasn't thinking clear. Shit happens. How about doing a solid for the Old People? Baker will give you back your daughter.

"Why is it I don't believe anything you're saying?"

You're not going to help me?

"No. I don't believe you're Jeremiah McNally."

People grow into who they always were. I got it on with Spotted Horse. It was quite a ride.

"You're a liar."

She was asleep. I made her come. That's what an incubus does. Ask her.

I step backward and close and bolt the door, then go down to the basement and open a burlap bag and drop a big-battery flashlight and four emergency flares in it, and pick up a mattock and a two-gallon plastic container of gasoline, and head out the back door.

Chapter Thirty-Three

THE POWER IS still out in Lolo, the night jet black. I open the barn doors so the chickens will have a shelter, then throw open the chicken house door and scatter them outside. I place the flashlight on the floor in the corner so its beam will flood the room. Then I save out one of the flares and pop the remaining three alight and spike them hissing and burning like a welder's torch in the middle of the yard, so no one can jump me out of the dark. I sink the mattock into a plank on the floor and rip out a strip of wood that looks like it was torn from the heart of the tree.

I no longer care that my time on earth is coming to an end. What better way than in hot blood? Would you rather meet the grim reaper at Roncevaux or between bedsheets stiff with your own fluids?

The chickens have run for the inside of the barn, and the horses are in my secondary barn down by the river. A crooked bolt of lightning splinters a tree on the far bank, turning my house into a silhouette. Inside those two seconds of electric glimmer, I see the telephone wire flapping from the second-story eave. There are no trees around it. It was obviously cut.

I pry and tear the planks loose from the two-by-eight joists that support the floor, and can smell the dirt and manure and rotted feed below. I hope Ruby gets my messages; I hope to see her before I die. I ask no help from the authorities because they will not believe the preternatural events I have witnessed in the last few months. The issue is not that the events challenge credulity; people believe what they wish to believe and often close their eyes and open their hearts to the worst people in the human race. The shame is theirs. Let them drown in their complacency.

I brought no gloves and my hands are starting to blister. I put down the mattock and wrap my right hand in a bandana, then work the mattock under another plank and prize it off of three nails that are newer than the others and hammered unevenly or hooked over.

Something is happening that I didn't anticipate. The temperature is dropping, the rain turning to snow, although the forecast was for drier and warmer conditions later tonight. I hear noises up on the hill that make no sense: rocks rolling down the slope, clattering sticks, feet running through undergrowth.

I tear the plank loose from the three nails and fling it aside, then wedge up two more with the mattock and tear them loose with my hands and stick the flashlight down in the hole. Four feet away I see a suitcase on its side; I also see two metal army-surplus ammunition cans. I hook the mattock on the handle of one can and pull it toward me. The weight seems greater than anything the can could hold. The wind is stronger, shaking the walls. I hear vehicles turning off the dirt lane and into my drive. My heart is racing, my head pounding. I get to my feet and stare through the doorway at the sky and do not believe what I see. The clouds are smoke-colored and forked with electricity and have formed into a dome. The rain has turned entirely into snow, stippling the ground, stiffening the grass, sliding off flowers that have just started to bloom.

I hear the dirty roar of motorcycles, the doors of cars or pickup trucks slamming, and the cacophony of voices I have heard all my life. To my shame, I sold tickets in 1948 to a barbecue and election rally for United States senator Strom Thurmond, who, as a South Carolina judge, sentenced to death a seventeen-year-old Black boy who may have acted in self-defense when he killed a white man. I was in Bogalusa, Louisiana, in 1965, when Confederate flags flew all over the city and Klansmen fired guns into Black homes and churches; I was in Little Rock in 1957, when Black children had to be protected by National Guardsmen. I can go on and on with it. The degeneracy of a mob has no equal. It combines the mentality of the bigot, the coward, the sadist and the molester and the rapist. If there is an exception, I've yet to see it. I would love to line up a few of the participants in my sights.

Now they are surrounding my home, both the living and the dead. I know Grandfather's Peacemaker will not get me out of my troubles. However, the other weapons in my gun cabinet would not avail me, either. I suspect the peak of Roland's life was the morning in the year 778 when he rode up Roncevaux Pass with Charlemagne in the thin air of the Pyrenees and realized he had unknowingly gone through the metaphysical eye of the needle. He had entered immortality, and from that moment on, death could lay no claim on him.

That is why I have always tried to emulate my father, who went over the top five times. He was in the same zone as the Brits, who took sixty thousand casualties in a day. He said the wind carried the stench for three miles. I loved my father just as I did my grandfather. They came from different bloodlines and backgrounds, but their ethos was the same, and it made them members of the same private club. They were brave but they were kind. They were heroic but humble; they gave voice to those who had none. Is there a better ethos to wear on your shield, particularly when it's your time to sign off?

I pull one of the ammunition cans from under the boards I've splintered and almost tear my arm loose from the socket. Then I pull out the second one and release the clamp that holds down the top and push it on its side and let its contents fall heavily on the floor. I have never seen a gold bar. There are three in the can. I do not know a great deal about the international price of gold. My understanding is that the price of a single bar of twenty-eight pounds hovers in the range of half a million dollars.

I try to get the suitcase out by pulling the handle with the mattock, but the fabric catches on a nail and wedges the suitcase between the floor and a post and the concrete foundation of the barn. I tear another board loose and open the four-inch blade on my Swiss Army knife and slice the nylon side of the suitcase, then work my hand inside the hole and touch a lumpy, tightly taped package that's bleeding white powder on the packages around it. I take one taste and have no doubt of the suitcase's contents. Jack and Clayton have stung me good.

I rip up two more planks and pull the suitcase free and drag it up on the floor, then slosh it with gasoline and throw it out the door onto the ground.

All the players are there and many others I don't know. The temperature has continued to drop. I see no headlights on the highway. The clouds are swirling in a circular fashion and have changed in color from black to purple and red and streaks of orange. The snow continues to fall, thick and streaming and wet. Fog puffs from the mouths of Ginny Stokes and John

Culpepper and Jimmie Kale, but none from the mouths of Jeremiah McNally and Major Baker and his men and others whom I don't recognize. The bikers are booted and covered with tats and wear greasy blue jeans and leather vests and have beards and hair like Visigoths; the chains in their hands tinkle in the wind.

The bridge across the river is gone, including the pilings. I look to the north and the south of my property. I see no structure of any kind. The woods are thicker, the sandy stretches along the riverbanks free of any concrete boat ramps or rest stations or telephone or light poles or warning signs about buried power lines. The year could be 1870.

I must make a confession here. It is not easy to die alone. I hoped Ruby would be with me. Dying is like moving to another country, except we have no passport and no preparation for the experience we are about to have. The last word of many a dying soldier in a battalion aid station is "Mother."

However, I have to free my mind of these concerns. I accept that I have to die this evening. But the manner in which that death comes is of enormous importance. Maybe those who die between fouled bedsheets are braver than the warrior who charges into the face of death. A feverish and degrading and debilitating death burns up the energy that physical courage and spiritual courage require. And dying by torture, as Saint Joan did at the stake, can be much worse. My stomach curdles when I look at the men with chains dripping from their hands.

Oddly enough, I address the major first, probably because his vanity requires him to practice a semblance of military discipline. "It's awfully cold for you fellows to be out, isn't it?" I say.

The brim of his hat is coated with snow. *Not really,* he replies. *We've had a go at this quite a few times.*

"Tell me, Major, do you feel comfortable with an entourage of moral imbeciles?"

I don't think it wise to speak of these lads in that way.

"What do you think I should do with this suitcase full of drugs?"

Give unto Caesar what is Caesar's.

A man pushes his way through the group. He's hunched inside a heavy coat with fur around the collar, hands stuffed in the pockets. His teeth are chattering, from either the cold or fear. It's Ray Bronson, Ruby's ex, probably wired to the eyes.

"You're not walking out of here, Broussard," he says. "That flare in your pocket won't save you. Do the smart thing."

"What is the smart thing?" I ask.

"To give up all hope."

"Unlike some of these others, you're alive, Bronson. Before I check out, I'd like to plant one in your forehead."

"You think Ruby is gonna show up?" he says.

"Why shouldn't she?" I reply.

"I killed her this morning."

I feel a cold hand squeeze my heart, and I have to swallow before I can speak. "What about that, Major? Is this man lying?"

The major lowers his eyes.

"Don't be coy with me, Major Baker," I say. "This man does your dirty work."

I did not order him to do that. He did it on his own. I'm sorry.

I feel my eyes watering. Ginny Stokes and Jimmie Kale and Jack Wetzel are standing side by side. Kale picks up a rock and throws it at me. It hits my forehead, right above the eye. Blood trickles through my eyebrow and down my cheek. Sister Ginny's arms are folded on her chest, her brow creased. Jack has his hands clamped under his armpits, staring at nothing, as though his face is composed of mismatched parts.

"Where is my daughter, Major?" I ask.

He nods toward the hills at the top of the slope. *Up there. She slipped away.*

"Why there?"

I have a feeling you'll find out soon enough.

"You own all these people?" I say.

They gave up their souls. It's their misfortune and none of my own.

"Look me straight in the eye and tell me that Ruby Spotted Horse is dead."

She is, sir.

"How did she die?"

Bronson went into her house with a knife. I think he set fires, too. Listen, Mr. Broussard, release the contents of the suitcase to Mr. Kale, and I'll try to do what I can for your daughter.

"You can do nothing for yourself—how can you help my daughter?"

He doesn't answer and even looks hurt. I feel numb all over, perhaps because I'm traumatized, perhaps because of the cold. The grass is completely white now, the river running dark and rippling in the center, the backwater on the far bank forming into sheets of ice.

"What's your stake in all this, Mr. Culpepper?" I say. His AR-15 hangs upside down from his shoulder.

"You meddled in our business and cost my boy his life," Culpepper replies. "Blood is blood. You spilled mine. I'm fixing to spill yours."

"I see."

I pull the cap off the flare and strike the rough surface of the cap on the end of the flare, not unlike scratching a kitchen match. I drop the flare on the suitcase. The gasoline-soaked contents burst into flame, the sparks spinning into the sky. I hear a moan from the crowd.

"Come here, Officer Bronson," I say, pulling Grandfather's revolver from my coat. "I'm going to tell you a story about Bonnie and Clyde. When it's over, you'll be as dead as they are."

But words are cheap, and threatening an unarmed man is even cheaper. Besides, the hill above my main pasture just lit up.

Chapter Thirty-Four

THE HILLSIDE IS strung with deer trails that zigzag through the trees in long angles up to the crest and have been compacted and smoothed by the hooves of wild animals for centuries, and now stick figures are building bonfires on them and dancing around the flames, while at least a dozen drums are pounding in the background. At the bottom of the hill, another bonfire leaps into the air, crisping the needles in the fir trees. I can see the dancers clearly now, impervious to the cold, bodies slick with greasepaint, feathers in their hair, and round deer-hide shields on their arms, the shields hung with scalps.

They whirl in individual circles as they collectively rotate around the bonfires, raising their knees, rattling gourds and animal skulls filled with loose bones. Some hold stone clubs; some trade axes sold to them by the white man, others brown bottles of whiskey that glitter in the firelight. Some carry Spencer or Henry rifles or spears mounted with a steel point. The song or prayer they chant is repetitive and hypnotic. The fires grow bigger and more intense, and the tree trunks are filled with dancing shadows as well as people. Then the drumming stops, and the dancers raise their arms and weapons toward the heavens. The effect upon my visitors is harrowing.

"What's happening, Mr. Broussard?" Sister Ginny says.

"We're on the other side of the veil," I reply.

"What?" she says.

"Look around us. Except for my house, the twentieth century isn't there."

"I don't understand."

"It's been airbrushed off the painting, Miss Ginny. We're in the past. We're among the unborn."

Her eyes are full of confusion. "I just wanted to help Jack."

Save your sympathies for yourself, madam, the major says. *That misplaced piece of semen is the cause of all this. He and his brother stole the drugs and gold from Kale after they helped Kale kill his own employees. Then they hid it under the scribbler's chicken house. I thought you knew all this.*

"Jimmie told me. He wanted to make up with my boy."

Jimmie Kale is a fucking liar, madam. What were you doing with a cretin like that?

"I was in his band. I was gonna have a career in the movies."

I think you've fucked yourself with a garden rake.

"I'm going back home now," she says.

You're not going anywhere, madam. Those are savages out there, not actors in a play. They'll stake you out. A three-day experience if you're fortunate.

"That's not true, Major," I say. "Those are Heavy Runner's people. They harmed no one."

Don't give me your shite, Mr. Broussard. I'm bloody sick of it. I'd like to round up all you bleeding hearts and flay you alive.

"Don't speak to me like that, sir," I reply.

He pulls his revolver. *I'll strike you across the face.*

I step closer to him. His body seems to tremble, as though it's an image projected on mist. "Why do you fear me?" I ask.

He's breathing heavily, his eyes as black as coals. Then I realize he's not looking at me. I turn around and see hundreds of Indians working their way down the hill, the women walking with the men, many of them carrying babies. They flow through the tree trunks and around giant boulders and off the trails and back on them and through the gullies and sinkholes, breaking down underbrush and saplings and fallen cottonwoods that crack apart like rotten cork, finally stamping flat the smooth-wire back fence on the pasture. They are led by an Indian who I believe is Heavy Runner. At his sides are Ruby Spotted Horse and Fannie Mae.

Ruby is dressed in a white beaded deerskin robe. The area around her left breast is soaked in blood. She has a trade ax in her hand. Fannie Mae carries no weapon and is wearing jeans and a train engineer's cap and a bomber jacket with Bugs Bunny on the front. I'm happy she has no weapon. Perhaps I should feel otherwise. But to my knowledge she has never deliberately harmed a person or an animal in her entire life. Her pacifist attitude was not even a virtue; she was simply incapable of hurting anyone or anything.

The others do not share her view. The first I see die is Culpepper. His AR-15 has jammed and he's beating on it with the flat of his fist, yelling, his mouth open wide. An arrow sails out of the dark over the heads of the mob and into his mouth and embeds in the back of his throat, the shaft shaking between his teeth, the steel point protruding from the back of his neck.

The Indians are in the corral and all over the back and side yards now. They show no mercy. They slash and gouge and fire point-blank into the faces of people on their knees. Ruby's legs and moccasins are drenched with blood from walking through the dead. Her hair is streaked with it, her face aglow.

I wade into the midst, Grandfather's Peacemaker back in my pocket, my arms in the air, trying to pacify mothers whose infants were murdered and pregnant women who were shot through the stomach and old people who were left to freeze in the snow and whole families who drowned in the ice floe on the Marias. Then Fannie Mae is at my side, pulling my arms down, yelling in my face. *Not ours to change, Pops. They signed up with Baker. They're stuck with the bastard forever.*

"Where are we going?"

Chief Joseph already said it. "The place where I go is the place where I will be."

"What about Jack Wetzel or Sister Ginny?"

What about them?

"They're not all bad."

Don't count on that.

THE SLAUGHTER IS spilling into the front yard, through the maple trees and across the dirt lane and past my secondary barn and onto the sandy banks of the Bitterroot. Sister Ginny is by the veranda, rolled into a ball, her hands clamped on her head and her knees tucked under her body, as though surrendering herself to a storm, arrows sticking from her back and neck like quills on a porcupine. Jimmie the Digger is screaming inside a circle of Indians whose axes and knives and spears rise and chop several minutes before his screaming stops. His arms and legs have been severed but not pulled from the torso, causing his clothes to sag on his body, like a broken mannequin. Someone has set his severed head in the fork of a maple tree.

Major Baker's men and some surviving bikers and women I've never seen are being clubbed and shot and pushed into the water. They sob and try to bargain with their arms outstretched, the current and ice surging up to their chests, their faces pinched with cold. The fortunate are shot through the head and float around the bend, their clothes puffed with air. The major is standing on a sandbar in the middle of the river, shouting incoherently, his pants tucked inside his cavalry boots, his saber raised to the sky. Ray Bronson lies at his foot, half in the water, staring at the top of the vortex, his genitalia stuffed in his mouth.

Fannie Mae takes my arm. *We have to go, Pops.*

"What is Baker yelling about?"

He says he'll be back.

"You haven't told me where we're going."

In your house. Your home. Where else would you want to be?

I know the answer to that question, but I will not tell her. "Then we had better go there," I say.

Chapter Thirty-Five

I WAKE IN THE morning on the couch. The sun is shining through the windows. I walk into the kitchen, perhaps expecting to see Fannie Mae. But the house is empty. I open the back door and walk into the yard. The grass is green, the breeze warm, the horses playing in the pasture. The suitcase of meth is a circle of ash. The chickens have reestablished themselves inside the chicken house, the destroyed floor is as I left it, and the gold bars still reside in the ammunition cans.

I walk to the hillside and back again. None of my fences are broken. I continue to the front of the house and the secondary barn and the dirt lane where I first met Ginny Stokes, Leigh and John Culpepper, and Ruby Spotted Horse. Downstream, I can see the concrete bridge over the Bitterroot and traffic going back and forth. The surface of the sandbar where Major Baker swore at the world is smooth and damp and clean and unmarked by any impressions except the feet of birds. My front lawn is immaculate, and there is no sign or tire print of Ginny's Ford F-150.

I search through the house a second time and open up all the windows, calling Fannie Mae's name, then Ruby's. The only sound I hear is the wind. I know the present date and the present year and the name of the new president. I know where I'm standing and who I am and what I am and what I am not. I open the cap on my prescription bottle and pour its contents down the drain. I swear to myself I will not let the events of last night drive me mad.

Then I hear a scraping sound under the house. I go out the front door, to the end of the veranda, and lean over the rail and peer down the side of the house just as Jack Wetzel crawls out from under it.

"What are you doin' there, partner? You look like a chimney sweep."

"Where is everybody?" he asks, blinking in the sunlight.

I determine not to participate anymore in the grief of others. "Don't know what you're talking about, bub."

"Everybody's gone. Miss Ginny, too."

"You want something to eat?"

He looks at the empty yard and the river and the sandy bank and the stretch of water where dozens were drowned or shot. "I guess," he says.

I hold the door open until he comes inside. He smells like grave dirt and gunpowder. "Was that hell we were in?" he asks.

"I suspect that depends on how you look at it." I start coffee in the kitchen.

"I changed my mind," he says. "Forget the food. I'm gonna do like she says."

"Like who says?"

"Fannie Mae. She told me I got lucky and I'd better not blow it."

"When did you talk to her?"

"A couple of hours ago. I was too scared to come out."

"That's all she said?"

"No, she said to tell you goodbye. She didn't want to wake you up."

My legs are so weak I have to sit down in a chair.

"You okay?" he asks.

"That's what she said? She didn't want to wake me up?"

"She said it wasn't her choice or something like that."

"*Think.*"

"I am, Mr. B. It's not my fault."

No, it is not his fault, and shame on me for indicating that it is. "Give me a few minutes, Jack, then we'll take a walk."

I go into the bathroom and sit on the side of the tub with my head in my hands, then finally get up and shave and brush my teeth and rejoin him in the kitchen.

"You look okay, Mr. B.," he says. "I didn't mean to sass you."

"You didn't. You're a good kid."

"No, not really."

"If I say you're a good kid, you're a good kid."

We go out in the backyard. The sun is high in the sky now, and our shadows are short and seem somehow diminished and unimportant on the grass. I retrieve a gold bar from one of the ammunition cans and wrap it in a paper bag and hand it to Jack. "This is worth around sixty thousand dollars. You do with it whatever you wish. Just don't let anyone take it away from you, and don't buy dope with it. I'm also giving you this set of keys. They belong to that old Toyota pickup down by the barn. I'll take care of the paperwork. Call me and I can mail you the title or you can come by the house."

"You're giving me all this?"

"Like Fannie Mae said, don't blow it."

"The *fuck*," he says. "I don't believe this."

"Don't use profanity on my property, if you don't mind."

AFTER HE'S GONE I load the Avalon with my camping gear and a rackful of winter and summer clothes and a lever-action Winchester and Grandfather's Peacemaker and the ammunition and boxes of canned goods from Costco. I leave one gold bar and a note for my wrangler caretaker in the kitchen and put the other gold bars in the Avalon's trunk and drive up Evaro Hill and onto the res.

In my time on earth I've learned nothing. The mystery of creation and its beginning and end remain a mystery. I believe the great sin is to depart the world without discovering the raison d'être for one's existence. I love Ruby Spotted Horse, but I believe she was an ethereal entity before I met her and, for good or bad, wanted me to become one of the "Guardians." Unfortunately I don't believe that's the answer for people like Major Baker. He's not the problem, the people above him are, and few of them will ever be brought to task.

I follow the Jocko River up to Ruby's house. The March winds are up, and the air is filled with huge clouds of cinnamon-colored dust that seem to rise from the ground to the heavens. Through the windshield I can see the pumpkin field next to her house, the irrigation rows eroded and blown away. The ruins of the house are like an amber-tinted photograph taken during the War Between the States.

I park the Avalon in the trees and get out. I can smell the ash, the charred wood, the heat-cracked bricks, the cloth furniture and mattresses and clothes that are half-burned or ruined by fire hoses and the cans of food and preserve jars that have exploded in the flames.

The animals are gone, and tumbleweed is already bunching up inside the outbuildings. Much of the house's second story has collapsed on the stairwell that leads into the cellar. I suspect machines with big claws will tear down the remnants and load it into trucks, and bulldozers will flatten the rest and pack the cellar with wreckage and dirt. The men operating these machines will have no idea of the subterranean world they are burying. And when all is done, birds and night animals will peck and scratch at the dirt, and rumors and legends about supernatural occurrences will spread through the indigenous community, but few whites will pay attention to them, just as few whites pay attention to the ghostly appearances and sounds that have occurred at the site of the Baker Massacre.

I want to call out to Ruby, but I know she's not here. I was supposed to take her place. I didn't. And she left, and that's it. I get back in my car and drive to the nightclub located close to the spot where Clayton Wetzel was ripped to pieces.

THE RODEO-RIDER BARTENDER is sitting on a stool at the bar, eating a hamburger. He sets it down and wipes his mouth with a paper napkin. "How you doin', Mr. Broussard?"

"I've never gotten your name," I reply.

"Mangas Coloradas Dunlevy. Just call me Mangas."

"That's an Apache name."

"My old man thought Salish names weren't warlike enough."

"I need a favor."

"You name it."

"Drive me and my car up in the Missions, then keep my car for me."

"It's still pretty cold up there."

"I'll pay you two hundred dollars."

"You don't have to do that. When do you want to go?"

"Now."

I LET HIM DRIVE. In no time it seems we cross miles of mead-owland and find the dirt road that takes us high up into the Missions, where the clouds are so dense and wet we have to turn on the wipers. I mention the rapid passage of time be-cause with each breath I draw, I feel that another part of my life is behind me, gone so quickly I cannot remember what it looked like. We pop out on a piece of broken, rock-scattered road that overlooks the valley and the teardrop lake where Ruby Spotted Horse and I made our troth.

"Jesus Christ," Mangas says.

"Yeah, it's a special place."

"How'd you find it? I've hunted in the Missions since I was a boy. I didn't know it was here."

"Keep it special, will you? Like it's a private club."

"Yeah," he says. "Yeah, I'll do that."

We descend into the valley, past rockslides and splintered and rotted tree trunks, then we're in bumper-high green grass that rakes under the Avalon like a hairbrush. Mangas helps me unload and put up a tent. When we're finished, he starts to leave.

"Hold on." I take two hundred-dollar bills and a business card from my wallet.

"How about an autographed book instead?" he says.

"Are you and your friends still running a rehab program for teenage addicts?"

"Yeah, and we'll be doing it for a long time."

"This is my attorney's card. He's going to transfer the Ava-lon to you. Behind the spare, you'll find several gold bars.

Those are for your program. Regarding the gold bars, I'd go easy on the paperwork."

"You're kidding."

"Nope. Take care, bud."

"Son of a bitch."

"That's the second time today someone used profanity because I gave him something."

I WATCH HIM DRIVE away, then ascend the dirt road that barely clings to the side of the mountain. In a few minutes he disappears inside in a cloud, rivulets of gravel tumbling from the edge of the road.

I unfold a canvas chair and start a fire and erect a grill and put a can of beans and two bean patties on it and watch the beans bubble in the can. This is the place where Ruby and I swore we would return if one became separated from the other. But she's with her people now, and I don't begrudge her the decision she may have made. The real issue is Fannie Mae. In a short story written by Andre Dubus, the protagonist says God had a son, but He never had a daughter. I have thought about that statement many times. It says something that language cannot. It defines the undefinable. It also suggests a level of pain for which no human solution seems applicable. In this instance, I feel deserted by her. Poor Jack could not remember Fannie Mae's final words with any exactitude. That means I will go over his words again and again, trying to find solace in a conversation that was written on the wind.

At sunset the frozen waterfalls in the distance look like they're on fire. The shadows on the cliffs, the haze on the lake, the insects clouding over the cattails, the trails of webbed-foot creatures swimming across the surface somehow become a reminder of death, and I wonder if I have made a mistake by bringing firearms with me. I may have struck Jack and Mangas with the impression that I am in control of my destiny. The opposite is true. I have no plan except for the possibility of striking out for the north country, hiking through an unsecured ravine into Canada, and disappearing north of Jasper, where the animals are as big as cars and the creation of the planet is still unfinished.

It's not a fantasy. It's there, and the despoilers of the earth would like to get their hands on it. So to be a defender of the earth seems a fine way to go out. I put on my canvas coat and walk out on a sandbar in the lake to wash my pan and cup and fork and spoon. As I bend over on one knee and skim the surface with my hand, I see Fannie Mae's reflection rather than mine.

You've been hard to find, Pops, she says.

I drop my pan, which settles to the bottom without disturbing her reflection. "Are you determined to scare me to death?"

I wanted to leave you something.

"You're leaving again?"

I'll be around one way or another. Then one day you'll see me forever.

"I wish you'd stay."

The party is just getting started, Pops. You've got to have faith.

"Do you see Ruby?"

She's standing right behind you. That's where I'll be. You just won't see us.

Then she's gone. That fast. I wade into the lake, calling her name. The walls of the canyon are royal purple, the snowy peaks of the mountains blazing in the sun's last rays. The water is as cold as death, and my feet are sinking into the silt.

I call her name again and again and hear it echo in the distance. Then I give up, defeated and forlorn, trembling inside my clothes, wondering if indeed I'm delusional and cannot deal with the permanent loss of my daughter.

The campfire is whipping in the wind. I kick it and topple the grill and send ashes and sparks flying into the gloom, then go inside my tent. On my cot is an old album of Janis Joplin's songs, one I gave to Fannie Mae on her thirteenth birthday. Dated with today's date and written with a felt pen across the cover are these words:

You are the best dad in the world. I'll love you forever.
Your daughter,
Fannie Mae Holland Broussard

Acknowledgments

Sᴘᴇᴄɪᴀʟ ᴛʜᴀɴᴋs ᴛᴏ my editor, Sean Manning, and his assistant, Tzipora Baitch, and the rest of the staff at Simon & Schuster. They have helped me in every way they could with what I consider my best and certainly my most personal novel, *Every Cloak Rolled in Blood*. I am also indebted to my copyeditors, E. Beth Thomas and Jonathan Evans, whose dedication and literary knowledge and talent I can always depend upon. And also special thanks to Erin Mitchell, my sidekick and publicist and movie representative and daily helper, who can fix almost any problem in the world.

I also wish to thank the Spitzer Agency, which has represented me for more than forty-three years and includes Anne-Lise Spitzer, Kim Lombardini, Lukas Ortiz, Mary Spitzer, and Philip Spitzer, who passed two days ago. When Philip and I met, he was driving a cab and running a one-man agency in Hell's Kitchen. At the time I was out of print and couldn't sell ice water in the Sahara. Philip kept my novel *The Lost Get-Back Boogie* under submission for nine years. It received 111 rejections before it was accepted by LSU Press, which nominated it for the Pulitzer Prize. No agent in the history of the publishing industry has a comparable record. Philip will be dearly missed.

I also wish to thank my wife, Pearl, and my children Jim, Andree, and Alafair for sticking with me. And I want to thank my daughter Pamala, who died one year ago. I think she is still with us and will always be. I also believe she helped me write the last few pages of this book. I mean that literally.

Lastly, thank you for reading my work. I think the readers of my books are the best people in the world. You're intelligent and kind and decent and patriotic, and it's always an honor to be in your presence.

That's it. We don't care what people say, rock and roll is here to stay.

One big union,
Jim